The Great Sand Fracas of Ames County

Terrace Books, a trade imprint of the University of Wisconsin Press, takes its name from the Memorial Union Terrace, located at the University of Wisconsin–Madison. Since its inception in 1907, the Wisconsin Union has provided a venue for students, faculty, staff, and alumni to debate art, music, politics, and the issues of the day. It is a place where theater, music, drama, literature, dance, outdoor activities, and major speakers are made available to the campus and the community. To learn more about the Union, visit www.union.wisc.edu.

The Great Sand Fracas of Ames County

A Novel

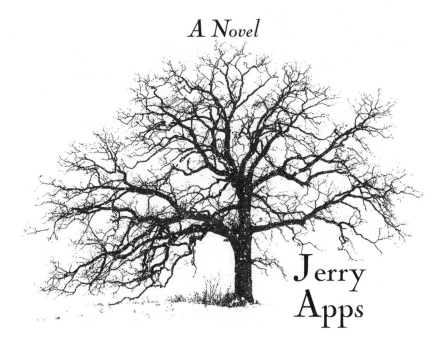

Jerry
Apps

Terrace Books
A trade imprint of the University of Wisconsin Press

Terrace Books
A trade imprint of the University of Wisconsin Press
1930 Monroe Street, 3rd Floor
Madison, Wisconsin 53711-2059
uwpress.wisc.edu

3 Henrietta Street, Covent Garden
London WC2E 8LU, United Kingdom
eurospanbookstore.com

Printed in the United States of America

Library of Congress Cataloging-in-Publication Data

Apps, Jerold W., 1934–, author.
The great sand fracas of Ames County: a novel / Jerry Apps.
pages   cm
ISBN 978-0-299-30070-8 (cloth: alk. paper)
ISBN 978-0-299-30073-9 (e-book)
1. Sand and gravel mines and mining—Wisconsin—Fiction.
2. Conservation of natural resources—Wisconsin—Fiction.
I. Title.
PS3601.P67G74   2014
813´.6—dc23
2014012643

To

Steve, Sue, Ruth, and Kate—

all had a hand in creating this book.

Contents

Contents

Contents

Acknowledgments

The idea for this novel came from a discussion my son, Steve, and I had when we were canoeing and fishing the Boundary Waters Canoe Area Wilderness of northern Minnesota three years ago. The fish weren't biting and Steve put up with (and had some great responses) to my "what if" questions as the foundation for this novel emerged.

Along the way, my wife, Ruth, offered her usual excellent comments. She reads all of my writing, both fiction and nonfiction. If my writing doesn't get past her, it goes nowhere. Once again, my talented daughter, Susan Apps-Bodilly, who also is an author, read and critiqued several drafts of this novel and offered many useful suggestions. Kate Thompson, editor extraordinaire, has an uncanny ability to spot weaknesses that I don't see and a structure that is less than satisfactory. She gave me several pages of suggestions of what to leave out, what to add, and how to arrange things so they made sense. Much thanks to all of those who read, reread, and helped this project through its many revisions and rewrites.

I especially want to thank Sheila Leary, press director; Raphael Kadushin, executive editor; and Andrea Christofferson, marketing and sales manager, all with the University of Wisconsin Press, for their continued support of my work. It is very much appreciated.

The Great Sand Fracas of Ames County

Prologue

*T*he whine of a chain saw assaulted the quiet of the new day as the mists rising from the waters of Link Lake slowly drifted west and the sun's first rays broke the horizon, illuminating the brilliant autumn colors of the maples and the aspens, the oaks and the birches that clustered on the hill-sides around the lake. Three men walked from their truck. One carried a chain saw; the other two carried axes. The chain saw operator, a burly man in his fifties, his face hidden under an orange safety helmet, revved the machine a couple of times like a teenager with a new driver's license and permission to drive his father's car alone for the first time. The men, all professional loggers, walked the short distance from their truck. The chain saw operator held the saw well in front of him, the saw sending off little spurts of chain oil. As the trio approached the old bur oak tree that they were ordered to cut this October day, they saw something emerging from the mist—something that surprised them. The chain saw operator shut off his machine and fished a cell phone out of his pocket to call his supervisor. "Boss, we've got a problem."

1

Ambrose Adler

The Previous April

Driving his team of horses on his way home from one of his infrequent visits to his doctor, Ambrose Adler was thinking that old Doc Stevens was right. The doctor had told him, "Ambrose, you keep doing what you're doing and you'll have a heart attack. And that will be it." He said it without the hint of a smile, so he obviously meant it.

Ambrose Adler was born in 1933 on a hilly, sandy farm located a mile west of the Village of Link Lake. For his entire life, he refused to be caught up in the wave of technology that began to sweep through Ames County in the 1950s and continued to this day. He raised a big garden and sold fresh produce during the summer months at a little stand he operated alongside the country road that trailed by his farm on the way to Link Lake. He had no electricity and no telephone, but he did have a battery-operated radio. He heated his ramshackle house with a wood stove, had no indoor plumbing, and continued to plow his hilly fields with a sturdy team of draft horses. He did not own a car and drove his team to town or most often walked there. Ambrose's long scraggly hair was white, his knees were bad, and he had arthritis that flared up especially on cool damp days, but his gray eyes were clear—and so was his mind.

When Ambrose arrived home from the doctor, Ranger was at the door to greet him. Ever since he was a young boy, Ambrose had kept a pet raccoon. The one he had now he had named Ranger because, with his little mask, the animal reminded him of the Lone Ranger, one of Ambrose's heroes when he was a young lad.

"Hi, Ranger," said Ambrose. "Miss me?" The little animal rubbed up against Ambrose's leg. Ambrose had stuttered since he was a boy and still stuttered today, but when he was alone with his dog or with his pet raccoon, he could speak clearly. He never understood why that was the case, but he enjoyed talking to animals, and they seemed to understand him and enjoyed "talking" with him as well.

Ambrose started the fire in the wood-burning cookstove and soon he could hear the snapping and crackling of the pine sticks that he used for kindling. Ranger sat at his feet, looking up at him, his head cocked to the side.

"You wanna hear what I learned from the doctor, Ranger?"

The little raccoon made a purring sound.

"Doc Stevens said I'm not so young anymore, and I guess he's right because I'll be eighty-two next year. He said I should slow down a little, but you know, Ranger, if I stop doing what I've been doing, I might as well die." He poked at the fire and thought for a minute. "There's something else that's been bothering me. You wanna hear about that, Ranger? You interested in hearing about what I've been thinking?"

Ambrose reached down and petted the little animal on the head.

"I've got a secret that I've told only one other person. I've been thinking that I really don't want to go to my grave with it—but how do I let people know about it, and even more important, I suspect, is when should I let them know? When should I let the cat out of the bag?"

Ambrose reached down and petted the raccoon again, then sat back in his chair. Oh, how he enjoyed sitting by his woodstove on a cool spring day, listening to the snapping and crackling of wood burning, smelling the wood smoke that escaped from the stove, hearing the subtle sound of steam rising from the teakettle. As he sat there, soaking up the warmth, his thoughts went back to the many years when he felt worthless because of his inability to speak properly. He remembered when he began doing this one thing, and how it had given him the self-confidence he had never otherwise known. Only his beloved Gloria, whom he had not seen in years, knew his secret. She had vowed to tell no one, and she hadn't.

Over these many years, he had kept people in the dark—people who thought they knew who he was but really didn't. People who thought they knew what he was doing but didn't know at all. He wondered what would happen when people discovered that there was a lot more to Ambrose Adler than a stuttering old man who grew vegetables and had ignored taken-for-granted technology such as telephones, automobiles, indoor plumbing, tractors, and central heating—and who talked to a raccoon.

2

Marilyn Jones

Marilyn Jones sat in her cramped little office located in the back of the Link Lake Supper Club. A small window to her left allowed her to see the waters of Link Lake, sparkling in the early morning sun. A mirror hung on the opposite wall, where she checked her appearance every time she left the office and entered the spacious dining room. She always wanted to make a good impression, no matter how she really felt at a given time.

This morning when she glanced in the mirror, she saw a woman with graying hair and puffy eyes from not enough sleep. But she still had a face and figure that caused men to turn their heads. The desk in front of her was piled with invoices and assorted pieces of paper that were part of running a business, especially one as successful as the Link Lake Supper Club. She was tired. Things had gone late last night as the Link Lake Wild Turkey Club—the Struttin' Gobblers—held its annual dinner meeting at the supper club. Several of the members intent on making the most of the celebration had stayed until the bar closed at 2:00 a.m. It was good for business, but Marilyn, now sixty-one, was bone tired when she came to work at 8:00 a.m., as she had done every day since she became owner and manager way back in 1973.

On Mondays the place was closed; otherwise, running a supper club was an everyday job. The place didn't open until 11:00 a.m., but she and her longtime employee, Joe Jensen, showed up each working day at 8:00 a.m. Joe cleaned up the place and she did the bookwork and handled all the details necessary to keep the Link Lake Supper Club afloat during these tough economic times.

An hour after Jensen arrived, Jonathon Frederick, Marilyn's chef of twenty years, arrived. Always right on time. Jonathon was responsible for the food orders, supervised all the cooking and baking, and was the never-challenged supervisor of the menu and the kitchen. No one questioned his decisions. No one, not even Marilyn. Over the years Jonathon had become ever crustier, but he was a good chef, one of the best, if not topping the list of all the restaurant chefs in Ames County. Marilyn knew that, but so did Jonathon—and he was quick to remind her of it when she questioned him about something involving the menu and the kitchen.

Marilyn enjoyed these early hours at the club, when the place was closed and quiet, except for the occasional squeaking of moving chairs and tables as Joe mopped the floor, and the subtle sounds and smells that came from the kitchen after Jonathon arrived. The last couple years, during these quiet moments, Marilyn often thought about how she wanted the community to remember her. She knew that one of these days she would retire—and she didn't want to be forgotten. She wanted to be remembered for more than merely being a successful businesswoman. She wanted people to remember her as a woman who cared about the community and worked hard to improve it. That's one of the reasons she had decided to help form the Link Lake Economic Development Council five years earlier and agreed to head it up when the mayor asked her to do it. She wanted people to remember that she, as president of the council, had sparked outside investors' interest in coming to Link Lake and providing much-needed jobs. If the economic council's negotiations with a mining company out of La Crosse panned out—well, it would surely add to her legacy. She smiled when she thought about that prospect.

She was also pleased that she, the Reverend Ridley Ralston, and Lucas Drake, a large commercial farmer, had been able to organize the Eagle Party, a political group with members throughout Wisconsin and beyond that was committed to bringing forgotten values back to government, including supporting business development with few rules and regulations.

The Link Lake Supper Club had demanded a lot of Marilyn Jones, but it had made her a wealthy woman. She never flaunted her wealth. She lived in a modest home on the lake only a few blocks from the supper club.

These days she often thought about how her life might have been different if she had a partner to share it with. She had several opportunities for marriage but turned them all down. She could never determine if her various suitors had the passion she had for running a business, and running a supper club surely required passion as well as untold hours of time, including every weekend. So she remained single, and even though there were always people around her, employees as well as customers, she had almost no close friends. Being a business owner and operator can be a lonely job.

3

Emily Higgins

*E*mily Higgins had presided over the Link Lake Historical Society, the oldest organization in the Village of Link Lake, for so many years that people couldn't remember when she was first elected. Higgins was a short, thin, white-haired woman in her mid-eighties, with a voice that carried to the far corners of any room where she spoke, no matter how large the room. One thing people liked or disliked about Emily Higgins was that she was a supporter of local history and the preservation of Link Lake's historic structures. She never wavered, no matter how much pressure she received from those who opposed her position and accused her of standing in the way of Link Lake's economic progress. Emily Higgins knew what she believed, and she wasn't at all shy about sharing those beliefs with others—especially when the discussion turned to local history.

Most people in Link Lake remembered when Emily Higgins took on the then newly formed Link Lake Economic Development Council five years earlier. The council, with Marilyn Jones at the helm, had convinced the Big R fast food chain to open one of its restaurants in Link Lake. Prior to that time, the only eating establishments in the village were the Eat Well Café and the Link Lake Supper Club. A fast food restaurant seemed a good fit, especially since the village was trying to attract more summer visitors to the area. Both the Economic Development Council and the Big R siting representative had agreed that an excellent place for a Big R establishment would be the abandoned Chicago and Northwestern depot site. The trains had stopped running in the 1980s; the tracks had been torn up and a bike trail had been established—quite a popular one, too. The Big R people and the Economic Development Council both agreed that the old depot, badly in need of repair, should be torn down to make way for a new Big R restaurant. Of course, no one had bothered to let Emily Higgins and the Link Lake Historical Society know about what the Economic Development Council and Big R were cooking up, and Emily didn't know a thing about it until an article appeared in the *Ames County Argus* announcing the potential arrival of Big R to Link Lake and the razing of the old depot.

When she saw the article, Emily immediately called an emergency meeting of the historical society, and soon Marilyn Jones discovered that the Link Lake Historical Society was not near as irrelevant as she thought it was. At the Economic Development Council's next meeting, which was supposed to be a celebration of the decision to bring a new business and new jobs to the community, everything hit the fan. The entire historical society membership, all forty of them, were in the audience, plus another twenty-five people who sometimes attended historical society meetings but never took the time or had the inclination to become members of the organization.

Marilyn Jones and the mayor knew something was up when they saw all those "old-timers," as Marilyn referred to them, in the audience at the community room at the Link Lake Library. She had no more than begun her opening remarks when Emily Higgins's hand shot up. When Marilyn refused to recognize her, Emily asked in her loud voice, "Is this deal with Big R final?"

"Miss Higgins, I believe you are out of order and that I have the floor," Marilyn replied.

"You may have the floor, Miss Jones, but as you know, I represent the Link Lake Historical Society and you haven't once bothered to let our organization know about this proposal to bring a new restaurant to town and to locate it on the site of the old railroad depot, so my question deserves an honest answer."

"Well, Miss Higgins," Marilyn Jones said, smiling. "I thought your group had better things to do than worry about a dilapidated railroad depot. We didn't want to bother you with this rather minor undertaking."

"Not bother us? Not bother us?" Emily said with an even louder voice. "I understand the plans are to tear down the depot for this new fast food place."

"Well, yes that's likely to happen. The Big R group prefers to put up new buildings. They like the depot's location, but the old building is in the way."

"In the way, huh?" said Emily, her face getting ever redder. "Are you saying that history stands in the way of your plans? Is that what you are saying?"

"Of course not, Emily. You know how much everyone on the Economic Development Council appreciates and supports Link Lake's history." She said it with a straight face, but it evoked several groans from the historical society membership, which included Ambrose Adler, who sat in the back row with a big grin on his face as he listened to the give and take between Emily and Marilyn.

"Have you suggested that Big R might renovate the depot so they could save the building but still have their restaurant on the site?" asked Emily.

"We did, but Big R rejected the idea."

"I suggest you talk with them some more," shot back Emily.

The meeting continued with the rift between Emily Higgins and Marilyn Jones deepening, and a new distrust between the Link Lake Economic Development Council and the Link Lake Historical Society developing.

The week after what turned out to be one of the most contentious meetings the citizens of Link Lake could remember, a well-known nationally syndicated environmental writer, Stony Field, wrote a column about the situation. For more than three decades, Stony Field had been widely known for shining a light on local communities across the United States, focusing on local matters but then showing how what happens in one place has application in many other places. Field's column was carried each week by hundreds of newspapers across the country, including the *Ames County Argus*.

Emily Higgins

FIELD NOTES
Local Historical Society Challenges Development
By Stony Field

Hats off to the Link Lake Historical Society in little Link Lake, Wisconsin, for taking on the village's Economic Development Council and challenging its members to consider more than money when looking at the future of the village. My research tells me that the Economic Development Council, led by supper club owner Marilyn Jones, and Link Lake's mayor, Jon Jessup, struck a tentative deal with the Big R fast food company to build a new fast food restaurant on the site of the former Chicago and Northwestern depot. Big R's plans included quietly tearing down the depot and replacing it with a new, modern Big R standard-planned building.

When the Link Lake Historical Society president, Emily Higgins, heard of the plans (the historical society had not been informed before a recent public meeting) she immediately rounded up 65 citizens who believed it was important to save the depot because, as Higgins said, "It's a part of our village's history and has a rather unique design."

My sources tell me that Big R has pulled the plug on the whole effort and is looking elsewhere in central Wisconsin to build a new fast food place. Good riddance, I say.

What can a village, no matter where it might be located in the country, learn from this? Several things. While economic development in a community is surely important, it is not the only thing that is important. History is important, caring for the environment is important, education is important, and the arts are important. Has Link Lake's Economic Development Council learned a lesson? Let's hope so. What is needed is for the council to work in tandem with groups like the local historical society and come to a common agreement before charging ahead with the agenda that "the economy and jobs are all that is important."

4
Fred and Oscar

Good morning, Henrietta," said Fred Russo, as he greeted Eat Well Café's regular morning waitress.

"And top of the morning to you, Mr. Russo," said Henrietta, who bowed a bit when she said it. Henrietta O'Malley was pushing sixty, her once red hair was mostly gray, but her green eyes sparkled when she talked. She was proud of her Irish heritage; her grandfather had come to Link Lake in the mid-1800s, not long after the village was established. The O'Malleys had been in Link Lake ever since.

"And will that handsome Mr. Oscar Anderson be joining you this morning?" she asked.

"Well, he'd better," said Fred, "or I'll be slurping coffee all by myself."

Fred Russo and Oscar Anderson, retired farmers in their eighties and lifelong friends, met every morning except Sunday for coffee at the Eat Well. Fred settled into his chair at their usual table in the back corner as Henrietta poured a cup of coffee for him.

"A grand and glorious day," said the always cheerful Henrietta.

"Well, I wouldn't go that far," said Fred. "Not so grand and glorious when your arthritis is kickin' up."

"Oh, I'm sorry," said Henrietta.

"Don't be, just one of those little extras that comes along after you've accumulated a few years."

Now, Oscar Anderson, with his ever-present cane, was making his way toward the little table where Fred was sitting.

"About time you showed up," said Fred by way of greeting. "You're late."

Oscar glanced at his watch. "Nope, you're early," he said.

Fred and Oscar

"Can I pour you some coffee?" Henrietta asked. She was smiling as she enjoyed the good-natured banter between the two old friends.

"Might's well, now that I'm here," said Oscar as he hung his cane over a chair and sat down.

"So how's my ornery old friend?" he asked Fred, smiling broadly.

"Old Arthur is kickin' up again this mornin'. Must be a change in the weather—some rain on the way," answered Fred.

"So what's new with you?" asked Oscar.

"Not much. Did pick up a couple rumors though. Always got my ears open to what is going on and what might be going on."

"As bad as your hearing is, you do manage to hear a lot," said Oscar.

"Just trying to pay attention, trying to stay awake and alert. When you're in your eighties that's sometimes a challenge."

"Ain't that the truth," said Oscar.

Both men sipped their coffee and were quiet for a bit. The Eat Well was filling up with breakfast customers, mostly older folks who had retired in the area and needed to get out of the house on a cloudy spring day.

"So Fred, you gonna tell me something about these rumors you've been hearin'?"

"Oh, yeah, the rumors. Well, I think I've been pickin' up more than just rumors. You wanna hear the rumors or you wanna hear what else I've been hearin', or a little bit of both, or maybe you'd like to hear about what I saw the other day?" said Fred.

"Fred, you've got a way of makin' the most simple things sound so damn complicated. I just asked what's new."

"Well, what I've been hearin' and seein' is this." Fred paused and took another long drink of coffee and held it up for Henrietta to fill on her way back from serving another customer. "There is something going on in the park."

"Which park is that?" asked Oscar.

"You know damn well there's only one park in Link Lake and that's the one named after old Increase Joseph."

"Something happening in Increase Joseph Community Park in the month of April when it's usually too cold to have a picnic and school isn't out yet?" said Oscar, a bit surprised at what his friend was saying.

"Well, I can't be sure. But what I saw were some guys wearing those bright orange vests, like the highway workers wear, prowlin' around. One of 'em was walkin' around the old Trail Marker Oak, gawkin' at it this way and that."

"Prowlin' and gawkin', huh?" asked Oscar.

"Can't rightly say but it looked like they were surveyors."

"Maybe the village is planning to fix the road by the park—sure could use some fixin'."

"Nah, they were well inside the park. There was three of them. They came in a white van that they parked on the road just outside the park," said Fred.

"You get their license number?"

"Why would I do that? But I did notice that the van was from a car dealer in La Crosse."

"Might be some kind of crooks," said Oscar.

"Geez, Oscar, crooks don't look like surveyors, and besides crooks know better than to frog around in a park in broad daylight."

"So what's the rumor you've picked up?" asked Oscar.

"Somebody told me that something's goin' on in the park."

"Good God, Fred, you just told me you saw some guys in the park—that's no rumor, if you saw 'em with your own eyes."

"Calm down, Oscar. The rumor is that something big is planned for the park. Something really big."

"I suppose fixin' the road by the park would be something big—especially for Link Lake. A new flag at the post office was the biggest thing happening in Link Lake last year. I suspect fixin' the road past the park would rank right up there with a new post office flag," said Oscar.

"Oscar, I don't think they're planning on fixing the damn road by the park. If you'd have listened, I said they was working in the park, doin' survey work inside the park."

"Why was they doin' that?" asked Oscar.

"How the hell do I know—except I heard it was something big. Something really big in the works."

The men sat quietly for a bit, enjoying their coffee.

"You read the last issue of the *Argus*?" asked Fred.

"Yup, always read the *Argus* from cover to cover, page one to the last page. Read it every week. Pretty darn good paper, too, if I must say so. Papers are havin' problems these days, some of the big ones are goin' out of business. *Argus* seems to be doin' okay, though. Why'd you ask?"

"You read Stony Field's column, the environmental guy who stirs up all kinds of mischief around the country?"

"Yup, always read Stony Field. Sometimes I agree with him, sometimes I don't. Pretty fair writer though. Easy to understand what he's trying to say."

"You read about the fact that you're gonna have to stop smokin' that old pipe of yours?"

"Where'd you see that?"

"Was right there in Stony Field's column."

"To hell, I read them columns pretty careful and I didn't see no mention about pipe smokin'."

"Well, old Stony was writin' about climate change, remember readin' that column?"

"I do, but I don't recall that he said anything about pipe smokin'."

"Well, he didn't say it in so many words, but he did say that puttin' smoke in the air, smoke from power plants for instance, is one of the contributors to global warming. That's what he said."

"I read that too. But he didn't say anything about pipe smokin'."

"Oscar, it don't take no rocket scientist to figure out that smoke is smoke and pipe smoke sure as hell is smoke."

"So you think smokin' my pipe a couple times a day contributes to global warming?"

"Well, it might. It just might. That's what old Stony Field was implying anyway."

"I don't think so, Fred," Oscar said, smiling. "I don't think Stony Field cares that I smoke a couple pipefuls of tobacco a day."

"Well, you gotta believe he cares about smoke. And pipe smoke is smoke, and if a million people, old guys like you, was all smokin' their pipes that would be one helluva lot of smoke goin' up there to contribute to global warming."

"Drink your coffee, Fred. Might help your way of thinking a little."

5

Ambrose Adler

*M*any people in the Link Lake community thought Ambrose Adler was different; some people came right out and said he was strange. One thing that made him different was that he stuttered. His parents had told him that he stuttered from the day he was born, and that they had thought he would grow out of it—that he would eventually learn to speak normally. It never happened.

When he started school, his fellow schoolmates teased him relentlessly. They asked him to say his name and he couldn't get past "A . . . A . . ." Then they pointed their fingers at him and laughed and told him he was some kind of dummy because he couldn't speak properly. He felt just terrible. He so much wanted to be like everyone else and he just couldn't, as hard as he tried. When he tried to speak, even a word or two, he got all red in the face and messed up the words that were so clear in his head but wouldn't come out of his mouth.

When he was in second grade, one of the older boys, Albert, told Ambrose that his pa said Ambrose's tongue was stuck in his mouth and that's why he couldn't talk straight.

"We're gonna cure you," Albert said as he motioned to several other boys who had been listening. Before Ambrose knew what was happening, Albert and three other boys grabbed his arms and legs, laid him out flat on the ground, and began pouring water in his mouth.

"Water will loosen up your tongue," Albert said.

Ambrose didn't know if Albert really believed what his pa had said or he was just being mean. Ambrose tried to yell, but when he opened his mouth no words came out and water poured in. One of the girls, Judy, who was in eighth grade, came to his rescue.

"You're going to kill him," Judy said. "Let him up. Let him up."

Ambrose staggered to his feet, gagging and throwing up water as the boys who'd held him down stood laughing and pointing their fingers at him. Judy told the teacher what happened, and the teacher made the boys who nearly drowned Ambrose stay inside the schoolroom and miss recess for the rest of the week. But that was all the punishment they got.

Kids at school and people in the community all believed Ambrose was "slow"—mentally deficient. But his mother and father, Sophia and Clarence, knew better and they always supported him. Ambrose surely didn't consider himself "slow." He liked reading and doing math. He liked writing. He liked school, but he didn't care for his fellow students, who couldn't move past teasing him every opportunity they got.

When he was in seventh grade, and well past five feet tall, husky and strong because of all the farm work he had been doing, an eighth grader pushed him to the limit one day. They were both carrying in wood for the woodstove in the school. "D . . . d . . . n't know you . . . you . . ." He didn't finish his mocking sentence. Ambrose took a piece of wood and whopped the eighth grader over the head. The eighth grader fell to the ground in a heap, the wood sticks he was carrying spilling on the ground in front of him.

For that little outburst of temper, Ambrose missed two weeks of recess. He never enjoyed recess anyway, so he spent his time in the schoolroom reading books.

Ambrose's parents didn't say much about the trouble he got into at school. But later that week his mother gave him a little notebook and a new number 2 lead pencil. "Why don't you write down things that are happening around the farm?" she suggested. And that's what he did. He wrote about the weather, especially about storms that rolled through that part of Ames County regularly. Fierce summer thunderstorms and wicked winter blizzards that made farm life challenging and left farm families isolated sometimes for days on end.

He wrote about what it was like to be different from other kids, and how their teasing and constant reminders of his inability to speak like other kids never ceased to make him feel inadequate, some days downright worthless. It was as if what was bothering him and causing him so much unhappiness had moved from his mind to the page in front of him.

He wrote about farm life, the crops his father planted and the livestock they raised. He wrote about harvesting hay, mostly by hand as their team of horses did only the heavy work such as pulling the hay mower and the hay wagon on which they pitched cured alfalfa and clover. Ambrose described in detail how to chop and split wood with an ax, which he and his pa did every fall.

He wrote about the coming of spring and how he looked forward to it after winter had dragged on and on, never wanting to give up its grip. And as strange as it may seem, after a long, hot summer of never-ending work, and an equally busy fall with the grain, potato, and corn harvests, he wrote about looking forward to winter when everything slowed down and life was more pleasant—until a blizzard blew in from the northwest and made the Ambrose family miserable for several days.

He wrote about the seasonal cycles on the farm and his reaction to them. Somewhere he had read that all of life is a circle and that people return to earlier places again and again as they live their lives. That was surely true for people who lived on farms. Each year you did the same thing: spring planting, summer caring for crops, fall harvesting, and winter resting and planning for the next year. It was the same each year, but it was always different too, as weather, markets, and a hundred other things added spice and challenge to farm life and made what might seem predictable quite unpredictable.

His stuttering continued, especially when he was in a group and the situation was stressful, such as when the teacher called on him. Ambrose discovered that if he relaxed and was speaking with but one person, he could string several words together in a sentence—the stuttering was still there, and it took a while for him to say the words, but it certainly was an improvement. Ambrose guessed the teacher figured that if he could communicate with one other person, he could communicate with several. Of course she was wrong.

Something else made Ambrose strange in the minds of many people who knew him; they believed he could talk to animals. Ambrose first discovered that he had this gift, and he truly believed it was a gift, when he was seven years old. Felix, the Adler's collie, would look at Ambrose as if he understood exactly what Ambrose was saying. And Ambrose noticed another strange thing; when he was alone with an animal and talking to it, he didn't stutter. One day Ambrose found a raccoon by the side of the road. Someone must have hit it with a car. It had a broken leg, but otherwise the animal seemed in reasonable shape. Ambrose named him George and put a little wooden splint on his leg wrapped tight with cloth and tape. Ambrose talked to George all the while he was fixing his leg, expecting any minute that the animal would bite him or try to run away. But George did neither. The injured raccoon seemed to understand what Ambrose was saying. Ambrose was afraid that the raccoon and Felix wouldn't get along, that they might try to kill each other. But the dog and the raccoon got along with each other just fine. In fact they became good buddies. What a threesome they were: a big collie dog, a limping raccoon, and a stuttering farm kid.

Ambrose was afraid that his father would make him turn George lose once he healed. But his father never said a word, and while the little raccoon could have run off anytime he wanted, he never did.

When Ambrose finished high school in 1951, most folks didn't think he was smart enough to graduate, except his father and mother, who always believed he was "destined for great things," as Ma said. After high school Ambrose turned to full-time farming with his father, helping him take care of the twenty milk cows, growing fifteen acres of corn, fifteen acres of oats, ten acres of potatoes, and tending a large vegetable garden that provided much of the food for their table.

George was Ambrose's pet for almost twenty years, but one morning the raccoon didn't greet Ambrose when he went out to the barn to help with the morning milking. Ambrose crawled the ladder to the haymow and found George's body; sometime during the night he must have died. Ambrose figured in human terms George would have been eighty or even ninety years old.

Only a few days after George died, Ambrose heard a neighbor telling his father that he had shot a big female raccoon that had been raiding his sweet corn patch.

"That old coon had little ones; I could tell she was nursing," the neighbor said. "Probably got rid of a half a dozen of them raiding bastards," he concluded proudly.

Overhearing this, Ambrose immediately decided to go looking for the raccoon's den, likely in a hollow tree in a woodlot near the neighbor's sweet corn patch. Every evening, when the chores were done, he went searching for the raccoon's den, knowing that if he didn't find it in a couple days the little ones would all die of starvation.

On his third foray into the neighbor's woodlot, Ambrose found the den tree. Only one little raccoon in the litter was alive, and just barely. Ambrose fed the weak little fellow with milk that he dripped into his mouth with an eyedropper. After a couple weeks, the baby raccoon was drinking out of a bowl and growing like everything. Ambrose named him George II. And of course he and the little raccoon talked to each other every day. Felix had died several years earlier, and Ambrose's father had replaced him with another collie named Fanny. Fanny and George had never much liked each other, but Fanny and George II became great buddies, and together with Ambrose they often had a three-way conversation: Ambrose sharing his thoughts, Fanny making a little whining noise, and George II making a purring sound. Ambrose couldn't understand what Fanny and George II were saying, but from the way they looked at Ambrose, they seemed to know exactly the meaning of what was coming out of his mouth.

Ambrose had grown accustomed to not being able to speak well when he was with people. He enjoyed farm work, appreciated having a chance to work with his father, who never once lost his patience when Ambrose had trouble trying to tell him something. About the only social contact Ambrose had was when he went to Link Lake for supplies, driving their trusty team and tying them up behind the Mercantile in a parking lot that still had a place to tie a team of horses, a hitching post left over from an earlier era. When he finished his brief shopping, using a list his mother provided, he often stopped at the Link Lake Library, where he spent an hour or so reading or deciding on a book or two that he would check out and take home with him. While at the library, he read several newspapers including the *New York Times* and the *Wall Street Journal*. He especially enjoyed reading books about nature—Emerson and Thoreau had become favorite authors of his.

He also generally planned his trips to town to coincide with the meetings of the Link Lake Historical Society. He sat in back of the room at the meetings, not saying a word but taking in every nuance of what went on. Some members of the historical society ignored Ambrose because they knew of his strange ways and his difficulty speaking. But not Emily Higgins. She made a point of talking with Ambrose each time he attended a meeting and tried to make him feel welcome.

6

Marilyn and Stony Field

As Marilyn Jones waited for a phone call from La Crosse on this cool April day, she read Stony Field's newest column, becoming more agitated by the minute.

FIELD NOTES
Fracking for the Future

By Stony Field

Have you heard about fracking? Neither had I until a couple years ago. Those who support the process see it as the answer to the United States' energy problems. Hydraulic fracturing, fracking, is a relatively new process for reclaiming natural gas. According to these same sources, the United States has more than 2,500 trillion cubic feet of natural gas just waiting to be fracked.

You are wondering how the process works? Well, as I understand it, all this natural gas embedded in gas-bearing shale deposits has just been sitting there waiting for these clever oil drillers to come up with a technology to release it from where it has been resting for thousands of years. For years oil drillers drilled straight down. With the new technology, they drill down and then make a sharp turn and drill horizontally. But there is more to it. All of this natural gas needs a little encouragement before it is released. And that is where hydraulic fracturing comes into play. Drillers inject millions of gallons of water, which is mixed with a special sand (more about this later) and chemicals into these vast underground formations. The pressure of the water, sand, and chemicals cracks the rocks (fractures them), allowing the gas to escape and flow into the wells.

As a result, we get an efficient energy source, a clean-burning fossil fuel, increase our independence from the Middle Eastern and other foreign suppliers of crude oil, enhance the country's energy security, and create jobs. Sounds like a pretty rosy situation, wouldn't you say?

But hold on before you begin waving the American flag and jumping up and down with we've-solved-our-energy-problem glee. First off, it's still a fossil fuel, and no matter what anyone says, one day we've got to wean ourselves from these older fuel sources. With too much enthusiasm about natural gas production, it will be easy to push wind and solar power and all the other alternative energy sources into the background with an attitude of "who needs this new stuff, we've got it figured out."

We also must be concerned about the dangers of hydraulic fracturing, and there are several. As I mentioned, the process requires millions of gallons of water, which can draw down local surface and groundwater resources. Also, the slurry of chemicals mixed with the water and sand are toxic and if not handled properly can contaminate local water supplies. The gas itself, when released, can travel through the ground and enter nearby water wells, which can present a safety hazard, as the gas is highly flammable.

And what about all the sand that is needed for the fracking process? What is its source? Guess what? Wisconsin and Minnesota are prime sources. I'll be writing more about this later.

Marilyn slammed the paper down on her desk. She thought, *The audacity of this jerk, Stony Field. What right does he have to shoot off his mouth about something that shouldn't concern him?* She wondered if he had somehow gotten inside information about what was being proposed for Link Lake—the subject of the phone call that she was patiently waiting for.

The phone on her desk rang loudly. "Link Lake Supper Club, this is Marilyn." She already knew from the caller ID that this was the call she was waiting for.

"This is Emerson Evans with the Alstage Sand Mining Company. How are you this morning?"

"I'm just fine. I've been waiting for your call."

"I have good news for you, Marilyn, and for the citizens of Link Lake."

7

Link Lake Historical Society

*T*hank you all for turning out on this rather chilly April day," said Emily Higgins as she called the regular monthly meeting of the Link Lake Historical Society to order. "I'm told spring is just around the corner, but I'm wondering what corner it's hiding behind." A few groans came from the audience in response to Emily's rather uncharacteristic attempt at telling a joke.

"Today is our annual planning meeting as you all know, and by popular demand, especially from some of our newer members, Oscar Anderson will make a presentation on the history of the Trail Marker Oak. The old oak is an important symbol for our community from the days when Native Americans lived here and when the village was first founded. And it remains an important symbol for our community today. But first we need you to sign up for one, two, or all three of the major activities we have planned for this summer. As you know the cemetery walk is coming up fast, and I need to see some names on this sign-up sheet." She began passing the sheet around the room. She was smiling when she asked—everyone liked Emily and even if she could be a bit pushy at times, no one doubted her love for history and fondness for the Village of Link Lake.

*T*he Link Lake Historical Society traced its beginnings to 1860 when the first group of settlers in this part of Ames County met regularly and wrote down what they remembered of the days when they lived in upstate New York. They talked about their trip on a steamship that sailed from Buffalo and eventually reached the port of the Sheboygan, where they disembarked and began their long trip overland. They recalled how they spent their first

26

night in Wisconsin at Wade House on the old plank road, and their second in Fond du Lac, a bustling city on the southern end of Lake Winnebago. Finally, they arrived at Berlin on the Fox River, took the ferry across, and found themselves in newly surveyed Ames County, after the treaty with the Menominee Indians was signed and the area was ready for settlement.

These many stories were written and stored in files in the old Link Lake State Bank building, long ago replaced by a more modern bank on the outskirts of town. The old bank building now served as the main offices for the historical society, which housed a small gift shop as well as the Link Lake Historical Museum. It held many memories, especially for the older citizens of Link Lake. The gift shop and museum, open from April until October, attracted hundreds of visitors during the summer months and busloads of schoolchildren in April and May and again in the fall while the museum was still open. The museum and the historical society were both operated entirely by volunteers—all under the direction and constant encouragement of Emily Higgins, who lived and breathed Link Lake history.

Membership in the historical society had remained constant for more than fifty years, with forty people on the membership list and from twenty-five to thirty who attended the regular monthly meetings, now held in the meeting room at historical society headquarters.

The meetings generally included a business meeting, much of it devoted to discussing and planning historical society events and activities, followed by presentations from those within the organization or speakers associated with other historical societies, the Wisconsin State Historical Society, or historians teaching at one of the University of Wisconsin campuses.

The organization had its own popular speakers. Oscar Anderson and Fred Russo topped the list. Several years back, Oscar and Fred had photographed every old barn within twenty miles of Link Lake, interviewed barn owners, dug into old records, and discovered the stories behind each barn. Their presentation, "The Barns of Link Lake," had proved to be the most popular presentation in many years. Now, at least once a year they were asked to repeat it—they of course continued to research these old barns and added new information each time they were asked to speak.

The Link Lake Historical Society also worked hard to involve the entire community by sponsoring major events that brought hundreds of people to the area. Each year historical society members designed a float for the Fourth of July parade and were actively involved in the summer's Trail Marker Oak Days.

They also sponsored three major events each year designed to attract tourists and locals interested in rural history. Each spring the group organized a walking tour of the cemetery with historical society members assuming the roles of past Link Lake notables. In May they reenacted the bank robbery that happened in 1900, and they organized an enormous thresheree each August at Ambrose Adler's farm. The thresheree attracted thousands of people from throughout Wisconsin and from several other states and was the main moneymaking activity for the historical society. The thresheree also served as an economic boost for the restaurants, taverns, the motel, and the gift shops in Link Lake.

This year, with the assistance of the Link Lake High School Nature Club and the Wisconsin Department of Natural Resources, historical society members worked with high school students to erect a video camera pointed toward a bald eagle nest in Increase Joseph Community Park. This "eagle cam" operated twenty-four hours a day, with streaming video of the nest available on the Internet for all to watch. The eagle cam had attracted viewers from all over the country.

Anyone have any new business before I turn the meeting over to Oscar?" asked Emily. She paused for a bit. "Hearing none, Oscar, let's hear about the Trail Marker Oak."

Wearing a new pair of bib overalls and a red plaid flannel shirt, Oscar slowly got to his feet and, with his cane, made his way to the front of the room. He was clutching a yellowed newspaper clipping in his hand.

He cleared his throat, looked out over the audience, and began.

"I believe you all know about the Trail Marker Oak, but some of you may not know its history, how it is that it stands today at the entrance to Increase Joseph Community Park. Back in 1952, the *Ames County Argus* ran a story about that famous old tree. If you'll bear with me, I'll read it." Oscar began reading the article in his deep baritone voice.

Trail Marker Oak

It's believed that this special bur oak tree saw the first light of day about 1830, when a tiny shoot pushed up through the prairie soil and sent forth its first leaves to capture the sunlight. It would be six more years before Wisconsin became a territory and 18 years before it reached statehood.

In 1830, these central Wisconsin lands that surround the body of water now called Link Lake were Menominee Indian lands and had been so for centuries. The Indians fished the waters of Link Lake, camped on its shores, and marveled at the lake's beauty. When the first settlers arrived, the land was mostly tall grass prairie with wild grasses—big bluestem, little bluestem, and several other varieties waving in the summer breezes. It was a quiet area with long, hot summers, cool, refreshing autumn days that carried on from September to well into November, snowy, cold winters, resulting in the lake freezing over from December to March, and then warm spring days with wildflowers, returning flocks of migrating birds, and Indians trailing by in search of the maple trees that grew near the lake. They tapped the maples for their sweet sap that they boiled down into maple syrup and maple sugar.

Oscar paused for a moment, turned the page of the newspaper, and continued.

As the bur oak tree grew through its infancy and began peeking above the tall prairie grasses that surrounded it, few people saw it. The occasional Indian passed by on the well-worn trail but a few feet from where the bur oak grew, and even a French fur trader hiked by once, apparently lost as he searched for the Fox River to the southeast. In 1839, a great prairie fire swept across this part of what was to become Ames County, sending up enormous clouds of acrid smoke that filled the air. During the midst of the fire, which finally stopped at the waters of Link Lake, the smoke obscured the sun. Many of the shrubs and trees died in the fire, but not the bur oak. Its corky bark protected it and the tree continued growing, even better than before, now more than a foot a year, as some of its competition for nutrients and water had been destroyed in the fire.

In 1840, a traveling band of Menominee Indians, who had regularly traveled the old trail, stopped in the scant shade of the 10-year-old bur oak, now some 12 feet tall. They walked around the tree, inspecting it from every direction. And they noticed that no other trees grew nearby. So this bur oak tree became a trail marker for them as they traveled from their trapping grounds to the trading post on the Fox River several miles to the south.

In 1848, when the bur tree was 18 years old and had been a trail marker for but eight years, the Menominee, heavily pressured by the federal government, negotiated a treaty that ceded all of their lands to the United States. After some serious discussions and a refusal of the Menominee to move to a reservation in Minnesota, an agreement was reached between the Indians and the government that the Menominee would be settled on a reservation near what is now Shawano, Wisconsin. As a result, thousands of acres of once Indian land was now ready for surveying and then for sale at $1.25 per acre.

In 1852, Increase Joseph Link, a preacher from New York State, along with a group of his followers called the Standalone Fellowship founded the Village of Link Lake and gave both the village and the lake the name of their leader. A year after the Standalone Fellowship founded the Link Lake community, Increase Joseph had a surprise visitor. A tall Menominee Indian appeared at his cabin door one day and introduced himself as Kee-chee-new. The two men shook hands. Kee-chee-new was a tall, fine-featured man with high cheekbones and a prominent nose.

The Indian said to Increase Joseph, "We camped by this lake for many years, our men and women and children. We camped by this big lake on our journey from the trapping lands to the west on our way to the river called Fox and the trading post there. Today I come to show you something. Something long important to the Menominee making the long journey from the valley of the great river to the west where we trap to the trading post on the river called Fox."

Increase Joseph followed the tall Indian to the top of a hill, just outside the Village of Link Lake.

"See this big tree?" asked Kee-chee-new. "See the trail nearby?"

"I've seen this bur oak tree many times," said Increase Joseph. "And I too have walked the trail that goes by it, a trail worn deep in the soil from the many hundreds who have passed this way over the years."

"This is a marker tree," explained Kee-chee-new. "It points the way to the trading post on the Fox River. Before the tree showed us the way, our people often got confused and traveled long distances trying to find the trading post. With the trail marker tree, they are shown the way."

Kee-chee-new ran his hand along the tree's corky bark.

"This is a sacred tree. It must always be protected. It has a special meaning for my tribe. You are a religious man; do you understand what I am saying?"

"I do," said Increase Joseph. "And I will do everything in my power to make certain that no one ever cuts down this tree or in any other way harms it."

Later that day, Increase Joseph stopped by the blacksmith shop in Link Lake. "I want you to make me a little sign," Increase Joseph said to the blacksmith. "I want it to read, 'Trail Marker Oak. A sacred tree.'"

From 1853 until the present time, the little metal sign has marked the location of the Trail Marker Oak.

"Well, that's it," said Oscar, as he folded the newspaper and reached for his cane that he had leaned against a chair. "That's the story of the Trail Marker Oak, a very special tree in our history, and in so many ways a very special tree yet today."

Emily Higgins stood up. "A round of applause for Oscar. We all need to be reminded from time to time about our histories and how important they can be for us today. Clearly, the Trail Marker Oak is one of those prized pieces of history for our village. That brings our April meeting to a close; we'll see you all at the cemetery walk. Bring your friends and hope for good weather."

8
Cemetery Walk

*W*WRI, the radio station in Willow River, ran public service announcements about the cemetery walk for a couple weeks. The *Ames County Argus* ran a long story with several photos in its most recent issue. One of the TV stations in Green Bay sent a reporter and film crew to Link Lake. They interviewed both Emily Higgins, who explained the history of the event, and Mayor Jessup, who said, "We must commend the Link Lake Historical Society for helping us remember the important people who made Link Lake what it is today."

Emily thought, *The mayor said the right words, but he really doesn't believe them.* Emily was quite certain the mayor, along with Marilyn Jones and the majority of the members of the Link Lake Economic Development Council, believed the historical society was made up of those opposed to change and was more of a hindrance than an asset to the community. But she also believed that beyond those who were members of the historical society, a goodly number of the residents of Link Lake and the surrounding communities appreciated the work of the historical society and supported its many activities and were especially pleased that the organization was helping people learn about the community's history and preserving historical buildings and other historical artifacts in the community.

The last Saturday in April dawned clear and sunny, one of those days that people talk about when they describe what spring can be like in central Wisconsin. It was an ideal day for a cemetery walk, or anything else outdoors, for that matter. Promptly at 10:00 a.m., Henrietta O'Malley, the head waitress at the Eat Well Café and a longtime member of the historical society, welcomed the fifty or so people who turned out for the walk, reminding them that they had a treat in store as they become acquainted with the historical figures who made Link Lake what it is today.

"Members of our historical society have taken the roles of the people we are commemorating, dressing as these people dressed and sharing something of their lives," she explained. "We will divide the group into three smaller groups, so people can hear and see more easily. And each group will have an opportunity to visit all the sites."

Henrietta quickly organized the groups—young people and older people, parents with children, local people and those from as far away as the Fox River Valley.

"Group one, please follow me to the grave of Increase Joseph Link, the founder of the Village of Link Lake," said Henrietta as she turned and began walking to the first grave site on the walk. A historical society volunteer led each of the other two groups, who went to other locations.

As he had done from the time of the first cemetery walk, Oscar Anderson played the role of Pastor Increase Joseph Link. Increase Joseph, as he was fondly called, always dressed in black from his black shoes to his black hat, and that's the way Oscar Anderson was dressed today. When everyone had gathered around, Oscar began. He stood in front of Increase Joseph's headstone, a simple stone with the following words inscribed on it:

Increase Joseph Link
Born 1826
Died 1893
A man of the cloth
Founder of Link Lake, Wisconsin

Oscar Anderson held a red book in his hand, as was the style of Increase Joseph, who always preached while waving a red book. In a loud, deep voice that carried well beyond the confines of the Link Lake Cemetery, Oscar intoned:

"We are each of us like the giant oaks that we see just outside this meeting place. The oak lives in harmony with its neighbors, the aspen, the maple, and the pine, as we each must learn to live with those who are different from us.

"We must learn to live in harmony with the Norwegians and Welsh, the Swedes and the Danes, the Irish and the English, the Poles and the Germans, and the Indians, too, like my friend, Chief Kee-chee-new of the Menominee. All are our neighbors.

"We must learn to live with those whose work is different from ours. We must learn to live with those who worship in ways foreign to us. There is one God, and he is concerned about all of us, no matter how we choose to honor him. He wants us to prosper, wants us to get along with each other, but first he wants us to respect the land. We must always remember that the land comes first. We must learn how to take care of the land or we all shall perish."

When Oscar finished, the group clapped loudly. Several people had questions, and Oscar, staying in his role as Increase Joseph, answered them.

"What religious denomination did you belong to?"

"We called ourselves the Standalones, meaning we were independent of all other organized religions," said Oscar.

"How did you travel to Wisconsin?"

"By steamboat on the Great Lakes and then overland by wagon after we reached Sheboygan," answered Oscar.

Henrietta interrupted, "To stay on time, we must move on." The group next arrived at the grave site of Henry Bakken, the editor of Link Lake's first newspaper, the *Link Lake Gazette*. Billy Baxter, the middle-aged and balding editor of the *Ames County Argus*, wearing a striped vest, as Bakken had always done, took the role of the village's first editor. When people were all gathered, Baxter began:

"My name is Henry Bakken, and I came with Increase Joseph Link from Plum Falls, New York, arriving in the wilds of Wisconsin in 1852. I started the village's first newspaper, which everyone in the community read and enjoyed. Increase Joseph and I were good friends—we traveled throughout Wisconsin as Increase Joseph spread his message of taking care of the land. We traveled to the far corners of this great state, to the wheat growing areas and to where the great pine trees grew. We learned of the Underground Railroad and aided its mission of helping black slaves travel to Canada in the late 1850s. We visited Peshtigo during the time when the great fire killed so many of their citizens in 1871. Increase Joseph Link was a great friend, a great preacher, and a man of the land."

Once more a rousing round of applause as the group moved on to the next grave site, that of Fred and Barbara Jones, the original owners and operators of the Link Lake Supper Club and the parents of Marilyn Jones, current owner of the supper club. Fred Russo played the role of Fred; Emily was Barbara Jones.

"My name is Fred Jones, and I was born in 1919," began Fred Russo, who was dressed in a suit and tie. "My wife, Barbara, and I," Fred gestured toward Emily, who was standing next to him, "opened the Link Lake Supper Club in 1955. She will tell you something about the history of the supper club, which was not much to look at in 1955 and had been closed for several years when we bought it. Barbara and I had vacationed in Link Lake before buying the supper club. In fact we were married in Increase Joseph Community Park in 1943 — in the midst of World War II. Both of our daughters, Gloria, who was born in 1944, and Marilyn, who was born in 1954, helped us at the supper club. Unfortunately we had a family squabble in 1966 and Gloria moved to California. Marilyn continued working with us and took over the operation of the supper club in 1973, after we were both killed in a car accident. At the time of our deaths, I was 54 and Barbara was 53. We were both active in the Link Lake Historical Society from the time we moved here in 1955 until the time of our deaths. And now, let's hear from my wife, Barbara, to learn her side of the story."

Emily, wearing a skirt and a smart navy-blue blazer, looked out over the crowd. She began in her characteristic loud voice, "I was born in Chicago in 1920, and, like Fred and his family, we vacationed here in Link Lake when we were kids. It was here in Link Lake that I met Fred, and as he has pointed out, we were married right here in Link Lake, in front of the famous Trail Marker Oak.

"After we married we kept coming here on vacation, and we remember driving by an old building located right on the lake, an interesting looking building, but badly in need of repair. We stopped at the Link Lake Historical Museum and there met Emily Higgins, who told us the history of the old dilapidated building. Emily was in her early twenties at the time and a volunteer at the museum store, if I remember correctly. She explained that the old building had been a tavern, a roadhouse, and stagecoach stop on the way from Waupaca to Willow River. Once we learned of its rich history, we decided to buy the place, restore it, and turn it into a supper club. The supper club is steeped in history—more than most people know. Fred and I enjoyed our years at the supper club, and we especially enjoyed living in Link Lake, which is so rich with history."

Emily bowed deeply and everyone clapped. The tour continued, recognizing several other Link Lake citizens, each depicted by a current member of the historical society. The walk took more than an hour, as the three groups visited each site. When everyone had visited all of the sites, the entire group got together once more. Henrietta passed around a bucket into which those attending were encouraged to offer a donation. She thanked everyone for coming and invited them to come to the Link Lake bank robbery reenactment, which was planned for May. Then she said everyone was welcome to enjoy apple cider and cookies at the Link Lake Historical Museum.

9

Ambrose, Ranger, and Buster

Somewhat in response to his doctor's admonition to slow down, Ambrose had plowed and planted only five acres of oats this year. In past years he had put in ten acres. Now in May, with the oat crop up and growing, he worked at planting his garden; this time both his dog, Buster, and Ranger, the raccoon, were with him, "helping" him with the job at hand.

"Well, fellows, what's going to sell well in the vegetable stand this year?" he asked. Both animals looked at him like they understood the question. He planted a long row of radishes, another long row of leaf lettuce, and ten rows of potatoes—three of early red ones, and the rest of late potatoes. Ambrose had started about fifty tomato plants from seed back in late March, and he would hold off setting out the tomatoes until the end of the month, when he was reasonably sure that a late frost wasn't still up Mother Nature's sleeve.

After lunch and an hour's nap, Ambrose and his "helpers" were once more out in the garden continuing to plant cabbages, broccoli, sweet corn—three different varieties that would mature at different times—a long row of sunflowers, and an equally long row of ornamental corn, which always sold well. He would hold off on planting squash, cucumbers, and pumpkins until he set out the tomatoes. These vine crop seeds always germinated so much better when the soil was warmer.

As Ambrose worked in his garden, the question of his long-held secret nagged at him. "Okay, you guys. When do I let the world know that old Ambrose Adler isn't the strange, out-of-date, stuttering farmer that everyone thinks he is?" Buster wagged his tail, and Ranger held out his paws, as he often did when Ambrose talked to him.

"So you don't know either?" asked Ambrose. "How will I know when the time is right? I may not have that much time left." Buster continued wagging his tail, and Ranger looked straight at Ambrose. Ambrose bent over and petted both the dog and the raccoon.

"Well, if we're gonna finish planting this garden today, we'd better get back at it," said Ambrose. The two animals continued watching as Ambrose worked under the warm May sun.

10
Marilyn Jones

On a bright and sunny early May day, Marilyn sat in her office at the supper club, thinking back to when she first began running the place. She remembered so well the day her life changed completely: it was September 25, 1973, and she was a sophomore at Ripon College. As she left the lecture room that Tuesday morning, her roommate, Jesse, met her at the door. "Someone from the main office just called and said you should stop by the office as soon as possible."

Marilyn immediately wondered what she had done wrong. She knew that she had been partying a little too much, and that her grades weren't much above a C average. But what had she done to trigger a summons to the main office "as soon as possible"?

She walked across campus thinking about what kind of trouble she must be in and what the possible punishment might be. And she wondered how she would break the news to her parents, who were counting on her to do well and to help them manage the supper club when she graduated. The Joneses had spent all their savings on enlarging, modernizing, and refurbishing the supper club, turning it into a popular place for locals and tourists alike.

Marilyn had been helping out at the supper club ever since she was three or four years old, and by the time she was in high school, she was waiting on tables and doing all kinds of odd jobs around the place. During the summers she worked there full-time. It wasn't a bad summer job—her parents even paid her a salary. But she would have preferred going out with her friends and spending some time away from the supper club.

She pulled open the main office door, walked up to the counter, and in a quiet voice said, "My name is Marilyn Jones, and I was told you needed to see me."

"Oh, Marilyn, thank you so much for coming by so promptly," said the secretary behind the counter, a gray-haired and very friendly woman. "Dr. Sykes is waiting to talk with you. His office is the first one down the hall."

Marilyn's head was still filled with worry about what she had done wrong as she knocked on the closed door. "Come right in," she heard.

"I'm Marilyn Jones."

"I'm Dr. Sykes," the plumpish, round-faced man on the other side of a rather cluttered desk said. "Please be seated." He pointed to a chair that sat alongside his desk.

Dr. Sykes took off his glasses, put them on the desk, and then looked right at Marilyn and said, "I'm afraid I have bad news for you."

Marilyn steeled herself for the worst. Would she be placed on academic probation? Had her partying gone too far, and was she going to receive a reprimand of some type? But what she heard was beyond anything she expected.

"We've just learned that your parents have been killed in a car accident," Dr. Sykes said quietly. "It happened at nine this morning on Highway 22, just north of Montello."

"What did you say?" Marilyn asked, hoping she had not heard correctly.

Dr. Sykes repeated, this time a bit more slowly. "Your parents were both killed in a car accident this morning."

"Oh, no. Oh, no. That can't be true. It must be someone else. Are you sure?" blurted out Marilyn, her blue eyes filling with tears.

"It's true, Marilyn. I stand ready to help you in any way I can—you just need to tell me how."

"It's not true. It's not true," Marilyn cried, pounding her hands on Dr. Sykes's desk, knocking one of the piles of papers to the floor. But when she looked into Dr. Sykes's sad face, she knew it was true.

Late that afternoon she tried to call her sister, Gloria, ten years her senior, to tell her of their parents' death and to ask her advice on funeral arrangements and what she should do with the supper club. Since she left for California in 1966 after a big family fight, Gloria had not once called or written to either of her parents or to Marilyn—not on their birthdays, not at Christmas, never. Marilyn thought she had moved to Los Angeles, but that city and the suburbs had no listing for a Gloria Jones.

Three days later, after Fred and Barbara Jones's obituary was published in the *Ames County Argus*, Marilyn received a phone call.

"This is Gloria," the voice on the other end said, "your sister. I read about our parents dying in a car accident. I won't be coming to the funeral—you probably guessed that."

"I . . . I was hoping you'd come," said Marilyn.

"Well, I won't be there. If you are concerned about who gets the supper club, it's yours. I want no part of it. I assume you have an attorney. Have him send me the necessary papers and I'll sign them so you have clear title." Gloria then gave Marilyn a Los Angeles post office box number and hung up.

And so at age nineteen, Marilyn Jones arranged for the funeral of her parents with services at the Church of the Holy Redeemed, a church that they dearly loved and where Marilyn and Gloria had attended Sunday school. She thought long and hard about what to do with the Link Lake Supper Club and finally decided to drop out of school and take over the management of the place. After all, she knew the ins and outs of the supper club as well as her parents did, having worked there since she was a little kid. She shared this information with the family's attorney, William Glaser, when she met with him to discuss her parents' estate.

"Are you sure that's what you want to do? Running a business is not all fun and games," cautioned Glaser. "What about your sister? Is she interested?"

"No, Gloria said I can do whatever I want, that it's mine. She said to send the necessary papers to a Los Angeles post office number and she'd sign them giving me clear title."

"I'll do that and I'll also help you get started managing the place, especially with the legal work. And I won't charge you a dime. Your folks were excellent clients," said Glaser.

"Thank you, I'll need all the help I can get."

Now, forty-two years later, Marilyn thought about her parents as she saw the headline "Link Lake Cemetery Walk a Perennial Hit" in the new issue of the *Ames County Argus*.

What a bunch of foolishness, she thought. *Who cares about a bunch of dead people? Just who in the world cares? Certainly not me.* She knew her parents were recognized on these walks, but she never attended. In fact she disagreed with the whole idea. *When are these people going to quit focusing on the past and begin thinking about the future? It's the future we should be worrying about. Forget the past. We can't do anything about it anyway. But we can do something about the future.*

She could never understand or accept that her parents had once been active in the Link Lake Historical Society. *I'm sure they must have had better things to do with their time. I should tell Emily Higgins to remove them from the cemetery tour.*

As Marilyn read the article, it was mentioned that the Link Lake Historical Society's many activities attract people to Link Lake and remind the local citizens of their history and its importance. *How silly. How many people go on a cemetery walk, fifty or so? And half of them live here. How can anyone call that important?*

Yet for all her protests that people should forget about the past, a quiet voice in Marilyn's head reminded her that she too wanted to be remembered—that she had made important contributions to Link Lake, like her parents before her. That voice seemed to grow louder with each passing day. She was hoping that her hard work with the Economic Development Council would vault her to the top of the list of Link Lake's most important citizens.

The Link Lake Economic Development Council had met monthly since Marilyn and the mayor organized it in 2008 when the Great Recession was sweeping across the country. Unfortunately the meetings had yielded little. Since the defeat of the council's efforts to bring the Big R restaurant chain to Link Lake, the council had not accomplished much and seemed to be losing steam.

Marilyn Jones

On this cool and cloudy spring day, as she waited for the council's next meeting, Marilyn thought about how she had gotten to where she was. And she thought about how Link Lake had changed since she was a little girl growing up there and working for her parents at the supper club.

She recalled that the stores in town, the saloons, and the churches seemed to be thriving during the late 1950s and into the early 1960s—and the supper club, where she had spent so much time working with her parents, had done very well in those years. She remembered riding her bike past the village population sign that noted eight hundred residents then.

Today as she thought about the economy of the village when she was a kid, she realized it had depended on the farmers living in the area who bought supplies and equipment in town. And she also knew the farmers had depended on the village as a market for their milk and produce. By the 1960s, everything had begun to change dramatically. Farms got larger and more and bigger equipment arrived. The small farms began disappearing and young people left the country for work in the urban areas. Electricity, tractors, grain combines, forage harvesters, hybrid seeds, commercial fertilizers, and chemical pesticides arrived on the farm. Television, indoor plumbing, and central heating made farm life comparable to what city folk had long taken for granted. Today only a handful of active farms remained in the Link Lake community. Marilyn's friend Lucas Drake and his wife owned and operated one of them—a one-thousand-acre corn and soybean operation. Unlike those large commercial farms, Ambrose Adler's farm remained at 160 acres and had embraced almost none of the agricultural and cultural advances that were sweeping across the country. But Marilyn thought Adler was a strange old man who was trying to hang on to the past. She had nothing but disdain for him.

Marilyn remembered when the old gristmill ceased operation, and soon after that, the cheese factory closed. Then it was the hardware store and the lumber yard and feed store that slammed shut their doors. Soon the Link Lake Mercantile stood empty, as did the pharmacy and meat market. The churches struggled to survive. Marilyn recalled attending one-room country school Christmas programs with her parents and watching the little farm kids perform on a makeshift stage—some of them quite good, many not so much. By the mid-1960s all of these schools were closed, and the Christmas programs were no more. Marilyn remembered farm kids in her Link Lake Elementary School classes, bussed in from the country after their community schools closed.

Two small manufacturing industries moved into the village sometime in the 1960s; one made plastic toys—the kind found in vending machines—and the other manufactured premium airplane propellers for the growing private plane owners. But still the village mostly depended on the nearby farmers for most of its economy.

Once again, Link Lake was in transition, even though some of the residents had difficulty accepting the changes. The businesspeople surely were feeling the results of the revolution in agriculture that was occurring. Even the Link Lake Tap felt the pinch, especially during the winter months when the tourist trade was slim to none. But their businesses picked up again in summer as Link Lake moved from a farm service center to a tourist town.

One of the outstanding features of the village was its location on Link Lake, some eight miles long and a mile or two wide and rich with natural beauty, not to mention northern pike, bass, and assorted pan fish. Today it seemed like every month a new condominium appeared on the shores of Link Lake, or a vacation home for the well-to-do from the cities. These developments were good for Marilyn's business, as many of these new people often ate at her supper club.

In some ways, Link Lake's draw for tourist money kept it alive, if not thriving. Some of the former businesses had been able to change with the times. The Mercantile became an antique store. The former pharmacy became the Eat Well Café, the once hardware store a gift shop, the old bank a historical museum, and the lumberyard a furniture and carpet store catering especially to those with high-end second homes on Link Lake and other lakes in Ames County and beyond.

But when the twenty-first century arrived, the business climate in Link Lake was once more severely challenged. The plastic toy factory, without warning, closed and laid off the thirty people who worked there, leaving behind a vacant building. Six months later, the airplane propeller factory closed and another twenty people lost their jobs. Today, Marilyn knew that the only major employers left in Link Lake were the nursing home and the assisted living center, the school system, and her Link Lake Supper Club.

By 2007 the Great Recession had begun to take hold, and Link Lake felt it as much or more than most communities. Many of those former employees of the defunct propeller and toy factories had gotten jobs in the Fox Valley, making the long commute each day, but now they were out of work again, surviving on unemployment payments and food stamps.

Marilyn Jones had seen a 20 percent drop in her income at the supper club as well. But rather than wring her hands and lament the bad luck she and everyone else seemed to be experiencing, she and the mayor called a meeting of the remaining business leaders in the community and organized the Link Lake Economic Development Council.

"God helps those who help themselves," she proclaimed at an early meeting of the council. "We will bring jobs to Link Lake, no matter what it takes." She received a rousing round of applause from the group with these words, which at least suggested some hope for the dire situation in which the village was mired. She was unanimously voted chair of the council that same night.

But Marilyn was disappointed that the Economic Development Council had had little success bringing jobs to Link Lake. Indeed, she knew it would not be the council's successes or future plans that most people would re-member and talk about, but its failures—in particular the defeat of the council's efforts to bring a fast food business to Link Lake. Up until that fiasco, Marilyn and the other council members had mostly ignored the Link Lake Historical Society or saw it as a social outlet for the older people in the community, who had little else to do than reminisce about earlier days. To a hard-charging businessperson, which was how some people described Marilyn Jones, the Link Lake Historical Society was irrelevant to the community. Marilyn had learned differently in 2009.

Now Marilyn was ready to call a special meeting of the Economic De-velopment Council, one open to the public. She was about to make an announcement to the world, as she would tell everyone something that would have far-reaching positive effects on the community.

11

Economic Development Council

Marilyn walked into the community room at the Link Lake Library with her head high and confidence in her step. "I have good news for you," she said as she called the regular monthly meeting of the Link Lake Economic Development Council to order. "It's been a long struggle to bring jobs to Link Lake and put our community on a stronger economic footing," Marilyn continued. She paused for a moment. She wanted the full impact of her words to be heard by the small collection of businesspeople, large-scale farmers, and other interested people in the community who were in attendance. For the last several years, the only words the council members had heard over and over were "We're open for business"—to the point that some businesspeople simply didn't attend anymore.

"Mayor Jessup and I have had extended conversations with the Alstage Sand Mining Company of La Crosse," Marilyn said, speaking slowly and loudly enough so all could hear.

"Yesterday I heard from Emerson Evans, vice president of the company. Alstage engineers found a sizable seam of high-quality sand right here in Link Lake that will prove profitable to us, bring jobs to our community, bring much-needed money to the village's coffers, and, I must say, put Link Lake on the map."

Emily Higgins quickly raised her hand.

"Why haven't we heard about this mining company before? Where are they planning to locate their mine? When? And is a mine what Link Lake needs? I've heard sand mining can be rather hard on the environment and there are potential health hazards as well," she blurted out in rapid-fire fashion.

"Well, Emily," Marilyn began, trying to avoid showing her disgust with the questions, "the reason you or no one else has heard about this is because the mayor and I just learned yesterday that the mine is a real possibility for our community. We didn't want to talk about it until we knew for sure that they were interested. Now we know they are."

"And what about where and when?"

"Those answers will have to wait a bit—until we negotiate a bit more with the Alstage people."

"When will we know?" asked Emily, her face a little redder than it was before."

"Soon, Emily. Soon. Be a little patient, okay?"

Emily sat down, but from the look on her face, she was clearly not happy with what she was hearing, or how Marilyn Jones had responded to her inquiries. Most members of the development council knew the long, difficult history between Emily Higgins and Marilyn Jones. Each had quite different ideas of where Link Lake ought to be headed and how it should arrive there. Nearly twenty-five years separated the two women—Emily was born in 1930, Marilyn, in 1954. Emily remembered when Marilyn was a little girl helping out her folks at the supper club that they had opened when they moved from Chicago. Emily considered Marilyn a spoiled, mouthy brat when she was a little kid—and had never changed her opinion of the businesswoman who earned a handsome living from the supper club that she now owned. And Marilyn considered Emily an old woman lost in the past and a troublesome menace to any forward-looking ideas the community might explore.

Marilyn had tipped off Billy Baxter of the *Ames County Argus* that he might want to attend the meeting, as the council had some important news to share with the community. Baxter raised his hand next.

"I hate to share my ignorance," he began, "but I don't know much about sand mining. About all I know is that 'fracking sand' has become quite a valuable commodity. By the way, I use the word 'fracking' advisedly as with only a slight slip of the tongue another rather popular F word slips out."

Baxter's last comment evoked a chuckle from the group, which for the most part was nearly completely humorless.

"I do have some information that the Alstage Sand Mining Company has shared with the mayor and me," Marilyn replied. "Are you interested in hearing some of it?"

"I'm all ears," said Baxter, as he flipped open his notebook.

Marilyn turned, retrieved her briefcase, and extracted several sheets of paper. She glanced through the notes and then began.

"This special sand is used for a process called hydraulic fracturing, which is a way of releasing natural gas from shale deposits. The process is not new—it goes back to the late 1940s." She looked up before continuing. Council members as well as Billy Baxter appeared to want more information.

"The fracking process, as it is called," she said with just a hint of a smile on her face, "has recently been used in eastern states such as New York and Pennsylvania as well as in North Dakota, Colorado, and Wyoming. The process uses enormous amounts of a special sand that we have in Wisconsin and have right here in Link Lake. Sand mines are flourishing in La Crosse, Barron, Chippewa, and Monroe counties. And talk about jobs: a sand mining operation near Tomah employs forty-three workers earning $18.00 an hour." Marilyn put her notes back in her briefcase.

"The Alstage Sand Mining Company operation here in Link Lake has the potential for being larger than the one in Tomah. We could have as many as seventy-five new jobs coming to our community," she said.

Council members were looking at each other and nodding their heads in approval.

Marilyn summarized, "After several years of misfired attempts of bringing economic development and jobs to Link Lake, it appears our community is on course for a brighter future."

A round of applause greeted the comment. Emily Higgins was not clapping. Lucas Drake held up his hand.

"Yes, Lucas," Marilyn said as she recognized her longtime supporter and friend.

Drake stood up. "I want to personally commend you and Mayor Jessup for your interest in the future of the Link Lake community and especially for promoting the community's economic health. Nothing is more important to a community than its economic health—said more plainly, lots of jobs. Everything else must take a backseat. History, environmental concerns, historic preservation—all are of lesser importance. Without a strong economy we have nothing."

Members of the Economic Development Council clapped as Lucas Drake sat back down. Emily Higgins shook her head in silent disagreement.

12

Ambrose and Gloria

Ambrose Adler sat on his porch with Ranger and Buster, thinking about what might have been. He remembered that summer day when he stopped at the library after making his purchases at the Link Lake Mercantile. He noticed a new assistant librarian working behind the checkout desk. At first he didn't recognize her, but then he realized that it was Gloria Jones, daughter of the owners of the Link Lake Supper Club. He remembered Gloria as a skinny, rather unattractive girl, whom he had seen on occasion when he came to Link Lake. A few years ago, he'd read in the *Argus* about Gloria graduating from Link Lake High School and then attending the University of Wisconsin in Madison with majors in journalism and English.

Gloria, now twenty-one and newly graduated, had just been hired to work at the library. She had grown up to be a beauty, at least in the eyes of thirty-two-year-old Ambrose Adler.

"How are you, Ambrose?" Gloria asked when he approached the desk to check out a couple books. Like everyone else in Link Lake, she knew Ambrose by sight, if for no other reason than he was the only person who traveled to town with a team of horses to do his shopping.

"I . . . I . . . am okay," said Ambrose, his face red both from his efforts to speak clearly and because he was overwhelmed by this beautiful young woman standing in front of him, with her short black hair, slightly turned-up nose, and the most beautiful brown eyes he had ever seen.

"Do you do a lot of reading?" Gloria asked.

"I . . . I . . . do," said Ambrose, trying his best to speak but finding it even more difficult than usual.

Ambrose and Gloria

In the weeks that followed, when Ambrose came to town, sometimes with a few sacks of corn and oats to be ground at the mill for their few milk cows or to pick up some supplies at the mercantile, he spent an increasing amount of time at the library, talking with Gloria. One sunny spring day Gloria asked Ambrose if he would like to share lunch with her. She had packed extra sandwiches with the hope that they might eat together.

"I . . . I'd like that," said Ambrose, who had discovered that when he was with Gloria, he stuttered far less than usual. At a picnic table under a big maple tree that shaded the library, Ambrose and Gloria shared ham sandwiches, dill pickles, and apple pie. Ambrose could not recall when he had ever been happier—he had been rejected and shunned by nearly everyone except his parents, yet he was now in the company of the most beautiful young woman in Link Lake.

A week later, when Ambrose stopped at the library, Gloria asked him if he'd like to see a movie at the outdoor movie theater in Willow River. "*The Sound of Music* is playing, with Julie Andrews," she said.

"Y . . . yes," Ambrose stammered. "But I don't have a car."

Gloria laughed. "I know that. But I've got one, and I'll pick you up at seven on Saturday night. Would that be okay?"

"It would," said Ambrose, smiling. He had never gone to a movie with a girl before and had never been to an outdoor theater. Promptly at seven on Saturday, Gloria pulled into the driveway at the Adler farm, where Ambrose was standing on the porch waiting for her arrival. He wore his best pants and shirt.

"You look nice," Gloria said when Ambrose climbed into her car.

"So do you. Nice car," Ambrose said.

"Got it as a present from my parents when I graduated from college. It's a 1965 Ford. Do you know about cars, Ambrose?"

"N . . . no, we never had a car."

When they arrived at the drive-in movie, Gloria pulled up to the ticket booth, bought two tickets, then drove her car in a parking place pointed out to her by the parking attendant. She removed the little speaker from the post near her parking place and hung it on the edge of the car window.

"Well, we're all set," said Gloria, sitting back in her seat.

"B . . . big screen," said Ambrose as he looked up at the expanse of white fifty yards or so in front of them that was attached to a metal framework.

"You want some popcorn?" Gloria asked.

"Sure, but let me pay," said Ambrose as he dug in his pocket for some money.

Soon Gloria and Ambrose were eating popcorn and listening to "The hills are alive with the sound of music." Ambrose glanced at the car parked next to them and he saw a young couple that was clearly more interested in each other than in what was happening on the screen. He glanced at the car in the other direction and he noted the same thing, a young couple with their arms around each other, kissing. Then he felt Gloria's hand on his neck; it was warm and oh so pleasant. Gloria slowly moved her arm around his neck and then she was kissing him. It was the most wonderful feeling Ambrose had ever experienced. It was more wonderful than watching the most beautiful sunset, more wonderful then hearing the rain drumming on a barn roof in July, more wonderful than the smell of newly mown hay, more wonderful than anything he had ever experienced.

Driving home from the movie, they talked little. Gloria drove with one hand the entire way, her other hand on Ambrose's. When they arrived at the Adler farm, she pulled in the driveway, turned off the car's engine, and once more kissed him. Never before had he had feelings like this. How much he wished he could speak better so he could express himself.

"Thank you so much," he said when he got out of the car. He watched as Gloria backed out of the driveway and headed back toward Link Lake.

Gloria and Ambrose's courtship continued throughout that summer and into the fall of 1966. The young couple saw several more movies at the outdoor theater in Willow River, spent time swimming in Link Lake, and even went fishing once, something that Ambrose had done many times before with his father. Gloria had a small apartment, where she regularly cooked meals for Ambrose and entertained him on Saturday nights and often on Sunday afternoons when the library was closed and there was no farm work to command Ambrose's attention. One Saturday night, during a terrific rain and windstorm that knocked down trees and shut down the power in Link Lake for several hours, Gloria said it was too dangerous to drive back to the Adler farm and that Ambrose should spend the night at her apartment. Ambrose agreed and said he would sleep on the couch, but she insisted that he share her bed, which he did.

The following Sunday, Gloria fixed a special dinner for Ambrose. Gloria said she would drive out and pick up Ambrose, but he said he enjoyed the walk into town. When he arrived at her apartment and they were both enjoying a before-dinner glass of wine, Ambrose said, "I . . . have something to ask you."

"Yes, Ambrose?" Gloria replied, not knowing what his question would be.

"W . . . will you marry me?"

From his pocket, Ambrose retrieved a diamond ring. He held it up for Gloria to see.

"Oh, Ambrose. I will. I will," she cried, overwhelmed with the moment.

"It . . . was my grandmother's ring."

"It's beautiful." Tears of joy streamed down Gloria's face. She wrapped her arms around Ambrose and kissed him. "You have made me so happy."

Gloria and Ambrose told his parents of their plans to marry. The Adlers were thrilled with the idea. Just the opposite happened with Gloria's parents. Gloria knew that her parents, as prominent Link Lake businesspeople, had been concerned that their oldest daughter was "dating this strange man who couldn't speak and likely had a mental disorder." Gloria's father had also been listening to his younger daughter, Marilyn, who at age eleven had regularly informed him of Gloria and Ambrose's activities— and said she couldn't understand what her sister saw in this old guy who couldn't even speak his name properly.

At the dinner table one evening, the one time during the day when Marilyn and her parents sat together, Marilyn said, "Do you know what I heard from my friend Janie whose folks have an apartment in the same house where Gloria lives?"

"So what did Janie tell you?" asked Marilyn's father, Fred, who was accustomed to hearing all kinds of tales from his young daughter.

"It's about Ambrose and Gloria."

"Yes?" He stopped eating and looked at Marilyn.

"Ambrose spends lots of time with Gloria."

"Yes, your mother and I know that. I wish it wasn't happening. It's certainly not good for her reputation to be seen with that old dirt farmer."

"Remember that bad storm we had last week?"

"Sure, but what's that got to do with Ambrose and Gloria?"

"Janie said that Ambrose spent the night with Gloria. That she didn't drive him home like she usually did."

"She said that, huh?"

"Yes, and Janie never fibs either."

Marilyn's parents looked at each other, but said nothing.

"Thanks for letting us know," said Marilyn's father.

When Ambrose and Gloria told her parents of their plans to marry, Fred Jones lost his temper and yelled, "You'll marry that stuttering idiot farmer over my dead body."

Gloria burst into tears. Ambrose just stood silently with his head down and his hat in his hand, for he had heard comments like this since he was a little boy.

Gloria's father turned to Ambrose. "If you so much as come close to my daughter again, I will shoot you. Do you hear me?" Ambrose remained silent.

Since meeting Gloria for the first time in his life he had known happiness and the joy of being close to another person. Now, like a candle flame blown out, it all changed. He walked to the door, opened it, and started the long walk home. He hadn't felt this low since he was in first grade and his schoolmates taunted him about his speech defect.

The next day, Gloria drove out to the Adler farm, all of her belongings packed in her car.

"I am so sorry," said Gloria when Ambrose came to the door. "I'm afraid Dad meant what he said about hurting you if we stayed together, so I'm leaving."

"W . . . where are you going?"

"As far away as I can. To California," Gloria said between sobs. "Will you come with me?"

Ambrose said nothing for a long time. "I . . . can't. Pa needs me here. This is my home."

"Oh, Ambrose. I will miss you so much," said Gloria, choosing not to question his decision.

"Goodbye," said Ambrose, tears running down his face.

They embraced one final time. Ambrose watched as Gloria's car disappeared down the Adler driveway. A cloud of dust remained for several minutes.

After a few weeks in California, Gloria got a job as an entry-level reporter for the *Los Angeles Journal.* She never told her parents or her sister where she worked. And she planned to never return to Link Lake.

The sound of an automobile turning into his driveway broke into Ambrose's thoughts about Gloria. He saw Emily Higgins get out of her 1985 Chevrolet and march up to his porch door. It was clear she had something serious on her mind. Ambrose opened the door for her.

"I can't stay to talk, Ambrose, but I've called a special meeting of the historical society for tomorrow afternoon. I hope you can be there."

"I . . . I can." Ambrose wondered what was going on but didn't have a chance to ask.

Emily turned, walked quickly back to her car, and was on her way.

Wonder what that's all about? thought Ambrose.

13

Historical Society Meeting

More than thirty-five members of the Link Lake Historical Society filled the museum's meeting room when Emily Higgins called out in a loud voice, "May I have your attention, please?" In an instant the room was so quiet that you could hear a chair squeak.

"Most of you who read the *Argus* are aware that our Economic Development Council has been in discussions with the Alstage Sand Mining Company of La Crosse, and that the company has its eye on the Link Lake community for the development of a new sand mine."

Heads were nodding. The news of Alstage's interest had spread rapidly throughout the community. As was typical, about half of the people in Link Lake thought it was a great idea and the other half had concerns about having a sand mine so close by.

"I have just learned," Emily said, catching her breath, "that the Alstage Sand Mining Company plans to open their sand mine in Increase Joseph Community Park."

A gasp went up from the audience. Members of the historical society knew the park's history and couldn't imagine that any commercial development would ever take place there.

"And even worse," she continued, "rumor has it that the company plans to build a road into the park and they want to cut down the Trail Marker Oak, which would stand in their way."

"They can't do that," said someone from the back of the room.

"I'm afraid they can," said Emily, "if the village board votes approval of building a sand mine in the park. Why, for heaven's sake, locate a sand mine in the park in the first place, you might ask? Why not somewhere else? Well, word is that the village will not only gain with more jobs, but they will receive a percentage of the revenue from sales of the sand. Since the Great Recession, the village's budget has suffered. The village board sees the sand mine as solving all of their problems." Emily had a heavy tone of sarcasm in her voice, for she had little faith in the village board and, in her mind, their often misguided decision making.

The meeting went on for more than an hour with people lamenting the possibility of losing the Trail Marker Oak and several suggesting strategies to save the famous old tree.

"Let's hold off a bit until I learn more," Emily said. "I plan to meet with Billy Baxter at the *Ames County Argus* tomorrow as a first step." With that she adjourned the meeting, although several people stayed on to talk about the possibility of a sand mine coming to Link Lake and what that would mean for the future of the village.

*E*mily Higgins showed up at the offices of the *Ames County Argus* in Willow River the next morning. Her face was red and she had fire in her eyes. In recent years Baxter had gained a renewed respect for older people who stood up for what they believed and weren't reluctant to speak their minds. Emily Higgins surely fit into the category.

"Have you heard the latest about the Alstage Sand Mining Company?" she blurted out. There was no hello, no good morning, no how are you.

"Good morning, Emily," Baxter said. "And how are you this fine morning?"

"You hear where they're going to locate the sand mine?" she said, as if she had not heard Baxter's greeting.

"Well, I did hear that the village of Link Lake plans to lease part of their park to the mining company," Baxter said, wondering what else he didn't know about the mining company's plans and deciding he'd better get busy and find out more.

"They are planning to cut down the Trail Marker Oak," Emily cried. "They . . . are . . . planning . . . to . . . cut . . . down . . . the . . . Trail Marker Oak," she repeated slowly.

"I must say I don't know much about the Trail Marker Oak," Baxter said.

"You don't know . . . you don't know the history of the Trail Marker Oak?" Emily could scarcely speak, she was so agitated.

"Should I?"

"Well," she said, lifting her eyebrows. "Your paper ran a long story about that famous and very historical tree in 1952."

"That was a bit before my time," he said quietly.

"Well, don't you read back issues of your paper?"

"Well, no, not often. I have lots of other stuff to do."

"Well, you'd better dig out that 1952 issue and bring yourself up to date, Mr. Billy Baxter, because whether you know it or not, there's a big story brewing and the Trail Marker Oak is the heart of it."

"And why do you believe that?"

"Because . . . because that damned Alstage Sand Mining company wants to cut it down. That's why," she said. Her face was even redder than when she first entered the *Argus* offices.

"Oh," is all Baxter could think to say. He was not accustomed to being challenged by red-faced older women.

"I shall keep you informed of developments," Emily said as she turned on her heel and exited Baxter's office, leaving him feeling like he did when a windstorm ripped the roof off the newspaper offices a few years ago.

He poured a fresh cup of coffee and took the stairs to the basement, where he kept the newspaper archives. In a few minutes he was reading the 1952 issue where the story of the Trail Marker Oak appeared on page two. *I wonder if the Alstage Mining Company knows all of this history,* he thought as he read about the old oak.

14
When Ambrose's Life
Changed

*A*fter returning home from the historical society meeting, Ambrose un-
hitched the team from the wagon, removed the harnesses from his horses,
and led them into their stalls in the barn. He put some fresh hay in front
of them and then returned to his house. He started the cookstove in the
kitchen and brewed a fresh pot of coffee. He was furious with what he had
learned at the historical society meeting. *What was the village board thinking?*
Don't they know the potential hazards of having a sand mine so close to a
village? And have they no respect for history? To think that they are considering
cutting down the Trail Marker Oak, a major piece of Link Lake's past.
Questions swirled around Ambrose's mind as he listened to the coffee pot
heating up on the cookstove.

As if able to sense his master's anger and frustration, Ranger rubbed up
against Ambrose's pant leg, making a purring sound.

"What do you think, Ranger? Would this be a good time to let people
know who I really am and what I've been doing all these years besides
farming and selling a few vegetables during the summer? The village seems
split right down the middle about a sand mine coming to town, with the
clear possibility that we will lose the Trail Marker Oak."

The raccoon looked at Ambrose and held out its paws.

Ambrose thought back to another time when he had to make a major
decision in his life, a decision forced on him by circumstances over which
he had no control. He remembered that July day in 1971 so well. He was
thirty-eight years old then and had never recovered from losing the love of
his life. The Link Lake community received a much-needed thunderstorm
the previous night, so when Ambrose walked toward the barn to help his

father with the morning milking everything smelled fresh and clean, as it does after a rainstorm. Ambrose's father, Clarence, arrived at the barn before Ambrose to feed the animals before the two of them milked their herd of fifteen cows. Clarence Adler was not much for modern ways of doing things, and the Adlers milked cows by hand even when their neighbors had long ago accepted electricity and modern milking machines.

Ambrose enjoyed milking cows by hand. He had done it since he was a kid and his hands were tough and strong, yet gentle. His father insisted gentle was the only way to milk a cow without getting your head kicked off. It was quiet in the barn while they milked. Occasionally a cow would turn her head and rattle the stanchion that confined her in her stall, but it was a subtle sound that mixed with the "zing, zing" sound of milk striking the bottom of an empty pail when one first started milking. Contrasting smells surrounded the hand milker—the fresh, rich smell of fresh milk accumulating in the pail held between the milker's legs colliding with the sharp smell of cow manure and mellowed by the earthy smell of stored alfalfa hay strung out in the manger in front of the cows.

Ambrose heard his father yell before he had gotten halfway to the barn. Clarence never yelled; it was not his way. But now he was yelling, "Help, help," in a way that sent shivers through Ambrose. He rushed to the barn as fast as he could and there saw his father in the bull pen, with big Fred, their Holstein herd bull, bellowing in a way he had never heard before and pawing at his father with his front feet and goring him in the side with his long, black horns.

Ambrose grabbed a pitchfork and thrust it through the boards of the bullpen at Fred, drawing blood from the animal's shoulder. Fred bellowed loudly, lifted his massive head, and looked at Ambrose with eyes that were red and menacing.

"Get back," Ambrose yelled as loudly as he could, thrusting the tines of the pitchfork into Fred's massive neck, once more drawing blood. Fred backed away from Clarence's prone body, but Clarence was not moving, not saying anything. Ambrose could see a stream of blood trickling from the side of his father's mouth, and his right leg was twisted in a grotesque way.

Ambrose pushed open the gate to the bull pen, thrusting the pitchfork at the enraged animal that had retreated to the back of the enclosure. With the pitchfork now in one hand and one eye on Fred, Ambrose grabbed his father by the shirt collar and pulled him out of the bull pen as Fred continued to paw with his front feet and bellow in a low, frightening way.

Ambrose latched the gate on the bull pen, laid his father on some fresh straw, and ran to the house trying to yell to his mother what had happened. He was trying to tell her to help hitch up the team so they could take his father to the doctor, but she couldn't understand him, so he began harnessing the team himself. When his mother arrived at the barn, together they gently placed Clarence in the back of the wagon on some fresh straw that Ambrose had put there. He galloped the team all the way to the doctor's office in Link Lake, but his father was dead when they arrived.

For the first month after his father's death, Ambrose was completely lost. He did the chores around the farm, of course. Milked the cows, made sure they had something to eat, and tried to take care of the crops as best he could. The day after his father's death, Ambrose contacted the livestock trucker and hauled away the killer herd bull that bellowed all the way into the truck and continued bellowing as the truck drove down the Adler drive and onto the country road that led away from their farm. Ambrose never forgot the sound of the enraged bull bellowing, and whenever he heard a sound like it, his thoughts immediately returned to that terrible day when his father died.

Ambrose didn't realize it at the time, but his mother's grief was even worse than his. He was so caught up in his own misery that he didn't at first recognize that his mother's health was slipping downward and quickly. Six months after his father was killed, his mother died in her sleep. Neighbors said she must have died of a broken heart—Ambrose suspected they were close to the truth of the matter.

Now Ambrose was on his own, with only the farm dog and his pet raccoon to keep him company. He had many decisions to make. For several months, he worked in a daze. He decided to sell the dairy cows and turn solely to growing and selling fresh vegetables at a little roadside stand near his farm. With the cows gone, he now had more time to do other things such as writing. He found writing down his thoughts therapeutic as he grieved the loss of his parents, and it was a lifestyle that had become quite comfortable for him.

By 1971, Ambrose had a closet stuffed with notebooks, full of stories, memories, and tales of what it was like to be different from other people. After Gloria moved to California, she and Ambrose had stayed in touch, and he often included one of his stories along with his letters. Upon learning of the tragic deaths of Ambrose's parents, Gloria wrote, "I don't know what you'll think of my suggestion, but it's something for you to consider. You might find the idea interesting, even challenging, and it will surely help take your mind off all your troubles."

15

Ambrose and Stony Field

Ambrose," Gloria wrote, "I think you should try publishing some of your writing. How about writing a weekly column? If you are interested, I will help you."

By this time, Gloria had advanced to the position of assistant editor at the *Los Angeles Journal*. "Why don't you send me three or four sample columns?" she wrote. "I'll polish them up a bit—if they need polishing—and we'll publish them in our paper. I think our readers would enjoy reading about early farm life in the Midwest. And if it works out, we'll offer your column to other papers in our syndicate."

Ambrose had never thought about publishing his writing; he had been quite satisfied with just doing it for himself, as his spirits always rose when he was writing. But now he seriously considered Gloria's suggestion. He thought, *It would be interesting to see some of my material in print, and see how others reacted to it. And what a thrill it would be to see some of my work in such a prestigious newspaper as the* Los Angeles Journal.

But like his father had always said, "Before you leap into something, it's best to sleep on the idea first." And that's what Ambrose did. The next day he knew for sure—he was going to send several sample columns to Gloria and see what happened.

Ambrose spent all morning writing and rewriting, typing on his old Remington manual typewriter that he'd gotten when he was in high school many years ago. He decided not to use his real name on his writing—and not reveal that he was a lowly dirt farmer in Ames County, Wisconsin, without a college degree and with a serious speech impediment. *Who would read stories from such a person?* Ambrose thought.

But what name should he use? He looked out over the big field just west of his barn and saw the dreaded stones that had made tilling this field challenging and sometimes nearly impossible. The stones broke plow points, bent hay rakes, and one time destroyed his old McCormick hay mower. Then the obvious came to him. *I will use the name Stony Field.* Gloria had suggested using a simple title for the column, just a few catchy words. He didn't know how catchy "Field Notes" would be, but he decided to run it by Gloria for her opinion.

Ambrose had one request. With the sample columns he sent to her he wrote, "I hope you will abide by my wish to tell no one who Stony Field really is and where he lives—not even your bosses at the paper." He put the package in an envelope and dropped it in the mail to Gloria.

Gloria wrote back to say that she would keep Ambrose's secret. She loved the title "Field Notes" and was ready to submit the column to her editors.

That was the beginning of Ambrose's writing career. In his first columns he wrote about farm life during the Depression years, and how his family had scraped and skimped to pay their taxes and other bills, and how even with all the misery caused by those dreadful years, his family had enough to eat and a roof over their heads, unlike those who lived in the big cities and lost their jobs and sometimes found themselves riding the rails in search of something to eat. He wrote about the drought that swept across much of the central and western states, wiping out farms, sending farm families packing in search of a place to live where the wind didn't blow every day and where dust didn't thicken the air so that people couldn't breathe.

He wrote about farm life during World War II and how farmers dealt with rationing and a shortage of labor as all able young men had gone off to fight in the war. He wrote about how the war had finally ended the long, agonizing Depression, and he wrote how ironic it was that killing people in war had resulted in saving people from starvation. Some things simply didn't make sense, and this was one of them.

Stony Field wrote about how farm life changed after World War II, how farmers now had tractors and electricity, milking machines and grain combines, indoor plumbing, and by the 1950s, television. He wrote how rural life changed dramatically during these postwar years as farms got ever larger, and the small family farm that had been the background of rural America for so many years began disappearing, and the young people who had desired to farm found they were no longer needed on the land and moved to the cities to find work there.

Soon newspapers across the country were picking up the Stony Field columns, as reader reaction, no matter where they lived, was increasingly positive. When Gloria asked Ambrose where she should send the money he had earned from his column writing, he told her to put it in a bank in Los Angeles, which is what she did. "Donate the money to environmental groups," he had told her.

After a few years of writing what some people called "nostalgia columns," Stony Field began writing more edgy pieces—topics related to the environment and the need to protect it from the onslaughts of urban development, the lack of adequate soil and water conservation measures, and how to combat a general apathy toward environmental protection that seemed to sweep across the country starting in the 1980s.

In one column, which he titled "Saving Souls or Saving Soil?," he criticized fundamentalist churches for ignoring the problems of the environment. By now his column was running regularly in the *Ames County Argus* along with hundreds of daily and weekly newspapers across the country.

One of the letters to the editor in response to the saving souls/soil column was from the Reverend Ridley Ralston, pastor of the Church of the Holy Redeemed, in Ambrose's hometown of Link Lake.

To the Editor:

I have been a regular reader of Stony Field's column. Having just read his recent one, I am compelled to comment. Mr. Field goes on at length writing about the need for soil conservation, but I believe he stepped over the line when he set up a contrast between saving souls and saving the soil. He should well know that saving souls must take precedence over all else. What is of most importance for true believers is having a place in Heaven. The soil is here for our earthly needs and has nothing whatsoever to do with our preparation for life after we leave this dreary, earthly existence. Stony Field is making some dangerous accusations with his anti-Christian message. We can do without this kind of information, and I would remind Stony Field that those of us who are God-fearing followers of the Word are watching him and his rather misguided musings.

Signed,

The Reverend Ridley Ralston

Ambrose smiled when he read Reverend Ralston's letter. He sat back in his chair and decided that he would write more columns that evoked some controversy—maybe this was one way to move people toward matters that were of vital importance to this country. Maybe through his writing he could once more get people to worry a bit about the environmental future of this good earth and not merely its economic future, to think a couple of generations into the future, and not worry so much about quarterly earnings and short-term predictions, and the gathering of ever more wealth, power, and material possessions, which seemed the goal of many people.

As he reread the Reverend Ralston's letter to the editor, he thought, *It's time to get people thinking and discussing what's going on around them. Too many people rely on authority figures like the know-it-all Pastor Ralston for their ideas and perspectives. It's time I gave them something else to think about. It's time to push people toward thinking for themselves rather than having other people do their thinking for them.*

Since Ambrose had begun writing "Field Notes" in 1971, he wrote many thousands of words about the importance of history and especially the importance of taking care of the environment. He had enjoyed doing this anonymously, with only Gloria Jones knowing who Stony Field really was. He liked that he was evoking conversation in coffee shops, in retirement centers, in taverns, and wherever people gathered. The beginning of such a conversation often began: "Did you happen to read Stony Field's column this week?"

Yes, he had enjoyed his anonymity. But now, with the village board poised to approve the opening of a sand mine in Increase Joseph Community Park, Ambrose Adler thought it might be time to let people know that this stuttering old farmer who seemed to be living in the shadows of the past wasn't the person everyone believed him to be. Perhaps this was the time to let people know that Ambrose Adler was Stony Field and that he was mad as hell about the idea of a sand mine coming to town, and even madder that the village board would allow the cutting of the historic Trail Marker Oak.

Bank Robbery Reenactment

*P*eople from as far away as Milwaukee and Green Bay came to Link Lake to witness the famous bank robbery reenactment that was sponsored by the Link Lake Historical Society. It was held the first Saturday in May each year at Increase Joseph Community Park. People from the community played the parts of those most directly involved in the incident, which without a doubt was the most exciting thing that ever happened in the Village of Link Lake since it was settled in 1852.

Emily Higgins played the role of Abigail Johnson, proprietor of Johnson House, a stagecoach stop, tavern, and roadhouse that was now the Link Lake Supper Club. Oscar Anderson was One-Eyed Billy, a robber wanted in three states, and Fred Russo played his sidekick, Norman. Billy Baxter, *Argus* editor, played Marshal Jonas Gust.

On the hillside overlooking the clearing, a hundred people or so sat on blankets and enjoyed their picnic dinners as they waited for the early evening event to begin. It was a clear, warm May day.

A podium was set up under the giant Trail Marker Oak. A faded façade of the Link Lake State Bank was lashed to a tree to its right and a façade of Johnson House was tied to a tree to its left. Longtime announcer of the event Earl Wade of radio station WWRI, a balding middle-aged man who wore thick glasses, walked to the podium. Wade had a deep, easy-to-listen-to voice, and according to most people who listened to him on the radio, he looked not at all like he sounded.

"Welcome everyone," Wade began. "You are in for a thrill and at the same time you will learn just a bit more about this wonderful Link Lake community and its history."

In front of the Johnson House façade, four men sat at a table reading newspapers.

"You see this?" one of the men said.

"See what?" the second man asked.

"This story about an increase in bank robberies in Wisconsin."

"Bank robberies, huh? Never happen here in Link Lake. Not enough money in our bank for a robber to take notice."

The group laughed as the crowd's attention turned to a man on horseback who rode into the scene. The man wore a pearl-handled pistol on his belt and had a badge pinned to his shirt. He stopped his horse at the improvised hitching rail, climbed off, and tied his horse. He walked over to the four men sitting at the table, who looked up when he approached.

"Howdy, Marshal, what can we do for you?" one of the men asked.

"Well, it's this way," said Marshal Gust. "I don't want to alarm anybody, but I just got a telegram from Oshkosh that a bank has been robbed there and the robbers were last seen headed west."

"Well, this would be west," said one of the men at the table.

"Ain't enough money in the Link Lake State Bank for any robber worth his salt to care about. Don't think we have much to worry about. But thanks for the warning, Marshal."

The marshal climbed back on his horse and rode off toward the village. The table and the four men disappeared behind the Johnson House façade, while a woman with a broom appeared in front of the roadhouse. She proceeded to sweep off the imaginary front steps and looked up to see two riders approaching, both rather poorly dressed and wearing pistols on their belts.

"Howdy, ma'am," said the taller man. "Name's Billy, my partner here goes by Norman. We're looking for a room and a meal. We at the right place?"

"You bet you are," said Abigail Johnson. "We got clean rooms and some of the best beefsteak you'll find anywhere in this part of Wisconsin."

"Your steak from one of those skinny dairy cows we saw when we was ridin' this way?" said the older man, who smiled broadly when he said it.

"Nah, we don't feed none of that skinny dairy cow steak—that all goes to them packing plants in Milwaukee. Here we serve the best beefsteak you can buy anywhere. I'll bet my reputation on it."

"Well, I'm glad to hear it," said the tall man. "We're lookin' for work—heard there might be some call for a lumberjack or two in these parts."

Abigail laughed. "You boys are just about fifty years too late—the only lumberjacks left are those way up north, up there in the Hayward area—and maybe over toward Rhinelander. Might still find a few lumber camps there. But around here, well most of the folks are farmers and they've taken up milking cows. You boys know how to milk a cow?"

The taller man laughed. "Well, we might look like cowboys, but milkin' cows is one thing we don't do. Wouldn't be caught dead milkin' one of them smelly cows."

"Well, bring your things in and we'll get you checked into a room. Dining room's still open—we'll see if we can rustle you up something to eat."

"Mighty grateful, ma'am," said the taller cowboy.

*E*arl Wade picked up the microphone.

"And now, as the sun sets over Link Lake and the first lamps are lit and people sit on their front porches, enjoying the cool breeze that rolls off the lake, people think how wonderful it is to live in such a quiet place where life is simple and the people are content and well satisfied. By 10:00 p.m. the lamps are blown out and the town is dark and it's quiet, except for the call of a whip-poor-will that repeats its name over and over again, the sound echoing across the lake."

*K*ABOOM! An explosion caused everyone in the audience to jump and look in the direction of the Link Lake State Bank façade. Smoke from the explosion drifted over the crowd, adding realism to the scene. Through the smoke, the audience saw two men, each carrying a bag, running toward their horses. They quickly climbed on their mounts, galloped past the podium, and disappeared on a trail that led farther into the woods of Increase Joseph Community Park.

Earl Wade said, "The lamps of Link Lake are once more lit as people are awakened by the explosion. The first lamp lit is that of Marshal Gust, who quickly dresses, runs to the livery that is a block from his house, saddles his horse, and heads down Main Street in search of the source of the explosion."

As Wade talked, Marshal Gust, astride his horse, trotted in front of the podium on his way to the Link Lake State Bank façade, which had a lingering stream of smoke coming from it. The marshal tied his horse to the hitching rail and quickly noticed that the bank door was open. He hurried inside and a few moments later was back on the street.

"The bank's been robbed! The bank's been robbed!" the marshal yelled in a loud voice to the handful of sleepy-eyed people now gathering on Main Street.

"I need a posse to help find these desperadoes. Any volunteers?"

Several hands went up.

"Go home, find your guns, saddle your horses, and meet me right here in a half hour."

*E*arl Wade continued, "The good people of Link Lake are visibly shaken, as they rush from their homes to find out what has happened, and what possible danger they might be in. The fifteen men comprising the posse, each armed with a rifle or a shotgun and a few with pistols, join Marshal Gust, who believes he has located the bank robbers in the woods a short distance from Link Lake."

The crowd's attention turned to the men crouching on the ground, their firearms raised and pointing toward the woodlot to their right.

BANG, BANG, BANG. Three pistol shots came from the woodlot, followed by rifle shots from the posse members, each firing several times. The sound of the gunshots was deafening.

"Hold your fire!" shouted Marshal Gust. "Hold your fire!"

Once more it was quiet, as the smoke from the gunfire drifted across the audience. Through the smoke emerged two men, their arms high in the air. Marshal Gust, his pistol pointed at the two robbers, marched them up to the podium.

The threesome stopped in front of the podium as Earl Wade walked up to the marshal and his captives.

"Congratulations to you, Marshal Gust. Can you tell us how you managed to capture these dangerous criminals?"

"Well, I tell you it was this way. We managed to track these crooks from the bank to the woods over there, where we captured these guys, but not without a fight. I organized the posse with some of them on the south side of the woods, some on the west side, some on the north side, and some on the east side. When they tried to leave the woods and they spotted the posse, they commenced shooting. But we outgunned them. No question about that."

"Do either of you men have anything to say?" asked Earl Wade as he looked to the men with their hands still raised in the air.

"Well, I'm One-Eyed Billy and this here is my sidekick, Norman. And we're pretty darned disappointed that we got caught by this small-town marshal and his gun-slinging posse. What did us in was the sand. This dang country is so sandy that all the marshal had to do was follow our tracks to that there woods. And that's what they did."

*W*ell, that's it, folks," said Earl Wade, turning back to the audience. "That's the story of the famous Link Lake bank robbery. Let's give a big round of applause to our actors."

Emily Higgins, Billy Baxter, Fred Russo, and Oscar Anderson all joined hands and bowed. The extras then took their turn bowing to the audience.

*A*s the sun set in the west, casting long shadows across the waters of Link Lake, the audience began picking up their blankets and moving toward their cars. In the distance a whip-poor-will called, the sound echoing across the lake.

17
Village Board Vote

AMES COUNTY ARGUS
Link Lake Village Board Approves Sand Mine
By Billy Baxter, editor

On a vote of five to one, the Link Lake Village Board voted to approve leasing a portion of the village's Increase Joseph Community Park for the construction of a sand mine. The Alstage Sand Mining Company of La Crosse has signed a twenty-year contract with the village, with a percentage of the profits from the sale of the sand going directly to the village's coffers.

Marilyn Jones, president of the Link Lake Economic Development Council, said, "Mayor Jessup and I, along with all the members of the Link Lake Development Council, are extremely pleased with the decision. Alstage will bring much-needed jobs to our community and with a percentage of the profits from the mine going to the village, many of its budget problems will be solved as well. Alstage is an environmentally respected company with a strong reputation for responsible mining."

The Link Lake Historical Society strongly opposed the decision. Emily Higgins, president of the society, said, "I can't believe the mining company plans to dig up our famous park and cut down the historically famous Trail Marker Oak, which the company says stands in the way of the only practical road to the planned mine. Neither the village board of Link Lake nor the Alstage Sand Mining Company has any respect for history. The historical society will do everything in its power to save this famous tree and the sacred sand on which it stands."

Village Board Vote

Emerson Evans, a spokesperson for the Alstage Mining Company, indicated the company was extremely pleased with the village board's decision. "We look forward to working with the good citizens of Link Lake, and we are pleased that we will be able to offer several employment opportunities to this community," said Evans.

18
Fred and Oscar

*J*ust read in the *Ames County Argus* that the value of our farms has climbed up a notch," said Oscar Anderson, as Fred Russo joined him at the Eat Well Café in Link Lake.

"How's that?" replied Fred as he took his seat.

"Ain't you been keepin' up with the news, Fred? Everybody's talking about sand these days."

"Well, I got 160 acres of sand, sprinkled with more than a few stones too. Made life interestin' when I was still farmin'. No fun slamming into one of them damn stones with a plow or a disk or a grain binder or whatever I was workin' with at the time. Hated them damn stones. Every one of 'em. Hated every damn stone that I ever saw."

"Fred, I'm not talking about stones. I'm talking about sand."

"Why you talking about sand? Ain't you got anything more important on your mind than sand? Especially after we both tried to farm the damn stuff for fifty years. Fifty years is a long time to farm sand when you never know if you're gonna get a crop or not. Unless it rains regular. When it rains regular you sometimes get a crop, but never as good as those who farm on the heavy land. Never grow crops like that."

They both stopped talking when Henrietta refilled their coffee cups. She smiled when she did. "Anything else I can get for you boys this morning?" she asked.

"Nah, coffee is enough. Them big sweet rolls look mighty appealing, though. But we eat one of them and we'll just get fat." Fred laughed.

"Speak for yourself, Fred," said Oscar. "Who's the one that's put on a few pounds?"

Henrietta smiled once more and returned to the lunch counter, leaving the two old friends to themselves.

"Let's get back to sand," said Oscar.

"Boy, you are stuck in the sand," answered Fred.

"Guess I'm just gonna have to spell it out for you, Fred. Bring you up to date with the rest of the folks hereabouts."

"I kind of resist that comment."

"Resent, Fred. Resent."

"What? What'd you just say?"

"You hear about that big Alstage Sand Mining Company that's comin' to Link Lake?"

"Did hear something about it. Guy at the lumberyard mentioned it the other day. Sounded to me like another gravel pit. Got two or three gravel pits already in the county. Figured that this was another one."

"Fred, this ain't no gravel pit. It's a sand mine."

"A sand mine? What in hell is a sand mine?"

"See you ain't been keepin' up with the news. You gettin' that old-timers' disease that makes you forgetful."

"Oscar, I ain't got no damn old-timer's disease. I just been busy as hell out at my place—hardly got time to go the bathroom, I've been so busy."

"I suspect you ain't heard of frackin' either?"

"What was that you said—did you just drop that big old F word that'd get us in a heap of trouble when we was kids and said it?" Fred was grinning like he'd just eaten the last piece of pie at a threshing dinner.

"I said frackin', not what you think I said."

"Still sounds like you're trying to spit out the F word and can't quite muster enough courage to do it."

"Fred, I don't know what I'm going to do with you," said Oscar. He was smiling as he said it.

"Fracking is a shortened version of hydraulic fracturing, a way to spread apart rocks that have natural gas stuck between 'em."

"Well, why didn't you say so? Of course I have heard of draulic fracting," said Fred.

"Hydraulic fracturing, Fred. Hydraulic fracturing."

"Call it whatever you want. But what's natural gas got to do with sand and the value of our farms?"

"Here's the deal, Fred. Our sand is very special sand. It's tough and is just what those natural gas companies need for hydraulic fracturing."

"So?" Fred raised his cup and took a long drink of coffee.

"So the Alstage Sand Mining Company is coming to Link Lake and plans to mine sand in the Increase Joseph Community Park that they have leased from the village," said Oscar. "And I must say, I'm not very happy about having a sand mine in our park. That will put a kibosh on our annual bank robbery reenactment, to start with. To say nothing about all the people who simply like to walk in the park or maybe have a picnic there."

"Is that where they're gonna have that damn old mine?"

"That's the place. What're we gonna do to keep it from happening?" asked Oscar.

"Seems like it's a done deal."

"Does sound that way, doesn't it?" said Oscar. "You'd think so, but that's not what's gonna happen."

"You know what would be worse?" asked Fred. "They could start diggin' up that sandy farm of yours."

19

Ambrose's Reaction

Ambrose couldn't remember when he had been so upset about something. He turned to his pet raccoon, which was standing by the chair where he was sitting.

"Do you know what, Ranger? Those damn fools on the village board just voted to put a sand mine in our village park. And even worse, the mining company says they've got to cut down the Trail Marker Oak to make a road into the mine."

Ranger looked at his master with an apparent understanding of the torment Ambrose was feeling.

"How stupid could the Link Lake Village Board be to allow a mining company to tear up the village's only park, and quite a historical one at that? And the thought of cutting down the Trail Marker Oak makes me sick to my stomach."

Ambrose looked out the window of his old farmhouse, toward his garden that had begun to produce well as ample rains had come to Ames County in the spring and had continued periodically into early summer. He wondered again, was this the time to reveal his true identity?

In 2010, Stony Field had won the National Environmental Writer of the Year award. The National Association of Environmental Writers made the award, which in addition to the publicity included a $10,000 prize. The organization thought that surely the award would cause Stony Field to emerge from the shadows—who would pass up $10,000? But no one appeared at the awards ceremony and the $10,000 went unclaimed for the first time in thirty years. By now people wondered if there was such a person as Stony Field. Some suggested the column might be the work of several writers collaborating.

Stony Field remained a mystery, but nonetheless a well-informed, albeit controversial environmental writer not afraid to take a position, but who also invited those disagreeing with him to speak out. More than once he had written that his goal was to get people thinking about the environment and then acting responsibly. But he was highly critical of those who failed to produce arguments supported with facts and clear, critical thinking. Occasionally, and more often in recent years, he found himself taking on the loud-talking, fact-lacking radio and TV pundits who made a lot of noise, much of it directed toward him and other environmental writers who dared to stand up for the natural environment and argued for a balance between decisions that enhanced the economic well-being of a community and at the same time protected the environment, as well as a community's identity and history.

Ambrose opened the door to his little office, a door he kept locked for here is where he wrote his columns, kept his considerable collection of books (Gloria mailed him new and what were considered significant environmental books as soon as they came off the presses), scrapbooks of his published columns, a wall of awards he had won for his writing, and framed letters of congratulations from a variety of notables including Al Gore. He was proud of what he had accomplished, and perhaps even more pleased that he was able to do what no one thought he could—a stuttering person had become a nationally known environmental writer. How could that be? He chuckled at the thought of it. He sat down on his well-worn office chair, picked up a sheet of typing paper, and fed it into his old Remington manual typewriter. This typewriter had served him well; after all these years, he still enjoyed the feel of the keys beneath his fingers, and the ding that announced he should throw the carriage and start a new line of type. It took some work to type on a manual typewriter; each key required a definite push before a little lever rose up from its resting place and slammed against the paper with a definite "thunk."

He had not admitted this to Gloria, but it was when he was sitting at his typewriter, watching letters, words, and sentences line up on the paper in front of him, that he felt most useful, most wanted. His main loves these days were working his garden, smelling the fresh soil as he turned it, his pet raccoon and dog, walking the trails on his farm, and writing his weekly columns. And of course he had never gotten over Gloria, the one and only true love of his life. There wasn't a day that went by that he didn't think about her and the wonderful times they had together, now so many long years ago.

He began typing:

FIELD NOTES
Mining for Sand

By Stony Field

My sources in little Link Lake, Ames County, Wisconsin, have informed me that their village board has approved a sand mine to be opened in the village's Increase Joseph Community Park. They are offering a twenty-year lease to the Alstage Sand Mining Company of La Crosse, a company with several operating sand mines in western Wisconsin and in eastern Minnesota.

Alstage Mining has indicated that the only reasonable access to this proposed mine requires that a famous historical tree, known as the Trail Marker Oak, must be cut down. This old bur oak once pointed the way for Native Americans on their way to the Fox River and for the French trappers who followed the same route. The old tree has a rich and unique historical past, and I'm told a famous Indian chief once got the Village of Link Lake's founder, Increase Joseph Link, to pledge that the tree would never be cut.

Has the Link Lake Village Board lost its senses? Is the board so under the thumb of Marilyn Jones's Economic Development Council that all they can see is jobs and dollar signs? Do they not realize that when a community ignores its history that it loses its soul? Communities, like people, have histories, and when they forget their histories, they forget who they are.

Link Lake's historical society, under the able leadership of Emily Higgins, knows that history provides a foundation for a community and gives it life and a sense of place. Higgins and her group have worked hard to convince the Link Lake Economic Development Council and the Link Lake Village Board of the error of their ways—apparently with no success.

In addition to the Alstage Sand Mining Company's lack of interest in local history along with the village board's don't-let-history-get-in-the-way-of-progress mantra, I have heard no discussion about the impact of a sand mine on the environment. No one in Link Lake has mentioned the enormous amounts of water necessary for processing this special sand. No one has talked about the health dangers from the dust created by these mining operations. No one has mentioned the need to improve the roads in and around Link Lake to accommodate the hundreds of trucks that will haul the sand to the rail yards in Willow River, to say nothing about the increased traffic that will result. Are jobs so important that the creation of them trumps all other matters? It would appear so for Link Lake's Economic Development Council and the Link Lake Village Board.

Is there still time to reverse this awful decision? Let's hope so. It will be a sad day in Link Lake when the Trail Marker Oak comes down and huge heavy-laden trucks begin hauling Link Lake's precious sand to the rail line in Willow River, where it will become part of fracking operations in the west, where this dubious process of procuring natural gas and petroleum previously impossible to access is occurring.

But, as some of us are apt to say, it's never too late. Any decision made can be unmade. I am inviting readers of this column to write their thoughts to the *Ames County Argus*, one of the newspapers in which this column appears and one read by the majority of citizens in Ames County and the Link Lake community. Let the Link Lake Village Board know the error of their ways, and let the Link Lake Economic Development Council know that the future of a community depends on more than jobs.

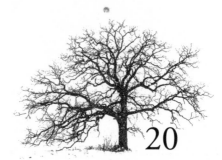

20

Editor's Response

AMES COUNTY ARGUS
Reaction to Stony Field Sand Mining Column
By Billy Baxter, editor

Never in my many years of editing the *Ames County Argus* has a column writer prompted so many people to write letters to this newspaper. More than 200 letters to the editor arrived at this newspaper since the column was first published, with more arriving each day. Most come as e-mails, but regular letters have filled our mailbox as well.

Stony Field, the award-winning but mysterious environmental writer, is prone to stir up people, but with his recent comments about a sand mine supported by the Link Lake Economic Development Council and recently approved by the Link Lake Village Board, he hit a hornet's nest. Letters are coming from throughout the country, from the east and the west coast, from north and south, from rural areas and major urban centers.

The letters run about two to one in favor of Stony Field's position—he argues quite convincingly that a community needs to attend to its history and be concerned about the environmental impact of a new development beyond merely supporting an idea because of the potential for additional jobs in the community.

We obviously do not have sufficient space in the *Ames County Argus* to print all of the letters we have received, so what I have done is select a sampling, trying to be fair in including those that agree with Stony Field and those that take issue with what he had to say. Some of the letters are so filled with angry invective and too often include words that cannot be

Editor's Response

repeated in a family-oriented newspaper that I have set them aside. Here is a sampling of the letters, both agreeing with and, often strongly, disagreeing with Stony Field's perspective:

Dear Editor:

What would this country do without a Stony Field and the other environmental writers who call to task the create-jobs-at-all-cost ilk that seems to be gaining traction these days? Here in Louisiana we have no sand mines, but we do have hydraulic fracturing taking place, and we know the environmental problems associated with it. Our country must get over its money, money, money attitude and become more tuned to what the planet will look like two and three generations from now. Hats off to Stony Field and his challenge to the Link Lake community to rethink its decision to build a sand mine in, of all places, a community park.

Sincerely,

John Reid, Baton Rouge, Louisiana

Dear Editor:

Stony Field reminds us, quite eloquently, of the error of our ways as we stumble into the future with dollar signs, and only dollar signs, on our minds. Mr. Field, wherever he lives, knows that for a society to survive and prosper in the future, it must know and accept its history as the foundation for all present and future activities.

He is so right in challenging our little community of Link Lake to give more thought to its recent decision to build a sand mine in our one and only park, Increase Joseph Community Park, named after the founder of our village.

Thank you, Stony Field, for telling us what we should have figured out for ourselves—that any economic development in a community must be seasoned with an ample amount of historical information plus clearheaded knowledge of potential environmental impacts.

One of your supporters,

Emily Higgins, president,

Link Lake Historical Society

Editor's Response

Dear Editor,

I often wonder why your paper continues to publish the trash written by an out-of-state writer who seems to relish sticking his nose in the business of small communities, such as Link Lake, Wisconsin.

Stony Field is clearly one of those save-the-environment-at-all-cost liberals who just doesn't get it. No jobs. No income. Nothing to eat. Who gives a rip about protecting the environment when they are out of work and don't know where their next meal is coming from? I doubt you'll find many hungry people carrying Save the Environment signs.

I would suggest your paper seriously consider dropping the Stony Field column. Those of us who live in rural communities, such as Link Lake, don't need to read the trash that Stony Field writes. I am a proud member of the Ames County Eagle Party. One of our goals is to put the kibosh on wild-eyed liberal writers such as Stony Field. They are a detriment to our society and are part of the trend that is dragging our country down.

Unless you drop the Stony Field column, I will find it necessary to cancel my subscription to your paper.

I hope my cancellation will not be necessary.

John Katz
Willow River, Wisconsin

21

Ambrose and Ranger

On this cool June morning, with dew sparkling on the hay field that Ambrose could see out his kitchen window, he sat enjoying a cup of coffee and reading the recent issue of the *Ames County Argus*. Ranger, his ever-present pet raccoon, stood at his side.

"Well, Ranger," said Ambrose, "it looks like old Stony Field got people thinking about putting a sand mine in Increase Joseph Community Park. Even got Bill Baxter at the *Argus* to sit up and take notice." Ambrose showed the newspaper editorial to the raccoon. "Know what Baxter said, Ranger? Here, I'll read it to you. 'Never in my many years of editing the *Ames County Argus* has a column writer prompted so many people to write letters to this newspaper.'"

The raccoon looked at the newspaper held in front of him and lifted a paw to touch the paper.

"And look at all these letters, Ranger, most of them agreeing with me. Just look at that. Maybe my writing is making a difference after all. Maybe there is still something we can do about stopping a sand mine from coming to Link Lake. Let's hope we can muster enough opposition to at least save the Trail Marker Oak. What a tragedy if that old tree came down."

Ranger looked at Ambrose and held out a paw for him to shake.

"We'd better get to work—lots of weeding to do in the garden, and our roadside stand needs a little sprucing up before we can be open for business. Wish I had more energy. Old age must be creeping up on me."

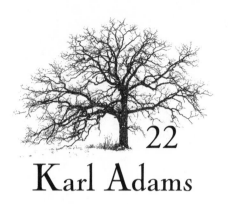

22

Karl Adams

*K*arl Adams arrived at the Appleton airport, rented a car, found Highway
10, and headed west toward Link Lake, some forty miles away. As a consulting mining engineer with offices in Portland, Oregon, he traveled the world,
helping mining companies set up new operations. The Alstage Sand Mining
Company had hired him to help them set up their mining operation in
Link Lake, Wisconsin. The company had set late October for the mine's
official opening.

Karl, a lifelong bachelor, was tall, thin, and had a full head of black
hair, deep penetrating eyes, and a personality that quickly won over people.
He was especially good at coming into a community where a mine was
planned to soothe over any negative feelings about mining, and, of course,
to emphasize all the positive features—especially the job creation and economic benefits that result when a mine opens. In the twenty-five years that
he had been a mining engineer, a community's acceptance of a mine had
become ever more contentious. Some people didn't want a mine in their
neighborhood, plain and simple. It didn't matter that the country needed
coal, or steel, or whatever else was dug from the ground; these people saw
mining as a way, to use their words, "to rape the environment." He also
had seen mining become a political issue, often tied to economic development and job creation with little concern for environmental protection.

In Karl's mind, bringing a mine into a community had its pluses. He
was also a realist and knew a mine had a downside as well, but if all the
rules were followed, a mine could be both an economic asset to a community as well as friendly to the environment. Increasingly in recent years, he
found himself doing more public relations in a community than technical

mining work. He was happy to do it and in fact rather enjoyed working with people, both those who applauded the coming of a mine as well as those who would never accept one coming even after a mine had been approved. As he drove over to Link Lake from the airport he thought about the only time he had been to Wisconsin, when a mining company had hired him to help with some exploratory work for a possible mine in Oneida County. That mine had never opened and the mining company decided to go elsewhere.

His contact at Alstage, Emerson Evans, had said little about the new mine in Link Lake, other than sending Karl some technical information about the quality of the sand there, and the fact that the mine would be located in a community park. The location seemed a bit odd to Karl, but it was not his job to question the site of a mine. He was to make sure the majority of people in a community were on board and supportive when the mine began operations. He had been in the middle of some really nasty situations where communities had chosen sides both for and against a mine's opening. He hoped that Link Lake would not be one of those places. Karl had read about the new iron mine in northern Wisconsin, and how it not only divided the northern Wisconsin community where the mine was to be located but also divided the state as it became a hot political issue with most Republicans foursquare behind the idea, and many Democrats raising serious questions about the mine's potential environmental impacts.

Karl Adams had done his homework. He had gotten the names of the members of the Link Lake Economic Development Council and names of the mayor and the Link Lake Village Board members. The latter group had negotiated the contract with Alstage. He especially wanted to meet Marilyn Jones, whom Emerson Evans with the Alstage Sand Mining Company praised as one of "the strongest leaders and most forward-looking persons" he had met in a while. Evans told him that she owned and operated the Link Lake Supper Club. He also had checked out the local newspaper, the *Ames County Argus*. Karl had learned many years ago that the local newspaper was a good place to start if you wanted to get a feel for a community, what was bothering it and what was making it feel good. Billy Baxter, editor of the *Argus*, was on the top of his list of people he wanted to talk with.

Arriving in Link Lake, Karl drove up and down Main Street, noticing the Eat Well Café, a couple of craft shops, an antique store, a furniture store, a dollar store, and, nestled against the lake, the Link Lake Supper Club. On the outskirts of town, he found the small but tidy-looking Link Lake Motel—the kind where you drive your car up to the door. It advertised "American Owned, Free Wi-Fi." Karl checked into the motel and then following the directions he had gotten from Alstage, he headed his rental car toward Increase Joseph Community Park. The park was only a mile or so from the motel and easy to find—one of the advantages of a small town is that almost everything is easy to find. He stopped at the park's entrance, where he spotted a massive bur oak tree. In front of the tree stood a concrete post with an attached old metal plaque that read, "Trail Marker Oak. A sacred tree." He wondered what that was all about. He spent the next hour exploring the park, using the technical information he had gotten to see exactly where the sand mine would be sited, the location of the processing facility, and the possible transportation routes in and out of the park.

The park was a beautiful, peaceful place. He noticed children playing on swings and a couple of families having a picnic lunch on tables organized under pine and oak trees with a fine view of the lake in the distance. The air was filled with the laughter of children and the sound of birds singing high in the treetops.

He made several notes in his pocket notebook and took photos with his phone. When he finished with his introductory inspection he headed toward Willow River, where he hoped to find Billy Baxter and gain some inside information about Ames County, Link Lake, and the coming of a sand mine to the community.

Baxter was in his office when Karl arrived, trying to decide what he should put in the coming issue of the *Argus*, and especially trying to decide how many more letters to the editor about the coming sand mine he should publish. The letters kept rolling in, still about two to one in opposition to the mine. Baxter was torn. If he kept printing the letters it would surely add fuel to the flame of opposition that was already burning brightly, and if he stopped publishing the letters he would be accused of selling out to the pro-mining group. He also had in the back of his mind ad revenue; he knew he should never make an editorial decision based on ad revenue, but it was ad revenue that kept his paper going, and a good number of his ads came from businesspeople who backed the coming of the mine and weren't at all bashful in reminding him of that fact.

Baxter heard a gentle knock on his door.

"Come on in," he said.

Karl Adams entered the tiny office piled high with newspapers, books, promotional materials, draft ads—an unorganized mess, at least to someone who liked things neat and tidy, which was Karl's preference.

"Name is Adams," Karl said. "Karl Adams. I'm a consulting engineer with the Alstage Sand Mining Company. You've likely heard of Alstage." He thrust out his hand to shake Baxter's.

"You bet I've heard of the Alstage Sand Mining Company. That's about all I've heard about for the past several weeks. Have a chair. You ever read the Stony Field column—that environmental guy?"

"Sure, his column is all over the place. I read it when I can. Haven't seen it in a couple weeks, though, been on the road."

"Here," said Baxter, tossing him a copy of the *Argus* with the recent Stony Field column in it. "Read this when you get some time. It's the one that stirred up people from near and far—he invited people to write letters to this newspaper, and write letters they did. Want to hear some reactions from people to a sand mine in Link Lake?"

"Sure, why not."

For the next half hour, Billy Baxter read letters he had received from all over the country either supporting the sand mining operation coming to Link Lake or lambasting it. Karl Adams listened intently but was not surprised. What he was hearing was typical. In one form or another he had heard all of this before, in all parts of this country and beyond. Mining, whatever form it took, had become an increasingly hot issue. Karl had hoped that sand mining, a relatively new type of mining, would not follow the same path as iron mining or coal mining. But that was obviously not going to be the case.

When Billy Baxter finished reading a sampling of letters, he looked up.

"So what do you think?" he asked.

"If it helps you to know, I've run into this same kind of buzz saw in every community where a new mine is proposed, especially in the last ten or fifteen years. People just don't want a mine in their backyard; it doesn't matter what kind," said Karl.

"Well, this sand mine has sure stirred up folks around here—and they don't stir up all that easy; most just seem to go along with the flow. Folks seem especially steamed up with the mine going into the park at Link Lake. And believe it or not, when you mention that an old oak tree is likely to be removed, well, some of them go ballistic."

"You're not talking about a certain tree with a little sign that says, 'Trail Marker Oak. A sacred tree,' are you?" This was the first time he'd heard that the mining company planned to remove the Trail Marker Oak. Evans hadn't told him about this little detail when he briefed him about the mine project. He made a mental note that he must talk to him about this.

"That's the one. You as much as steal a leaf off that old tree and you are in a mess of trouble," said Baxter, smiling.

"So what's the story?"

"You got time to hear it?"

"I do. If Alstage's sand mine is going to succeed, we've got to cover all the bases, including concerns about an old oak tree."

Baxter sat up in his chair and began sharing what he had learned about the Trail Marker Oak and its importance to the Link Lake community, especially to the members of the Link Lake Historical Society. When he finished he said, "Well that's what I know—and if you want to learn more, you surely must talk with Emily Higgins, president of the historical society. Believe me, it's an experience talking with her."

"I look forward to meeting her," said Karl.

"Well, be careful. She'll have you on her side of the fence before you can say, 'I didn't think old people had strong opinions.'"

"I'll take my chances," said Karl. He was thinking, *I've met people like this before. At least you know where they stand.*

"Of course you'll want to meet with Marilyn Jones over at the Link Lake Supper Club—she's the one largely responsible for convincing, at least she convinced the businesspeople in Link Lake, that bringing a sand mine to town was the right thing to do."

"She's on my list," said Karl, getting up from his chair. "Thanks for all the good information; I'm sure we'll be in touch."

"You want to take copies of some of these letters along—to see what's got people all revved up?"

"Nope, I've seen my share of hate letters. Comes with the job. Not easy being the front person for a sand mine—but I kinda like it. At least I'm never ignored," said Karl as he opened the door and left.

23

Karl at the Eat Well

*O*n his way back to Link Lake from the *Ames County Argus*, Karl Adams scratched his head. *I thought this was going to be an easy one. Wrong again. So the local historical society is involved? Usually it's some environmental group that takes the lead in opposing a mine—should be easy dealing with a bunch of oldsters with history on their minds. Some of those environmentalists are just plain kooks—they're walking time bombs.*

He opened the car windows to let in some fresh air as he traveled down Highway 22, past a few fields of overgrown Christmas trees, a reminder of the days when fresh farm-grown and nicely sheared Scotch pines were on everyone's list for the holiday, past a farmer baling hay (he could smell the sweet smell of hay curing), past several fields of corn that was dark green and a foot or more tall, past a farmer whose cows were out on pasture— something he seldom saw on the West Coast anymore. As he rounded a gentle turn and drove down a long slope toward the Village of Link Lake, he saw the lake itself shimmering in the distance. He could see boats clustered in the inlet near where the village was located, probably fishermen, he thought. He could see fine homes, huge homes some of them, lined up on the opposite shore. In doing his homework, he discovered that one of Link Lake's principal income sources came from those with summer homes on the lake, people from Chicago and Milwaukee who spent weekends and vacations on the lake—and contributed much to the economy. He had learned that during the Great Recession that began in 2007, income in the village from tourism had plummeted. He guessed that the community was actively seeking new revenue sources and new opportunities for jobs, and thus made the deal to bring a sand mine to town.

Karl at the Eat Well

As he drove along, he was considering what it would be like living in this community for the next several months while he helped Alstage establish their sand mine, solve the logistical as well as the technical kinks associated with opening a new mine, and above all move a majority of the people toward accepting a sand mining company as a good citizen in their community, one that brought jobs and taxes to an area that needed an economic shot in the arm.

He pulled up to the motel, unloaded his belongings, cranked up the in-window air conditioner, and sprawled out on the bed. He read the Stony Field column and thought, *Why can't a guy like this keep his nose out of little communities like Link Lake, Wisconsin? What he's managed to do is create a firestorm from what probably had been a few smoldering embers.*

Karl woke up early the next morning, feeling refreshed and ready to face the challenges of a job that to many, including Emerson Evans (who would never admit it), was nearly impossible. When Karl first signed the contract with Alstage, and he and Evans talked about possible problems with some people in a community not accepting the mine, Evans said, "The only way to bring a new sand mine into a community is through sheer power. Line up the votes, spend money to discredit the opposition, and charge forward. Power backed by money always wins."

But Evans knew Karl's reputation for bringing together people in a community through persuasion and friendly contact, and Evans was willing to give Karl a chance to do what he was good at doing—to not try to push people into a decision that the majority did not accept. The company's plan was to have Karl Adams live in Link Lake for a while before and during the early months of the mine's operations. But as Karl thought about the Trail Marker Oak, he was more than a little miffed at Evans, who had not told him about this old tree and the community's feelings toward it.

As Karl reflected on the Stony Field rant against sand mining, and the tremendous reaction he had evoked as evidenced by the hundreds of letters the *Ames County Argus* was receiving, he realized the Link Lake community had already been strong-armed and the camps for and against the mine had made their positions known. Karl was clearly starting in a deep hole.

He showered and dressed and drove the half mile or so from his motel to the Eat Well Café for breakfast. At 6:30 a.m. the place was about filled with customers, many of them fishermen, Karl assumed, and some of them old-timers who liked to get up in the morning for an early start on the day. The smell of bacon frying and coffee cooking filled the air. Karl saw a couple of older gentlemen sitting at a table toward the back of the little restaurant and decided to join them.

"You men mind if I join you? Place appears to be filled," said Karl.

"Nah, pull up a chair. You new to town? Ain't seen you around," said one of the men.

"Name's Adams," Karl replied, "Karl Adams. And you are?" he asked, as he thrust out his hand to one of the men.

"I'm Oscar Anderson," said the man closest to the window, as he shook Karl's hand. Karl noticed that he had big, calloused hands and his hand-shake was firm.

"Fred Russo," said the other gentleman, who also shook hands with him.

"Well, nice to meet both of you. I assume you both live here in Link Lake?" asked Karl.

"Nah, we're retired farmers. Neither one of us could live here in town. Place is just too big, too many people, too much noise. We like it quiet. Away from all of the stuff that takes place in a town like this."

Karl wondered what kind of "stuff" Oscar was referring to.

"So what's going on in Link Lake these days, besides the fishing looking pretty good out there on the lake?"

"Well, generally I could say, 'not much,' but I tell you things are heating up in little old Link Lake."

"How so?" said Karl with a straight face, as he knew full well what he was about to hear.

"You ever hear of Stony Field?" asked Oscar Anderson.

"The environmental writer?"

"That's the one. Well that Field guy hit a hornet's nest when he took on the Link Lake Village Board and their decision to allow a sand mine in the park. He just made a bunch of people mad as hell."

"So what do you guys think about a sand mine coming to the area?" asked Karl.

"Don't much like the idea. I just can't believe that stupid mayor, who has a ring in his nose and is led around by Marilyn Jones, steamrolled the village board into believing it was a good idea. Those guys on the village board—every damn one of them—they ain't had an original thought since they was elected. They're just stupid as hell."

Karl looked up as Henrietta asked, "What can I get for you?"

"How about two eggs scrambled, whole wheat toast, and a cup of coffee."

Henrietta scribbled some notes on her pad and disappeared.

"So Stony Field and the idea of a sand mine coming to town has got some folks riled up?" said Karl.

"That would be the understatement of the year," said Oscar. "Ain't seen folks, especially them of us who are members of the Link Lake Historical Society, so worked up about something—not since the movers and shakers tried to tear down the old depot and bring a fast food place to town. Historical society won the day on that one. That they did. Movers and shakers had egg on their faces." Oscar took another drink of coffee.

Karl Adams took all of this in, listening carefully to every word, but trying not to show any reaction. When he finished his breakfast, he picked up the bill, walked to the cash register, and paid.

"Wonder what brings that fella to town?" Fred asked.

"Who knows, maybe he's a poet coming to Link Lake to find something new to write about."

"Oscar, he ain't no damn poet. Poets don't write about sand mines. They write about sunsets and pretty flowers and birds that sing in the night."

24

Karl and Marilyn

After finishing his breakfast at the Eat Well Café, including writing down the names Oscar Anderson and Fred Russo and noting a summary of their comments about the upcoming sand mine, Karl Adams drove back to his motel. He punched in the number for the Link Lake Supper Club.

"Link Lake Supper Club, this is Marilyn."

"Marilyn Jones?" asked Karl.

"Yes, this is Marilyn Jones. Who's calling?"

"Karl Adams, with the Alstage Sand Mining Company."

"Karl, good to hear from you. Emerson Evans said you'd be coming to town to help us launch our new sand mine."

"Well, I'm here. Arrived yesterday. I'm staying at the Link Lake Motel. Any chance we could meet this morning?" he asked.

"Sure, come right over. We don't open until eleven, so park in the back and take the door to the right, which leads to my office."

"I'll be there in a half hour," said Karl. He punched the End Call button on his cell phone and put it back in his pocket. Next he sent an e-mail to Emerson Evans.

We've got big problems here in Link Lake. I'm not yet settled in—living in a motel until I find something better. I've been getting an earful from the citizens. It seems that our "friend" Stony Field is up to his old tricks. Somehow he got word of our plans to develop a sand mine here in Link Lake and wrote a column chastising the village board for deciding in our favor. The local newspaper received several hundred e-mails, most of them in opposition to the mine.

Karl and Marilyn

I had breakfast with a couple of old retired farmers this morning who seem to have a good take on what's going on—and it's not good. I'll have my work cut out for me.

Why didn't you tell me about Alstage's plan to cut down an old oak tree in the park? It seems this single fact has more people steamed up than about anything else. Sure would have helped if I'd had that little piece of information.

I've got an appointment with Marilyn Jones; as you know she's been the spark plug behind getting approval for the mine. I'll be interested in her take on the situation.

The sun was already high on this early June day as Karl drove toward the Link Lake Supper Club on a narrow road that fronted the lake. He saw a cluster of fishermen in the cove on which the supper club was located. Karl thought, *I wish I was one of them. It would be a great day to do some fishing. I haven't had a fishing pole in my hand since I got into this mining business. One of these days I've got to slow down a little, take some time to do the things I want to do rather than always doing what others want me to do.*

As Karl drove into the empty parking lot of the Link Lake Supper Club, he admired the beautiful, log-sided, well-kept building and the flowers growing along the walk to the front door. He noted the wonderful location of the supper club. It appeared a whole wall of dining room windows looked out on the lake.

He drove around to the back of the building, where three vehicles were parked. He noticed two back doors; he walked to the door on the right and knocked.

"Come right in," a friendly voice said.

Once inside and with a few pleasantries exchanged, Marilyn said, "I'm so pleased you're here. I've heard of your reputation of bringing communities together—and boy does Link Lake need bringing together. I thought we'd gotten over the hump after the village board voted to approve the mine. But then this guy Stony Field, who writes that stupid column, has screwed up everything. Sure wish we could get ahold of him and straighten him out."

"Well that's not likely to happen—Stony Field has a great national reputation. Anything we would say in our defense will help fuel his fire," said Karl.

"You're probably right. But he sure has got people all excited around here, especially that damned Link Lake Historical Society—now there's a bunch of busybodies with too much time on their hands. And that Emily Higgins, the old bat who runs the historical society, she is a piece of work. Got her long nose stuck in every piece of improvement this town tries to make. If everybody would listen to her, this town would be stuck so far in its past that nobody would have a job and all we'd do is run around and look at historical stuff."

Karl Adams was listening carefully, trying to think of a strategy that might bring the community together once again. Something that would take their minds off the sand mine that wasn't scheduled to open until October, which was five months from now.

"Perhaps I should talk to this Emily Higgins," he said.

"Wouldn't help. She's got her mind made up and when her mind is made up it closes tight. No room for a new idea, not unless it helps the Link Lake Historical Society."

"Think I'll talk to her anyway. She might give me some clues about what I can do to bring folks together."

"You found any housing yet?" asked Marilyn, changing the subject. "That old Link Lake Motel was built in 1950 and has made few improvements since."

"Haven't had time to look for another place," replied Karl.

"I know about a neat little cabin right on the lake. One of the few that's for rent. Here's a phone number to call." She wrote a number on a piece of paper.

Back once more at the motel, Karl called the number Marilyn had given him, reached Blue Waters Realty, and quickly arranged for a place to live. It was right on Link Lake and according to the realtor even had a dock with boat available for his use. *Maybe I'll have a chance to go fishing after all*, thought Karl as he loaded his sparse belongings and headed toward his new home for the next several months—or until the sand mine was operating well and everything was back to normal in the community.

25
Vegetable Stand

Ambrose Adler smiled to himself when he thought about all the reaction he'd gotten from his recent Stony Field column chastising the Link Lake Village Board. He was hoping that somehow, in a small way, what he had written would change enough minds that the decision to open a sand mine in Increase Joseph Community Park could be overturned. But he also wondered again, should he reveal that he was really Stony Field? If he did, he knew it would trigger a tremendous amount of publicity—and he knew he would hate every minute of the attention. But it could have positive effects: the national attention just might help stop the sand mine.

As he set up his vegetable stand alongside the road that trailed by his farm, he also thought about how successful his little stand had become as an increasing number of townspeople as well as tourists in the area stopped to buy fresh fruits and vegetables. Now, in early June, the strawberry crop was about ready, he had lush leaf lettuce, some of the best he'd grown in years, lots of broccoli, outstanding radishes, and in a week or so the first zucchini and green beans. People were listening to the national cry to buy locally: "See where your food is grown and try to avoid buying vegetables grown halfway around the country."

But he also knew that the tourists in the area found it interesting to visit this old bearded and stuttering vegetable farmer who had a pet raccoon and talked to it.

When Ambrose had everything in order, he straightened the green faded sign that read Homegrown Vegetables. He took one last look to see that his early-crop vegetables were properly displayed, and then he sat down and opened the book he had with him, Henry David Thoreau's

Walden, a book that provided a foundation for much of his writing, and a book that seemed to be more profound every time he turned to it. Ranger rested in the shade of a nearby tree.

He had no more than opened the cover of the book when he saw the neighbor boy, Noah Drake, pedaling along the road on his bike. Noah was now twelve years old and he often stopped by Ambrose's farm on his way to and from school. During the summer months, when school was out, he often pedaled over to Ambrose's place just to talk with him and play with Ranger. Noah's father, Lucas Drake, farmed his more-than-a-thousand acres just a half a mile west of Ambrose's 160 acres.

Noah liked Ambrose Adler. The old farmer took time to talk with Noah, something that Noah's father seldom took time to do. Ambrose would patiently listen while Noah shared what he was doing in school and what was happening on his farm. Noah had also become great friends with Ranger. Ambrose had taught Noah how to "talk" with Ranger—at least that's what Noah believed he was doing when he fed the little animal treats and it cocked its head to the side and held out its paws.

"Hi, Ambrose," Noah said as he rode up, climbed off his bike, and leaned it against the side of the vegetable stand.

"H . . . Hi, Noah," said Ambrose.

"Got your vegetable stand up, I see."

"Y . . . yup. Want a radish?"

"Sure," said Noah as Ambrose handed him a couple of big, red, freshly pulled radishes.

"Where is Ranger?" inquired Noah as he bit into a big radish.

"B . . . back there," said Ambrose as he pointed to a tree a few feet behind the vegetable stand, where Ranger was resting.

Noah walked over to the tree and the little raccoon, recognizing Noah, stood up and walked toward him.

"How are you, Ranger?" said Noah. "You doing okay?" The raccoon looked right at Noah and made a purring sound, its way of communicating.

"Got any treats for Ranger?" asked Noah.

Ambrose reached into his pocket and handed Noah a little treat, which he held in front of the little raccoon.

"What do you say, Ranger? Can you say 'please'?" Noah said.

The little raccoon purred more loudly and held out its paws.

"Good enough," said Noah as he handed the treat to Ranger.

"W . . . what's new?" asked Ambrose as he watched Noah play with Ranger. *I wish more kids were this interested in wild creatures*, he thought.

"Pa's pretty darn mad this morning," said Noah.

"What about?"

"There's this writer guy, Stony somebody. Pa says he's the biggest and most stupid jerk that he's ever known about. Pa says he is forever sticking his nose in the business of small towns. This Stony guy wrote about a town in Pennsylvania where they was doing something called fracking. I think that's what Pa called it. Anyway, this Stony guy wrote a story about that and got people out there all upset and wanting to stop the project."

"Is that r . . . right?" said Ambrose, trying not to show any expression.

"And you know what got Pa really steamed up?"

"What?"

"The story Stony wrote about a sand mine coming here to Link Lake and how stupid it was of the village board to approve such a thing. When Pa read that piece in the paper I saw his face get red and he slammed the paper down and said a couple of swear words that he told me never to use. Pa was so mad."

"R . . . really?"

"Yup, almost as mad as he was when this Stony guy wrote about how wrong it was for farmers to grow corn that was used for making ethanol. Boy that story made Pa almost as mad as the one about the sand mine coming to Link Lake. I suspect you know we grow 500 acres of corn on our farm, and most of it goes for making ethanol."

"I knew you grew corn but not that much."

"Yup, we grow lots of corn. Pa says without the ethanol market the price of corn would only be half of what it is now. Pa says he wishes, and he said some swear words, that this Stony guy could somehow be shut up."

"R . . . really," said Ambrose.

"Know what?"

"What?"

"Pa thinks somebody's going to shoot Stony someday and shut him up for good."

"Your pa said that?"

"Yup, he did. If I was Stony I think I'd watch out. Bunch of folks in this country are really mad at him and out to get him."

26
Karl and Emily

*T*he afternoon following his meeting with Marilyn Jones, Karl Adams drove over to the historical society's museum and parked his car on the street in front of the museum store. He wanted to learn about the historical society and its activities and he wanted to become acquainted with Emily Higgins, who was obviously, in addition to Marilyn Jones, one of the driving forces in the Link Lake community.

A little bell tingled when Karl pushed open the door of the museum shop. Karl was greeted by a slim, older woman standing by a little counter. Her name tag read Emily Higgins.

"Welcome to the Link Lake Historical Museum," said Emily. "Thanks for stopping by. Would you like a tour? Lots of history in this little village."

"I would," said Karl, surprised that this older woman was willing to tour but one person.

"Let me straighten up a few things here in the store, first," said Emily. Karl watched as she closed and locked the cash register and put up a little sign that said, "Back in a half hour."

Then she turned to Karl. "You ready?"

"I am," said Karl. He had not expected a tour, nor did he expect to be on one before he had scarcely a chance to say hello.

"Follow me," said Emily as she turned and headed toward the museum entryway. She stopped in front of the old bank vault, its door showing a big jagged hole in it.

"This bank was robbed back in 1900," she began. It was obvious to Karl that she had done this tour many times, as there was no hesitation. She continued, "Our village marshal and a local posse tracked the robbers out of town and had a shootout with them in the woods only a couple miles from here. We do a reenactment of the event each year in our park. Brings in hundreds of people. Our historical society is very active—new activity this year is working with the Link Lake High School Nature Club to sponsor an eagle cam—a chance to watch the big eagle nest we have in our local park."

"Very interesting," said Karl.

They continued out the back door of the bank, to a little one-room school that was moved to the museum site a few years ago. "This is the Progressive School that was located between here and Willow River. We moved it here so people, especially young people, could see what these country schools were all about," said Emily. "I attended this very school when I was a kid. With all eight grades in only one room and with one teacher, these little schools did very well in their day—thousands of one-room school graduates are still around."

"Sure different from the school I attended," said Karl.

They next toured the old blacksmith shop, where Emily explained to Karl how the bellows worked and how the blacksmith heated up metal with a forge and then pounded it into a variety of shapes with a hammer and an anvil, making such things as door hinges, kitchen knives, hooks, and an assortment of other iron products.

Then it was on to a shed, where Emily showed Karl a cradle that the early farmers in the area used to cut wheat, and a flail that they used for separating the wheat kernels from the straw. The shed also housed several wagons and buggies, including an enclosed buggy that early mail carriers used to deliver mail to the farmers after Rural Free Delivery became available in the 1890s, before there were automobiles.

"Where did you say you were from?" asked Emily.

"I didn't, but I'm from Portland, Oregon, and just moved to town. I'm living in the Smith cabin on the lake."

"I know the place. Know it well. In fact Gen Smith was an active member of our historical society. You'll like it there. Nice location."

"Seems to be," said Karl as they returned to the museum gift shop. "Thanks so much for giving me the tour. Very nice of you."

"My pleasure," said Emily. "I'm always pleased to show people around who are interested in history."

"Yes, I've always had an interest in history," Karl replied. He glanced around the museum shop and saw a variety of items for sale, ranging from T-shirts with an imprint of the lake on them, to reproductions of old photos of the village at different times in its history, to a softcover book, *Barns of Link Lake*, by Oscar Anderson and Fred Russo.

Karl spotted a large, framed photo hanging on the wall. It appeared to be that of a huge bur oak tree.

"What's this?" he asked.

"Oh, that's a photo of one of Link Lake's most famous historic artifacts. It's known as the Trail Marker Oak. The Trail Marker Oak guided the Indians who lived in these parts as they traveled to a trading post on the Fox River."

"Fascinating," said Karl.

"Got ourselves a problem with this famous tree, though," she said.

"What would that be?"

"Well, there's this sand mining company from La Crosse that plans to open a sand mine in our park, which is where this famous tree is located. Because of the rock formations in the park, the company says they've got to cut down this old tree to make an access road."

"Is that right?"

"It's got a lot of people pretty darn mad. You see we've got this Economic Development Council that's trying to bring more jobs to the area, something we need, I guess. But I don't think a sand mine is the way to do it. Bunch of folks are pretty upset about it—trying to reverse the decision."

Karl continued to stare at the photo of the old tree.

"So you're from Oregon. What's your name?"

"It's Karl, Karl Adams."

"And if I could be so blunt, what brings you to Link Lake?"

"Oh, I'm working on a special project here—so I thought I'd learn a little about the history of the place."

"Well, good for you," said Emily. "We need more people interested in our history."

Karl and Emily

After leaving the museum, Karl drove back to his cabin. He thought about Emily Higgins, a person obviously committed to Link Lake and its history. And also a person who was interested in putting the little village of Link Lake on the map. The eagle cam was a great idea. He fired up his computer, clicked on the village's website, and soon was looking at an enormous eagle nest—he saw a couple of little eaglet heads, their mouths open and one of the adult bald eagles feeding them. He watched the eagle cam for nearly half an hour—he could see why people were attracted to it. He thought about the Trail Marker Oak and wondered if the mining company had purposely not told him about it. Or if they just didn't know how important that old tree was to this community. He was willing to give them the benefit of the doubt—that they probably either hadn't heard about the tree or, if they had, didn't think it was important to mention to him. Yet he had a nagging feeling about it, because he knew that symbols, especially ones that you can see and feel, are extremely important to many people.

Karl changed his clothes and did something he hadn't done in years— went fishing. On his way back from the museum, he had bought an inexpensive fishing rod, a packet of snelled hooks, a big red bobber, a fishing license, and a container of red worms. He climbed into the boat that came with the cabin and rowed toward where several fishermen were fishing.

He dropped the anchor over the side of the boat, baited up a hook, set the bobber, and tossed the line out into the lake. He'd long forgotten how relaxing it was to fish, to sit in a boat on a sunny afternoon and watch a bobber bounce as a westerly breeze riffled the water. He needed time to think, to come up with a strategy that he could use to bring this bucolic little town back together again. He wished he had been here earlier, that Alstage had asked him to work with the people of Link Lake before the citizens had become so polarized.

But the company hadn't done so and he had to make the most of the situation that he faced. He remembered his conversation with Marilyn Jones. She appeared to have the best interests of Link Lake in mind, except her solution to the problems the village faced were obviously considerably different from those of Emily Higgins and members of the Link Lake Historical Society. He knew he had misled Emily about what he was doing in town, but he really hadn't lied to her—only hadn't told her who he worked for and what the special project was. With some effort, Karl thought he could work out some kind of accommodation between these two strong-minded women. The ringer in the entire effort would likely be the environmental writer Stony Field. *Who knows what he'll write about next?*

Karl soon found himself dozing in the warm sun and only occasionally glancing at the big red bobber a few yards out from his boat. His eyes flew open when he felt a tug on his fishing rod. He glanced toward where the bobber had been and it was gone, completely submerged. He immediately began cranking on his reel as the tip of his fishing rod bent toward the lake. He continued cranking and then a large fish broke the surface of the lake, its tail bouncing on the water before it once more dropped into the lake and continued tugging on the ten-pound test line that the operator of the bait store suggested he purchase.

After another couple minutes of cranking and tugging, Karl had the fish alongside the boat; it looked to be at least a foot and a half long. As he reached over to lift the fish into the boat, the fish shook loose the hook and disappeared into the depths of the lake.

Karl sat with the fishing rod and the limp line in his hand. *I hope this is not how things will work out with what I have planned for this community.*

27

Fourth of July

Over the next several days, quietly working with Marilyn Jones and Mayor Jessup, Karl Adams offered suggestions that he hoped would help heal the rift that had developed in the community over the opening of a sand mine in the park. Karl had gotten authorization from the Alstage Sand Mining Company to help finance his ideas "with a reasonable amount of funds," as Evans had said in a recent e-mail. The mining company had actually provided several thousand dollars for the Link Lake Economic Development Council to use for expenses and prize money to be allotted to organizations wishing to enter floats, old tractors, fire trucks, horses, or a band in the Fourth of July parade, and for any other event the community might plan during the summer. The company did not want to be recognized for their largesse and be accused of trying to buy off the community with good deeds, so they insisted that the fewer people who knew about their monetary contributions the better.

The Village of Link Lake had for many years sponsored a modest Fourth of July celebration with a parade and evening fireworks. This year, with the financial help from the Alstage Sand Mining Company, the community pulled out all the stops, starting with an eleven o'clock parade down Main Street. Better than any year in memory, even for the old-timers, the entries in the parade were outstanding. And there were more of them, in fact twice as many entries as the previous year. Those watching previous years' Fourth of July celebrations had often commented that if you arrive five minutes late for the parade, you would miss seeing it. That was surely not the case this year.

Neighboring communities Willow River, Plainfield, Pine River, Waupaca, and even little Saxeville entered floats, as did each of the four local 4-H clubs and the Link Lake High School FFA organization. Of course all the fire departments for twenty miles around entered their fire trucks in the parade. Fred Russo and Oscar Anderson, as they had done in previous years, drove their antique tractors. Fred drove a John Deere Model B that he had meticulously restored to like new, and Oscar Anderson, with his restored Farmall H tractor, which also looked as if it had just rolled off the factory floor, followed behind. Other retired farmers drove an assortment of antique tractors, a Ford 8N, a Massey-Harris 44, a Minneapolis-Moline; even an old Fordson tractor that predated all of them was in the parade. The event had been well advertised; an hour before the starting time Link Lake's Main Street was lined with people four deep. No one remembered such a crowd attending the Link Lake Fourth of July parade for the past forty years.

"Just like it was when I was a kid," said Emily Higgins, when asked what she thought about this year's parade.

The announcer for the parade—other years there had been no announcer—was Earl Wade from WWRI. People in previous years had often wondered who was who and what was what. Not this year. This year the parade was well planned, and well organized, thanks to Karl Adams's behind-the-scenes hard work—and experience organizing parades such as this in other communities.

The parade began promptly at eleven when Officer Jimmy Barnes parked his squad car across Highway 22, its blue lights flashing. Highway 22, which became Main Street when it passed through Link Lake, was closed with a detour around town until the parade had passed.

The Link Lake High School Marching Band, playing a rousing Sousa march, led off the parade as the crowd cheered and clapped.

A panel of judges consisting of Marilyn Jones, Mayor Jessup, and Emily Higgins sat on a raised platform in front of the historical society's museum taking notes as each float, tractor, and fire truck passed. Monetary awards were available for each category of entry as well as a huge trophy to be awarded to the best overall entry.

Earl Wade, following the script Karl Adams had prepared, commented, described, and otherwise gave new life to this year's parade. The parade was picture perfect. Almost, anyway.

Fourth of July

The Link Lake Fire Department not only had their three best and finest fire trucks in the parade, but they also entered their 1928 fire truck, which had not been driven for twenty years and had been sold for junk but not yet picked up. Volunteer Fire Chief Henry Watkins, himself a better-than-average mechanic, had spent a week of evenings working on the old truck in preparation for the parade. He assured his volunteer firefighter colleagues that the old truck was ready for one more run. He said, "I want to give this old truck that served us well one more chance to shine."

Chief Watkins also said that he wanted to drive the old truck himself, that it would bring back some old memories for him. The old truck was purring along the parade route, having no trouble at all keeping up with the entry in front of it, the Link Lake Historical Society float. As all entries were asked to do, Chief Watkins stopped the truck in front of the reviewing stand, allowing the engine to idle. As the crowd watched and listened, Earl Wade gushed on about the old truck, about the volunteer fire department and its good work, and about how Volunteer Fire Chief Henry Watkins had spent many hours making this old relic of a truck into the fine working fire truck it is today.

Then people heard a hissing sound, barely perceptible, that turned into a low and then a louder whistle. Some of the parade watchers thought it must be part of the performance, as Chief Watkins was known for doing unexpected things at times, even being a bit of a showman. But the look on the chief's face wasn't quite right; he wasn't smiling as was his usual demeanor but had a look of puzzlement.

Earl Wade motored on with his many words of praise for Link Lake and the support it provided its volunteer fire department. Along with the whistle, a trickle of steam lifted from the old truck's engine compartment, and it quickly turned into a gushing cloud that floated across the reviewing stand, making the judges appear as silhouettes in the cloud.

People were perplexed at what they were seeing, wondering if all of this had indeed been planned, that the fire department had come up with a special effects show to win the approval of the judges for the fire truck category. Emily Higgins was making notes. Mayor Jessup looked concerned. Marilyn Jones was trying to wave away the steam.

For an instant the gushing cloud of steam stopped and then, to the surprise of everyone, there was an enormous KABOOM that was so loud the babies in the crowd immediately began wailing and, for an instant, everything shook, including the reviewing stand. And if the explosion wasn't enough, yellow flames and heavy black smoke began pouring from the old truck's engine compartment.

Chief Watkins leaped from the machine, carrying a fire extinguisher in his hand, but the little extinguisher did little to quell the flames that were leaping ever higher. One of Link Lake's fancy new yellow fire trucks pulled out from its place in line a couple of entries to the rear of the burning truck, its siren wailing and its red lights flashing. Immediately Link Lake firefighters had the fire out. Their modern truck waited to take its former place in the parade and several Link Lake Fire Department volunteers began pushing the old fire truck down the street, but not before Chief Watkins climbed back into the truck and took charge once more, waving at the crowd as the truck slowly passed by. This time the chief had a wide grin on his face as the old truck proceeded along the parade route, now propelled by human power. The former bright red covering for the engine compartment was black and charred.

When the parade was finished, and while announcer Wade waited for the results from the judges, the Link Lake High School Marching Band entertained the audience with a medley of marches. Finally, Mayor Jessup handed a piece of paper to Earl Wade, who began announcing the winners in various categories—farm tractors, marching bands, floats, fire department entries, and so on. The winners came forward to claim their prizes and checks. Everyone eagerly wanted to know who was the grand prize winner. Which of the one hundred or so entries would walk off with the trophy for the all-around best entry in the parade?

The crowd grew silent as Wade unfolded a second sheet of paper. "On a unanimous vote, the grand prize and this beautiful trophy goes to . . ." Wade paused to add some suspense to the moment.

"The grand prize goes to the Link Lake Volunteer Fire Department's antique fire truck entry and their rather innovative way of demonstrating their abilities as firefighters."

The crowd applauded loudly and cheered as Chief Watkins and the entire contingent of Link Lake volunteer firefighters came forward to claim their prize. It was later learned that the judges couldn't decide if the entire smoke, explosion, and fire were planned—or they just happened. They finally decided it didn't matter; it clearly was the most exciting and entertaining, as well as informative, part of the entire parade. When someone asked Chief Watkins what really had happened, he would only say, "No comment."

Nothing the rest of the day, not even the free picnic on the lawn fronting the Link Lake Supper Club, where everyone enjoyed free beer, soft drinks, bratwurst, potato salad, and baked beans throughout the afternoon, could top the parade. Not even the fireworks shot up over the lake that evening, which by all standards were the best that anyone had ever seen in Link Lake. None of these events could top the parade and the "creativity and prowess of the Link Lake Volunteer Fire Department."

That evening, Karl Adams returned to his cabin, put his feet up, watched the eagle cam for a few minutes to see how the little eaglets were doing, and then sat down on the little deck overlooking the lake enjoying a bottle of Spotted Cow, a beer he discovered here in Wisconsin and really liked. *All this turned out better than I thought. What a huge crowd, and I didn't hear one word mentioned about the sand mine. And to think we managed to get Emily Higgins, the mayor, and Marilyn Jones on the same platform— and agreeing on something. That's got to be a step forward.*

Karl took a long sip of his beer.

28
First Protestors

On the day following the "widely successful and great fun" Fourth of July celebration, as someone described it, Marilyn Jones sat in her office at the Link Lake Supper Club. Out her window she could see several volunteers working at cleaning up the debris left over from the big event. A crew from the tent rental company was taking down the tent, and Joe Jensen, her maintenance man, janitor, and all-around handyman, was toting the big bratwurst grill back to its storage place in the shed in back of the supper club. After entertaining several thousand people on the supper club lawn the previous day, Marilyn was happy to rest and take a deep breath on this day after.

She was aware of Karl Adams's idea that if you brought people in a community together and they had a good time, some of the bitterness over a sand mine coming to their village might be put aside and perhaps even forgotten. But she wasn't at all sure about it. In her experience, when people decided they were opposed to something, it took more than a fancy parade, grilled bratwurst, free beer, and a fireworks extravaganza to change their minds.

She also was concerned about the protestors who showed up in town at the entrance to the park a few days after the newspaper announced the decision that a sand mine was on the way. Each day, a half dozen or so of them marched up and back in front of the park entrance with signs that read, "Stop the Mine!" She was quite certain that all of them came from out of town, but they still were a constant reminder to everyone in town that a mine was on the way.

Emily Higgins was thrilled with the success of the Fourth of July celebration. Her goal and that of the Link Lake Historical Society was to bring people to Link Lake so they could see what a great little village it was and what a rich history it had. She was also pleased with the wonderful turnout for the brat fry and fireworks that took place on the lawn of the Link Lake Supper Club.

Emily, of course, did not know that the Alstage Sand Mining Company had provided the money for parade expenses and prizes, as well as the entire food, beverage, and fireworks expenses. But Emily, ever suspicious, wondered where the money had come from. And Emily did not know that this was a carefully planned event to help soften the reaction of the community to sand mining and to bring a sharply divided community together.

Ambrose Adler, who had watched the parade, enjoyed the free meal, and watched the fireworks before walking back home, was also skeptical of what might be behind the event. In his many years attending Link Lake Fourth of July festivities, he had never seen one quite so well organized, so well publicized and indeed, so well attended. Ambrose had more than a sneaking suspicion that this event was a well-planned and well-financed event, likely with the Alstage Sand Mining Company pulling the strings. He had seen similar tactics used by big companies wanting to come into little communities where there was local opposition and then trying to overwhelm them with goodwill. He remembered that right here in Ames County a few years ago a company had tried to open up a big industrial hog operation over on the Tamarack River. They'd offered the community several things, including paying for a statue of a local lumberjack who'd lost his life when a log jam broke lose. Their big plans for the hog operation didn't pan out, and they pulled back their offers to the community.

Ambrose, like the rest of the community, was well aware of the out-of-town protestors showing up each day at the park carrying signs opposing the sand mine. He appreciated their passion—but he wasn't sure they were doing much to help the opposition to the project. Small-town folks aren't accustomed to out-of-town protesters in their midst. Ambrose was concerned that what they were doing might backfire in that more people would be taking the side of the village board, the Economic Development Council, and the Alstage Sand Mining Company.

Ambrose had asked Gloria to send him news articles from around the country on the topic of sand mining, and now he reviewed them carefully:

Opening and operating a sand mine is a fairly complicated process involving several steps, which begins with removing trees, grass, topsoil, stones, and whatever covers the sand to be mined. Depending on the geology of the area, the sand is then scraped free or blasted to loosen it. If blasted, the material generally needs crushing to reduce the size for later handling. Once loose, it is loaded on trucks and hauled to a processing plant for washing and processing. Processing involves washing the sand as it is carried over a vibrating screen to remove fine particles. When the washing is complete, the sand is moved to a surge pile where much of the water clinging to the sand particles goes into the ground. From the surge pile, the sand goes to a dryer and is then passed through a screening operation. Once dried, the sand is further screened and sorted. Sand particles of a similar size are stored for transport to hydraulic fracturing mining sites.

Upon finishing reading the steps in a sand mining operation, Ambrose sat back in his chair. *I wonder if the Economic Development Council and the village board would have been so quick to approve a mine in the village's park if they had known all of what I just read. What will people say when their dishes rattle and their houses shake when their new mine sets off a blast to shake loose the sand? Are they willing to have the air filled with dust so they can add a few more jobs to the area? Are they willing to put up with the constant roar of trucks hauling sand through the village? And are they willing to see the destruction of the Trail Marker Oak as a necessity for what some are calling progress?*

With all of this swirling around in his mind Ambrose walked out to his garden, Ranger and Buster following closely behind. He harvested the vegetables he thought he might sell that afternoon at his roadside stand. He ate a brief lunch, napped for a half hour, then hauled the vegetables with an old wagon out to the stand, where he spent the afternoon. But he was troubled. And he wasn't feeling all that well. Getting overexcited about the coming of a sand mine to the community surely didn't help his bad heart.

29
Free Wi-Fi

*W*ell, Fred, what'd you think of it?" Fred Russo and Oscar Anderson were having their regular morning coffee discussion at the Eat Well Café.

"Think of what?" asked Fred as he took his place opposite his old friend and waited while Henrietta poured his coffee.

"What everybody is talking about this morning."

"How am I supposed to know what people are yakking about? I've been home doing my chores, catching up on work that needs doin' before one more summer slips by," said Fred.

"The Fourth of July celebration. That's what everybody is talking about."

"Pretty good this year wasn't it?" said Fred. "Except one thing I didn't like."

"And what would that have been?" asked Oscar, a bit put out that his old friend didn't like everything about the celebration.

"It was the free bratwurst and beer."

"You didn't like the free brats and beer? What's the matter with you? You goin' senile on me?"

"I didn't say I didn't like the brats and beer—they were both pretty darn good, too good in fact."

"So what is your problem, Fred?"

"Problem was that they were free."

"And please tell me how that could be a problem?" asked Oscar.

"If I had to pay for the brats and beer, I wouldn't have eaten so many and would have downed a few less beers. Had me a bellyache and a headache when I got up this morning. Haven't had such a thing since I was twenty years old."

"You can remember when you were twenty years old?" asked Oscar.

"Yes, I can. In those days I may have put down a few more beers than necessary on occasion."

"Just a few more?" Oscar was smiling.

"Yup, that's about the sum total of it—had just such a headache this morning. Kind of refreshing to experience something when you're in your eighties that you experienced when you were twenty. Kind of a good thing, I'd say."

"Whatever it takes to make you happy," said Oscar.

"What'd you think of the trick that our esteemed fire chief pulled with that old fire truck—it blowing up and catching on fire right there on Main Street?" asked Fred.

"Tell you the truth, I don't think any of that was supposed to happen. I think that old fire truck, even with all the work the chief had done on it, was on its last tracks and it just happened to die during the parade. Chief handled it all pretty darn good, I'd say," said Oscar.

Both men concentrated on drinking their coffee, when Fred glanced at the new little placard that sat on their table. "Free Wi-Fi," it said. "What is this Wi-Fi?" asked Fred, "and why do you suspect it's free?"

"Don't have a clue what that means. Expect the Wi refers to Wisconsin—must mean something about Wisconsin is free and you can get it right here in this little restaurant," said Oscar. "Let's ask Henrietta, she'll know."

When Henrietta came by with coffee refills, Oscar said, "Henrietta, what's this free Wi-Fi?" He pronounced each of the letters separately.

"Something new for us, people stopping by have been asking for it—especially the tourists here in town. Locals want it too. They say the only place it's available is at the library."

"But what is it?" asked Fred.

"Well," Henrietta began. "Wi-Fi stands for Wireless Fidelity." She picked up the little placard sitting on the table and read, "We are pleased to provide free high-speed access to the Internet to our customers for their computer and cell phone use."

"Geez, Fred, we could have looked at the card and we would have known what it was," said Oscar.

"Ain't much for reading cards with small print. Eyes ain't that good anymore," said Fred. But then he added, "But I still don't know what it is. Where do you plug into this Wi-Fi thing?"

Henrietta laughed. "You don't plug it in, it comes through the air."

"Come through the air, huh? Well, show me some of this Wi-Fi."

"Fred, it probably works like the radio and the TV. You don't see those signals coming through the air."

Fred shook his head. "What will they think of next? Just can't keep up with all this stuff."

"Gotta try a little harder, Fred. Gotta try to keep up; otherwise folks will toss us old guys into the dust bins of history."

"There you go with that highfalutin language that I'll bet you don't even understand," said Fred.

"Maybe so, Fred. But at least now when somebody mentions Wi-Fi we'll know what they're talkin' about."

"Maybe you'll know, but I still don't understand how it works and why somebody would come here to get it like they might get a cup of coffee," said Fred as he drained his cup and looked around to see if he might spot somebody using this Wi-Fi thing.

30

Supper Club Remodeling

Marilyn Jones had been thinking about making substantial changes to the Link Lake Supper Club. Their schedule of being open from eleven in the morning until late in the evening had been in place for as long as Marilyn had owned the supper club. Everyone had become comfortable with the schedule and it was working well.

But when Marilyn saw all the new people in town for the Fourth of July celebration and she noticed the steadily increased use of the bike trail on the former Chicago and Northwestern Railroad right of way, she began thinking. She wondered if she was missing a bunch of business from people who were not likely to stick around for a good meal and the view of the lake, but merely wanted to stop for a cup of coffee, a fruit smoothie, a protein bar, or perhaps some pastry before they continued on their way along the bike trail. When she heard that the Eat Well Café had added free Wi-Fi and it was attracting an increasing number of bike riders, she made up her mind. She called a meeting of her chef, Jonathon Frederick, and her waitresses.

"You all know how much I appreciate your hard work and dedication to the Link Lake Supper Club. We are doing well, but we can do better. I've got some ideas for some changes, as everyone in business says, 'Unless you keep up with the times, you go backward.' We've been fortunate, especially since the recession, to increase our business a little. But I have an idea that will increase our business a lot and at the same time bring us up to date with the world."

Jonathon wondered what she was talking about. She hadn't mentioned any big changes to him and he was the one responsible for planning and preparing the food for many years.

"I believe all of you are well aware of the number of bicyclists that pedal through Link Lake every spring, summer, and fall on the bike path. That number is increasing. These folks are a market we are missing. The number of tourists coming to Link Lake has been on the increase as well—most of these folks are from the cities, where what I am suggesting is common to them. I propose we remodel part of our dining room into a coffee bar that opens at nine in the morning and is open all day, where we serve coffee, a limited selection of fresh-made pastries, and offer free Wi-Fi. That's what folks want these days. Some coffee, a little food, and a chance to check e-mail and send messages."

"So some of us are going to work longer hours," said Jonathon, appearing not at all happy with what he was hearing.

"And I will make sure that everyone who works longer hours is properly compensated."

"If I could ask," began Jonathon, "are we doing this because the Eat Well now has free Wi-Fi and the bikers are stopping there?"

"That's partly it. The Eat Well is really not our competition, but they surely are attracting a lot of bike riders since they began offering free Wi-Fi."

"Well," continued Jonathon, beginning to bristle, "I'm opposed to the idea. If we include a coffee bar with Wi-Fi, we will destroy our image as a first-class supper club with a long history and a great view."

"Our history and view won't change," said Marilyn, a bit taken aback by her chef's comment.

"But our reputation will. And a good restaurant's reputation is the most valuable thing it has," huffed Jonathon.

"Perhaps," said Marilyn, "but we still must try to keep up with the times."

The waitstaff sat watching and listening to the exchange, not thinking it wise to express their opinions one way or another as they had to get along with both Jonathon and with Marilyn—and this discussion was shaping up as a battle between two strong personalities.

"I want you all to think about this for a few days and let me know your reactions. I'd like to start the remodeling right away so we can capture some of the late summer and fall bikers traveling through town," said Marilyn.

"I'll give you my thoughts right now," said Jonathon as he pushed back in his chair and stood up. His face was red and the veins in his neck were throbbing. "I think it's an awful idea. I quit." He threw his apron on the table and stalked toward the door. "You'll have to do your own damn cooking and baking—and making coffee for these yuppie bike riders that pedal into town. Good luck with all of that." He slammed the door when he left.

"Didn't expect that," Marilyn said, a bit embarrassed that her staff had to witness the confrontation between her and the supper club's longtime and quite locally famous chef.

"I'll talk to him when he cools off and see if I can change his mind. I hope I will have your support for my idea—I believe it's the direction we must go if this place is to stay in business and grow into the future." Several of the waitresses' heads were nodding in agreement.

As it turned out, Jonathon Frederick did not return to his former position of head chef at the Link Lake Supper Club but went to work for a supper club in Willow River, at a major competitor of Marilyn's establishment. Marilyn began advertising for a head chef, and once she began searching she learned that she should hire two of them—one to be in charge of the food for the planned coffee shop and the other, she hoped someone with a good reputation as a chef, to take over the duties for the dinner crowd that expected a better-than-average dining experience.

These staffing problems took up much of her time, so much that she had little time left to think about the new sand mining company coming to town. She didn't have time to worry about the protesters at the park who appeared every day, rain or shine, and marched back and forth with their Stop the Mine signs.

31

Trail Marker Oak Days

Marilyn found time to meet secretly with Karl Adams, Mayor Jessup, and members of the village board to discuss further plans that Karl had for generating more community support for the sand mine due to begin operations in October.

After the Fourth of July celebration, Karl had posted on the bulletin board outside the village hall a large map of Increase Joseph Community Park showing exactly where the sand mine would be located. The plan showed how the mine would take up about half of the two-hundred-acre park, leaving the other half essentially untouched. The map did not include the Trail Marker Oak near the park entrance but did indicate the large rock outcropping that limited the access to the park and thus offered but one way in and out of the proposed mine site. Of course local people knew the park and the rock outcroppings well and knew where the special bur oak was located and realized it was in the way and would have to be taken down.

"Marilyn and I have been talking," Karl Adams began. "She told me about the annual Trail Marker Oak Days celebration held each summer in Link Lake. The Alstage Mining Company would like to help you folks expand this event—to make it the biggest and best Trail Marker Oak Days the community has ever seen."

"What are you suggesting?" asked Mayor Jessup, who was well aware of the irony of celebrating the Trail Marker Oak when the company planned to cut it down.

Karl went on in considerable detail outlining the several activities he had in mind to enhance the celebration, with all additional expenses covered by Alstage Mining. He suggested they hold the event on an early August weekend when the area would be filled with vacationing tourists, which would surely enhance the crowd.

In the past, Trail Marker Oak Days was held at the Increase Joseph Community Park, and although the sand mine was due to open there in a few months, the group decided it would be appropriate to center the event's activities there once more. They would not mention that this would likely be the last time for the event to be held in the park—especially since the Trail Marker Oak would no longer be there after the mine opened. They were well aware of the half dozen or so protestors who so far marched back and forth in front of the park entrance Monday through Friday, but not on the weekends. Of course the celebration would be held on a weekend.

In addition to the arts and crafts fair, with booths located in the park, Karl suggested two additional activities "to spice up the event." He suggested a cardboard boat race on Saturday and a bass fishing contest on Sunday morning. Both of these events would begin at the Link Lake Supper Club's pier, only a short distance from the park.

Although he was well aware of Emily Higgins's opposition to opening the sand mine in the park, and her vehement objection to cutting down the Trail Marker Oak, Mayor Jessup suggested they ask Emily to once more recite her "Ode to the Old Oak," as she had done for every Trail Marker Oak Days from the first time it was held.

Marilyn Jones was not too sure about this decision, for it would give Emily one more opportunity to engender opposition to the mine, but she held her tongue. Marilyn also realized that if Emily did not do the ode, a fair number of people would wonder why, especially members of the Link Lake Historical Society.

Publicity in the *Ames County Argus*, on WWRI, as well as in newspapers in the Fox River Valley, Madison, and Milwaukee announced Link Lake's annual Trail Marker Oak Days celebration scheduled for the first weekend in August. The news reports mentioned the annual arts and crafts fair but also emphasized that additional special features this year would include a cardboard boat race across the big lake's inlet in front of the Link Lake Supper Club on Saturday and a bass fishing tournament on Sunday.

*B*y six thirty on Friday afternoon prior to the big celebration, several artists, some of them coming from as far away as Chicago and the Twin Cities, had set up their booths in the park, showing off everything from paintings of horses and mountains to woodcarvings, block prints, and metal and leather crafts—a vast array of artistic creations for people to see and buy.

The parking lot at the Link Lake Motel was jammed with fishing boats in preparation for Sunday's bass fishing contest—and the Link Lake Supper Club was filled with customers, some waiting up to an hour for dinner.

By ten on Saturday morning, Increase Joseph Community Park was elbow to elbow with people visiting the art fair, chatting with each other and with the assortment of artists who had their work on display. Although not arts and crafts, Emily Higgins had encouraged her friend Ambrose Adler to set up a booth, where he sold fresh vegetables from his farm. His booth was quickly one of the busiest as people lined up to buy fresh vegetables: cucumbers, new potatoes, sweet corn, broccoli, beets, carrots, leaf lettuce, and green beans.

At eleven o' clock, the scheduled time for the brief program, Emily Higgins took her place on the little stage that had been erected in front of the famous Trail Marker Oak tree. The old tree looked as vigorous as ever with its rather massive trunk leaning in the direction of the Fox River to the southeast.

Emily welcomed the substantial crowd that had gathered to hear her annual recitation of the "Ode to the Old Oak." She was well aware that this might be the last year for the Trail Marker Oak—but she vowed to do the best possible job she could, with the hope that something as simple as her recitation might help save the old tree.

With a loud, clear voice she began.

Ode to the Old Oak

Long before the first white people set foot in this county called Ames and this place that became Link Lake, this tree, this old oak, this old bur oak tree, stood as it stands today. A reminder of who we are and where we've been, a reminder of those who traveled these parts before us and sought direction. Sought direction from this old oak. This old oak called the Trail Marker Oak.

It is believed this bur oak tree first saw the light of day in the year 1830, eighteen years before Wisconsin became a state, and twenty-two years before Ames County was settled. This was Indian country then, and this old bur oak served as a road sign that helped the Indians find their way to the Fox River and the trading post there. The French traders who followed them also knew this tree, as did the first white settlers who came to Link Lake in 1852. All used this tree as a direction finder.

The founder of our village, Increase Joseph Link, and a tall Menominee Indian named Kee-chee-new met one day, and it was Kee-chee-new who took Increase Joseph to see this old tree, at this very spot where we are standing now. It was Kee-chee-new who said, "This is a sacred tree standing on sacred ground." And it was Increase Joseph Link who responded, "I will do everything in my power to make certain that no one ever cuts down this tree or in any way harms it."

As the years passed, this old oak, this Trail Marker Oak, has been a symbol for this community and our people—a link to our past, but also a symbol for our future. We as individuals need direction in our lives. And so do communities. This old tree stands as a reminder of this and more. This old tree represents the history of our community; it represents our present, and it symbolically points our way to the future.

As many of you know, this old tree, this sacred tree standing on sacred ground, is destined to be destroyed so that the sacred sand beneath us can be mined and carted away to feed the ever-thirsty demand for our country's energy supply. What a tragic loss it will be.

Oh, sacred tree, how much we have adored you and benefited by your presence. Oh, sacred tree on this sacred ground. Oh, sacred tree.

Emily bowed as the audience clapped. Mayor Jessup whispered to Marilyn, "We should not have let her speak. Her words will only fuel more dissent and give these crazy protesters more ideas for their misguided actions."

By 1:00 p.m. people began gathering on the lawn of the Link Lake Supper Club for the cardboard boat race scheduled to begin promptly at 2:00 p.m. Most people had never seen a cardboard boat race, so many stopped by merely to see what it was all about.

People saw an enormous stack of cardboard boxes that had been broken down, and several huge rolls of gray duct tape standing on a nearby table. The idea of the race was for a team of three to construct a "boat" from the available cardboard, fastening the pieces together with the duct tape. The rules said the boat must be just large enough for one member of the team, usually the smallest person, to sit in it and paddle with the canoe paddle provided.

The event was in two stages: the construction of the boat, which was timed, and the race itself, which was not. The first cardboard boat to successfully paddle across the inlet in front of the Link Lake Supper Club would win and go home with a trophy and a crisp, one-hundred-dollar bill.

At 2:00 p.m., five teams of three waited for the starting pistol shot that announced the official beginning. Young people made up most teams; one team included Noah Drake, Ambrose Adler's young friend, and two of his school buddies. Another team appeared to be made up of college-aged women, each dressed in a rather skimpy bikini, at least not swimwear often seen in Link Lake. One team included three middle-aged men that appeared to have spent a little too much time in the Link Lake Tap.

The pistol shot echoed across the lake and the contest was on. Noah Drake's team immediately trotted to the enormous pile of flattened cardboard boxes. Two boys selected cardboard, the third grabbed a roll of duct tape, and they quickly began assembling a boat. They had obviously planned ahead of time what they would do. The college girls began sorting through the pile of cardboard, apparently searching for color-coordinated pieces. The slightly tipsy third group stood studying the pile of cardboard, clearly not knowing how to begin or even what to do. The remaining two teams, both made up of young people, boys and girls, hurriedly cobbled together structures that vaguely resembled boats.

The second pistol shot announced the ending of the time for boat building and the time to launch the structures into the water. A volunteer in a boat was located just offshore, watching to make sure that everyone was safe, that everyone in the boats was wearing a life jacket, that the rules had been followed, and that any loose debris was picked up. The three tipsy men dragged a mass of tape and cardboard toward the water. They pushed their "boat" into the lake; the man selected to do the paddling tripped and fell over the fragile structure, which promptly sank to the bottom of the lake. Everyone laughed and clapped. The two men remaining on shore fished their partner out of the lake, dragged out the wet cardboard, and bowed deeply to the crowd, which cheered and clapped even louder. The smallest of the three college girls left shore in the bright, multicolored boat with a gentle push from her partners. The young woman, with a big smile on her face, began paddling as slowly the boat beneath her disappeared and she was left holding only the paddle. She swam ashore, while the observer in the boat with a long pole with a hook on the end captured the cardboard. She garnered a round of applause when she walked up the beach.

The remaining three boats, considerably more seaworthy than the two that had preceded them, moved slowly across the inlet, which was about one hundred yards. Noah Drake's team's boat sank just before reaching shore. The man in the boat had trailed along behind them and picked up the young man, who had already started swimming toward shore. The remaining two boats arrived on shore at exactly the same time—the observer in the boat had carefully watched their progress. He picked up both of them and brought all three of them back to the starting place, where the dual winners were announced and a new hundred-dollar bill was handed to each of the winning teams. One of the winning teams had come from Willow River, the other one from Waupaca.

Sunday, the second day of Trail Marker Oak Days, dawned sunny and cool. The weather report said the high would be in the mid-seventies, ideal weather for almost anything one wanted to do outside. There was little or no wind, so the fishermen didn't have to fight rough water in their quest for a winning catch.

Contestants for the Big Bass Fishing Contest roared off in their fishing boats at dawn, to the far corners of Link Lake where they thought a big bass might be lurking. By noon, when the fishing contest was officially over, fishermen, who had to keep their catches alive and release them after they were measured and weighed, lined up to see who was the winner of the event that offered a prize of $500 for the biggest catch. Posted near the landing was a note that said Wisconsin's record largemouth bass was caught in 1940 and weighed in at eleven pounds. Bass fishermen always hoped they had an outside chance of beating the record as well as winning the cash prize for the largest catch of the day. As it turned out, a fisherman from Princeton caught a five-pound, ten-ounce bass, which proved to be the winner for the event.

The crowds visiting the booths in the park were the largest ever, according to Emily Higgins. Ambrose Adler's fresh vegetables sold out by noon each day. He told Emily that he sold more vegetables in these two days than he had the entire month so far.

A large screen had been erected in one of the booths sponsored by the Link Lake Historical Society that projected moment-by-moment activities of the new eagle family located some distance back in the park and thus not disturbed by the crowds. People stood watching the eagles from early morning until late afternoon on each of the two days of the celebration—it was clearly one of the most interesting of all the exhibits.

With the quiet backing of the Alstage Sand Mining Company, this second community event was an obvious success no matter who one asked. Karl Adams drove back to his cabin, snapped open a beer, and sat on his patio overlooking the lake. *I think all of my hard work is paying off. It was too bad that Emily Higgins had to mention the sand mine, but this one negative feature was surely outdone by all of the fun people were having. Besides, I doubt most people at the event cared one way or the other about that old crooked bur oak tree.*

Karl recalled the old grizzled man who sat at a little vegetable stand at the park. He remembered seeing him at the Fourth of July celebration. He talked with him for a bit at his vegetable stand—at least tried to talk with him, but he was difficult to understand because of his speech impediment.

He learned his name was Ambrose Adler and that he had a small vegetable farm just outside of Link Lake.

Now, as he sat on his patio sipping a bottle of Leinenkugel's, his thoughts returned to Ambrose. *There's something familiar about that old man. But I can't put my finger on it. Something about his eyes, those clear gray eyes that seem to look right through you.*

32
Lake Coffee Bar

The weeks following the highly successful Trail Marker Oak Days were quiet in Link Lake. These August days were mostly clear and warm, with the daytime temperatures reaching the mid-eighties and sometimes low-nineties. An occasional thunderstorm in the evening freshened things up and kept the farmers happy but did not dampen the spirits of the summer tourists, who reached record numbers in recent weeks.

By mid-August, workmen completed the remodeling of the Link Lake Supper Club, and the new Lake Coffee Bar opened. Bicyclists traveling the nearby railway bike trail began to find the place and passed the word along to their friends, who were also stopping by. Marilyn Jones had succeeded in hiring a new chef, Pierre Le Page. She hired him away from a top-shelf restaurant—mostly because he had once vacationed in Link Lake and liked the community. He spoke with a heavy French accent, which added a bit of mystique to the supper club. She promoted Shirley Noble, one of her longtime waitstaff, to be in charge of the Lake Coffee Bar.

Marilyn's life had once more become easier. Crowds at the coffee bar, though not yet outstanding, were respectable and growing. Customer numbers for dinner had increased considerably, even more than before the Great Recession. Pierre Le Page had added several new French items to the standard menu of steaks and fish. A favorite was *boeuf bourguignon*, a special recipe of Le Page's that included beef, dry red wine, Cognac, and several secret ingredients. It was fast becoming a favorite, especially among tourists.

Marilyn mused about how well Karl Adams's tactics of creating a series of events to take people's minds off the sand mine had worked. She had been highly skeptical, but she had to admit, he knew what he was doing. Of course it didn't hurt that the Alstage Sand Mining Company had poured several thousand dollars into backing the events, from paying for advertising and covering expenses to offering generous amounts of prize money for the various competitions.

She also had to admit that the eagle cam idea turned out far better than she had anticipated. She had a computer screen set up in the new coffee bar, which continued to attract considerable attention as the two eaglets continued to grow and could often be seen peering over the edge of the big nest.

She was also pleased that she had not heard anyone talking recently about the plight of the Trail Marker Oak. People had either forgotten about it, or they had accepted the fact that in the name of progress and bringing new jobs to the community, some minor sacrifices had to be made. She was becoming more certain that when she retired from operating the Link Lake Supper Club, she would be remembered for how she had turned the community around. The new sand mine would clearly put little Link Lake on the map, and she would be viewed as the person who made it happen, the person who brought economic security to a little backwater town that feared facing the future and resisted change at every turn.

Karl Adams was feeling good too about what he had achieved in the few short weeks since he moved to the Link Lake community. He continued to eat breakfast each morning at the Eat Well and listened to the banter. Trail Marker Oak Days were all the talk for several days, especially because of the large crowd the event brought to Link Lake. Karl overheard Henrietta say to one of Eat Well's regular customers, "Our little Link Lake is really doing well this summer. Never saw so many people in town since my years of living here. Lots of community spirit. Lots of good times."

Karl smiled to himself. His plan to take people's minds off the new sand mine was working beyond anything he had hoped for. He even noticed people stopping by to look at the big map outside of the village hall, where they could see exactly where the mine would be located. Sometimes two or three people stood in front of the map, talking to each other about it and pointing to various places on the map.

Karl read the Stony Field columns each week and observed that lately Stony Field had made no mention of sand mining or hydraulic fracturing. He was writing about climate change and how it was affecting the polar bears in the Artic; another column was about water problems in southern California. Karl thought, *At least we've got Stony Field off our backs. Guys like that can be a real pain.*

The Eat Well, like other Link Lake establishments, had a monitor where people could watch the eagle nest and the progress the eagle family was making. Karl found it fascinating—he watched it online for a half hour or so every evening when he returned to his cabin.

With everything going according to plan, Karl went fishing nearly every afternoon and was catching fish as well. One day he caught a bass larger than the one that took the prize at the recent bass fishing tournament. He was a catch-and-release fisherman—mostly because he really didn't know how to clean a fish and even worse, he didn't have the first idea of how to prepare one to eat. He could have asked Pierre Le Page at the supper club; Marilyn had introduced him to her new chef, but he was satisfied with the pleasure of hooking a fish, struggling to land it, and then letting it go. *A fish that fights that hard to live deserves another chance.*

In his weekly report to Evans at the mining company headquarters in La Crosse, he wrote:

Everything's going smoothly in Link Lake. No talk about the coming sand mine. People have turned to other matters. The money spent on the two major weekend activities appears to have clearly made a difference. Even the handful of protestors has backed off. People continue to talk about the good times they had, and how the events brought more people to Link Lake than they would have ever imagined.

Suspect your advance people will have no problems when they begin test drilling—when did you say? First week in September?

Karl

33
Busy Summer

Ambrose Adler couldn't remember when he had experienced a busier summer. Sales at his roadside stand had soared—in fact nearly every afternoon he sold out most of the vegetables and fruits he had available. He was thankful for a good growing season. The strawberry and raspberry crop had been outstanding. The sweet corn and new potatoes were excellent, and the cucumbers and zucchini continued to do well.

One day back in July, when Noah Drake had stopped by to talk and play with Ranger, Ambrose asked him if he'd like to help out with the stand. Noah said, "Sure, I don't think Pa will care; the corn crop doesn't need much attention now, nor do the soybeans. So sure, what do you want me to do?"

Ambrose explained that Noah could help pick strawberries and raspberries, gather the green beans when they were ready, snap off ripe ears of sweet corn, cut the leaf lettuce, wash it and put it in little bags, and dig some carrots and beets. Noah did all of this and seemed to enjoy doing it. He rode his bike over to Ambrose's farm each morning and worked with Ambrose until noon.

Noah appreciated the opportunity to make a little extra money, but he also liked spending time at Ambrose's farm. It was so different from the farm his dad operated with big diesel John Deere tractors, huge John Deere combines, tilling equipment, and all the rest that had become standard on large commercial farms. Ambrose had none of these things. He still plowed his big vegetable garden with a team of horses and a one-bottom, sixteen-inch walking plow. Likewise he smoothed the garden's surface with a horse-drawn disc, marked the rows with a person-powered marker, and controlled the weeds with a hoe and a strong back. He used no commercial fertilizer but did spread ample amounts of horse manure on the garden site each fall before plowing it.

Noah also found it interesting that Ambrose did not have electricity and lighted his house with a kerosene lamp that sat in the middle of the kitchen table and lighted his way to the barn with a kerosene lantern. Noah couldn't understand how someone could live without electricity, without a telephone, without a TV, and without an indoor toilet. Ambrose did have a battery-operated radio.

Noah had his own cell phone that he used regularly to call his friends and let his mother know where he was. He wondered how anyone could get by without having a telephone in his pocket.

Ambrose simply couldn't do all the work associated with his fresh vegetable stand by himself anymore and very much needed the help that young Noah provided. Ambrose discovered he was increasingly out of breath, and often, in the midst of doing a task such as digging potatoes, found he had to sit in the shade every few minutes and rest before returning to work.

Ambrose also enjoyed Noah's company. As they worked together each morning, he learned about Noah's interest in wild animals and that he planned to do something related to nature when he graduated from college. Ambrose encouraged him, telling him that these were great ideas and that he should let nothing get in the way of his dreams.

"Pa doesn't think much of what I want to do," Noah told him one day. "He says that people interested in nature stand in the way of those who want progress in the country. He says nature lovers are a bunch of ill-informed kooks."

"D . . . don't think so," said Ambrose. He and Lucas Drake had lived a half mile apart for more than forty years, but they really didn't know each other at all. Ambrose knew that Drake was chairman of the ultraconservative Eagle Party, but Ambrose didn't know until now how much Lucas Drake despised anyone concerned about nature and the environment.

"I started reading Stony Field's column every week after we talked about it in school," said Noah. "I kind of like what he has to say, most of the time anyway. Do you read Stony's column?"

"I . . . do," said Ambrose.

"Pa just hates him. He says that people should get together and shut him up. Pa says that if people listened to guys like Stony Field there'd be no jobs, everybody would be on food stamps, we'd all have higher taxes, and the country would just plain go to hell."

"P . . . retty strong words," Ambrose said.

"Pa gets all red in the face when I mention Stony Field, so I don't talk about him. But I still read his columns. Stuff like climate change, and how clean water is the big issue in much of the world today, and how some animals probably won't survive if we keep doing what we're doing."

The old man and the boy worked together quietly for a few minutes, each with his own thoughts.

"Did you see the eagle cam of the eagle family in the park?" Noah asked, breaking the silence.

"I . . . did," said Ambrose. "Saw it at the library the other day."

"Pretty interesting, huh?"

Ambrose nodded his head but then interrupted the conversation. "I . . . I think we've got enough vegetables for this afternoon," Ambrose said as they began hauling the produce to the little stand, where a car was already parked, waiting for the new day's fresh vegetables.

Once the vegetables were all nicely displayed in the little stand, and they served the waiting customer, both Ambrose and Noah sat down and in turn took long sips from the brown jug of water that Ambrose brought along. He was out of breath and welcomed the rest.

"You ready for the thresheree next week?" Noah asked. Big signs were posted all over Link Lake and the surrounding communities announcing the Link Lake Historical Society's annual thresheree, held each year at Ambrose Adler's farm in late August.

"M . . . mostly," said Ambrose. Noah noticed that Ambrose had cut the hayfield across the road from his buildings with his team and mower, a second cutting, and had hauled the sparse crop to his barn. That, along with the first cutting he had put in the barn in early July, was usually enough to feed his horses through the winter. The field would be used during the thresheree for parking cars.

That afternoon Noah watched when Ambrose hitched his team to the ancient McCormick-Deering grain binder that he stored in his machine shed most of the year and then cut the five-acre field of oats that he planted each year just for the thresheree. Oscar Anderson, Fred Russo, and other retired farmer members of the historical society would stand the oat bundles into shocks that were lined up in rows across the field, waiting to be threshed.

The next day Ambrose mowed the grass around his buildings, clearing a big area where the various exhibits, including the threshing machine, would be set up.

34

Thresheree

*T*he following Saturday, cars were lined up a half mile down the road, waiting to park in Ambrose Adler's field and attend the annual Link Lake Historical Society Thresheree, one of the largest events held in Ames County. The Ames County Fair was probably the only event that drew more people, and that was because it ran for four days, while the thresheree was only one day long.

Historical society volunteers wearing orange vests pointed people toward where they could park after they paid the two-dollar entrance fee. Soon scores of people were walking by the exhibits—gasoline engines that once powered farm water systems, Delco generators that provided thirty-two-volt electricity to farms before regular electrical service became available, exhibits of broad axes of various sizes, the kind used to fashion logs into barn and church and house beams before sawmills came to the community, lamps and lanterns of various shapes and sizes, reminders of the days before electricity.

Old-timers and kids, farmers and former farmers all enjoyed seeing history and chatting with each other. Grandfathers pointed out to grandchildren what various items were and how they were used. "See that barn lantern," an older gray-haired gentleman said to the young person with him who was fiddling with a cell phone. "I used to carry one like that to the barn. We milked cows with the light from one of those."

"How could you see anything with something like that?" the younger person asked.

The old man chuckled. "We could see enough. Could see enough to milk a cow."

Curious people from urban areas asked questions, "What's that? How do you use this thing? How did farm folks survive without electricity? What'd you do in winter? Did you have air-conditioning in the barn?" Some were dumb questions—whoever heard of air-conditioning in a barn when nobody had air-conditioning in their farm homes?

The lineup of antique tractors attracted considerable attention. A long line of old tractors was parked in a neat row starting with a big green John Deere R, then a John Deere A, a model B, and an H. The International Farmall tractors were lined up next, a super M, an H, a model B, and an A. Then several orange Allis-Chalmers tractors, made in Milwaukee. A gray Ford 9-N and an 8-N—the gentleman's tractor, it was called. Several Case models, also made in Wisconsin, three or four Massey-Harris and Minneapolis-Moline tractors, plus a couple of steam tractors that predated all of the gasoline models.

By eleven a long line of people waited to buy tickets for the thresher's dinner, which drew several hundred people each year. Chairs and tables were set up under the trees in front of Ambrose's house. The meal was prepared by members of the historical society, some of whom remembered helping their mothers with threshing dinners when they were children growing up on farms in the community. The meal consisted of two kinds of meat—roast beef and pork chops—mounds of mashed potatoes, bowls of thick brown gravy, carrots and peas, and thickly sliced homemade bread with fresh butter. The desserts included two kinds of pie, cherry and apple, as well as devil's food cake. Emily Higgins made sure the pies were cut in five pieces. "Nobody wants one of those skinny pieces of pie the restaurants serve," she said.

A portable generator sat off to the side, providing electricity for the big electric roasters filled with meats, mashed potatoes, and vegetables, as no electricity was available at the Adler farm. Historical society volunteers began serving the thresher's meal at eleven thirty, and continued until one thirty—in time so everything could be cleared for the signal event of the day, the demonstration of threshing grain with a J. I. Case threshing machine powered by a John Deere R tractor. The threshing demonstration was scheduled to start at 2:00 p.m. and continue until the five acres of oat shocks were threshed. The threshing machine was set up near Ambrose's barn, so the straw stack could be easily reached from that structure. Ambrose used the straw to bed his horses in the winter and to make things more comfortable for the few laying hens in his chicken house. He also used the straw as mulch for his vegetable garden, especially the tomatoes.

Oscar Anderson, as he had done in previous years, was in charge of explaining the process of threshing grain. Using a microphone so the enormous crowd could hear him, Oscar began by talking about how grain was threshed with a flail or having an animal walk over it before threshing machines became advanced enough to do the job. He explained how the early threshing machines were permanently situated and farmers hauled their grain to the machine for threshing, sometimes several miles from their farms.

"But when inventors like J. I. Case of Racine began manufacturing threshing machines like this one, everything changed. Now the threshing machine came to the farmer, instead of the farmer traveling to the threshing machine," intoned Oscar. Mr. Jerome Increase Case was also the first manufacturer to make a steel threshing machine, a vast improvement over the older, wooden models, which occasionally caught fire when a spark from a stone ignited them."

Oscar went on to talk about threshing bees and how neighbors helped each other as the threshing machine moved from farm to farm. He explained that the threshing bees were social events as well as a way for neighbors to help neighbors. He talked about the huge threshing dinner, reminding people that the dinner served here today resembled the threshing dinners of earlier days in nearly every way.

Karl Adams had never attended a thresheree, but as he listened to Oscar talk he found the idea of threshing bees extremely interesting. Karl had arrived at the thresheree early enough so he had a chance to walk around Ambrose's place, as other people were doing. He looked through the open door of Ambrose's barn and saw the stalls where Ambrose's horses stood. He walked by Ambrose's house, past the porch with a rocking chair, past a bed of old-fashioned orange day lilies. Everything was neat and tidy. Karl knew that Ambrose lived without any of the modern-day, taken-for-granted conveniences that almost everyone else had. He heard people describe him as strange, not only because he stuttered, but because he did not own a car, farmed with horses, and had no electricity. Karl thought, *This is someone I'd like to learn more about.*

*W*e are ready to begin the threshing demonstration," Oscar said when he saw the owner of the big John Deere R climb on the tractor and pull back on the throttle so the quiet "pom, pom, pom" of the idling machine became a much louder "POM, POM, POM." He slowly backed the tractor until the continuous belt that connected the tractor to the threshing machine was tight. Then he set the brake and engaged the tractor's belt pulley so the belt began moving and the threshing machine came to life with pulleys and belts turning this way and that.

Meanwhile the first load of oat bundles, stacked high on a wagon pulled by a team of Percheron horses, lumbered up to the machine.

"Whoa," the teamster said as he wound the harness lines around the ladder at the front of the wagon, grabbed up a three-tine fork, and motioned to the man on the tractor that he was ready to fork oak bundles into the machine.

The speed of the tractor pulley increased, the threshing machine began shaking a bit, and the man on the wagon began pitching oat bundles, heads first, into the machine. Soon straw was flying out of the blower pipe, landing on the ground, where there would soon be a straw stack. Freshly threshed oat kernels came tumbling into a container on top of the machine that when filled would send a stream of kernels into grain bags attached to the bagging device that thrust out from one side of the machine. Volunteers soon began carrying filled bags of grain into the oat bins in Ambrose's granary—winter feed for his horses and his small flock of chickens.

The oat crop had been good this year. The threshing machine worked through several loads of bundles hauled from Ambrose's oat field to the threshing machine. Everything was going well: the straw stack was growing in size, the oat bin in the grain bin was filling, and those watching were gaining an authentic look at what threshing from an earlier day, before grain combines came on the scene, looked like.

Noah Drake, who had been working in the granary and had come outside for a breath of fresh air, saw it first. "What's that coming out of the straw stack?" Noah asked.

"Looks like steam," one of the bag carriers said.

"That's not steam," the second carrier said. "That's smoke. The straw stack is on fire."

"Turn off the machine," the carrier man yelled to the man on the tractor. "The straw stack is on fire! The straw stack is on fire!" Someone called 911 to alert the Link Lake Fire Department as men scrambled to remove the drive belt connecting the tractor to the threshing machine. The tractor driver quickly turned the tractor around, and someone helped hitch it to the threshing machine so it could be pulled away from the now flaming straw that was threatening to engulf Ambrose's nearby barn.

Within ten minutes, a very long ten minutes for those watching the event unfurl, the Link Lake Volunteer Fire Department arrived and in another fifteen minutes the fire was out. More than half of the straw stack had been burned and that which wasn't had been ruined by the water. The old former dairy barn had been saved; its only harm was some blistered paint from the heat of burning straw.

Those who had been working on the threshing crew were muttering among themselves as to what might have started the fire. Someone suggested it probably had been a small stone in an oat bundle that caused a spark.

People trailed off to their cars, thankful that no one was hurt and that the only damage was to a straw stack. Ambrose shook Fire Chief Henry Watkins's hand when the fire was out.

"Th . . . thank you," said Ambrose. He had tears in his eyes. To lose his barn would be losing an important part of his family's history. For Ambrose, and for most farmers of his generation, a barn meant much more than merely a structure to house animals and store feed.

35
Problem Solved

A lazy summer sun slowly climbed above the horizon, making the waters of Link Lake sparkle. The sun awakened Karl Adams from a deep sleep. When Karl worried about something he didn't sleep well—and when he started on a new job by a mining company, sleeping was especially difficult. The first couple weeks he was in Link Lake the pro and con factions about the new sand mine coming to town had declared war on each other. He had to figure out how to smooth things over and so far he was making progress.

Karl had years of experience working with divided communities when a new mine came to town. As he sat on his patio, looking out over the lake, he felt good. He knew that with some of Alstage Sand Mining Company's monetary help, he had come a long way in taking people's minds off the sand mine through the various community activities held over the past couple months. People were smiling again, even laughing.

He climbed in his car and drove to Increase Joseph Community Park. Emerson Evans had informed him that morning that one of their new, highly sophisticated drilling machines ("It cost us more than a million dollars") had been delivered to the site yesterday. "They had a little trouble bringing the machine through the narrow entrance, where that old oak stands in the way," Evans told him, "but they made it okay. Next week we'll begin some test drilling so we know exactly what kind of sand we've got, and how difficult it will be to get at it." Evans had also asked if any problems were brewing, protests, that sort of thing.

Karl had replied, "Everything is cool here. Nice bunch of folks. I anticipate no difficulties."

Karl had a bad feeling, though, when he drove by the park's entrance and saw not a half-dozen protesters marching, which had been the earlier case, but at least twice that many, maybe more, walking back and forth carrying Stop the Sand Mine signs. He didn't stop to confront them, but he guessed they were out-of-town agitators who enjoyed getting in the way of a community's progress.

He drove past the village hall, where the big sign showing the exact location of the sand mine had been posted for several weeks. This morning he noticed a big red circle around the mine site with a line through it and the words "No Mine" scrawled on the bottom of the map.

Karl stopped at the Eat Well Café for breakfast and noticed the place was all abuzz. Others had seen the protestors as well and wondered what it meant. Someone said, "I saw a huge semi delivering a fancy machine at the park yesterday."

"Must be they're gonna start mining any day now," someone else said.

"Nope, they're not supposed to start until October."

"Wonder who them protestors are? Where they came from?" the first person asked.

Beyond talking about the protestors at the park, he also overhead a couple of fellows who were quite livid that someone had "messed up" the mining map, as people referred to it.

"Police ought to arrest whoever did that and throw the book at 'em. We don't do things this way in Link Lake. We don't run around spray paintin' things we don't like."

Karl Adams smiled to himself when he heard all of this, but he was concerned that people's minds once more had begun focusing on the sand mine, exactly what he did not want to happen. He did notice a few people watching the Eat Well's eagle cam feed. The two baby eaglets appeared nearly big enough to leave the nest. Karl caught himself watching the eagles as well. *A mature bald eagle is surely an impressive creature*, he thought.

36

Arrest the Protestors

*W*ith breakfast finished, and with an earful of comments about what had recently been transpiring in Link Lake, Karl called Marilyn Jones and arranged to meet with her within the hour. When Karl entered her little office, Marilyn said, "What in hell is going on, Karl? I thought you had everything under control. Do you know how many protestors are up there at the park? I counted fifteen. And did you see how they defaced your map at the village hall? The bastards. This has got to stop. What are you going to do about all this, Karl? This whole project is going to hell in a hand-basket unless we do something to stop it, and right now. I called the police department and told them to arrest those damn protestors."

Karl said quietly, "They can't arrest them; they've got a right to protest."

As if not hearing what Karl had just said, Marilyn continued, "Not a damn one of them is from Link Lake. What the hell do these people think they're doing? Messing with our little town when it's just none of their damn business." She pounded her fist on the table.

In the several months that Karl had been working with Marilyn Jones, he couldn't remember when he saw her more angry or heard her use profanity.

"So what do you suggest we do, Karl? This whole damn strategy of calming down the people was your idea. Now, all of a sudden, everybody is upset again. People are wondering what's going on. Somebody told me they saw one of your trucks delivering a big machine to the park yesterday. That right?"

"Yes, that's right."

"Well, why didn't you tell me about that, so at least I would know that somebody would see that machine and decide it was time to raise a ruckus?"

"I didn't think it was important . . . the company will be bringing lots of equipment during the next few weeks."

"Well, give me a heads-up so this kind of stuff doesn't come as a surprise. My new chef saw the protestors when he came to work this morning. You know what he said, Karl? You know what he said?"

"What'd he say?"

"Pierre said he moved from Madison to Link Lake with his family to get away from all this protesting. Said he thought this was a quiet, peaceful little community. He couldn't believe all those protestors were marching back and forth in front of the park's entrance. And he asked me what it was all about."

"And you told him about the new sand mine coming to town?"

"Of course I did. I told him this would be the best thing to happen to Link Lake in twenty years. That once the mine was up and running our business would prosper even more than it is now."

"And what did Pierre say?"

"He didn't say anything, other than thanks for letting him know. He just turned and went to work. For all I know he is against the sand mine. He didn't say where he stands."

"Maybe he doesn't care one way or the other," said Karl.

"I don't know what to think. I sure wish we could do something about those outside agitators. I think I'll call the sheriff in Willow River, have some of his deputies come over and work with our police to keep an eye on them. Just can't trust those protestors, don't know what they'll do next."

*E*mily Higgins smiled when she drove past the park entrance on this warm sunny morning and saw the protestors marching with their Stop the Mine signs held high. Emily had been in touch with the historical societies in the region and had informed them about the plans for the village to build a sand mine in the park and destroy the Trail Marker Oak in the process. She had asked if their members would volunteer to march—but only when she gave the word. When Emily learned that the mining company had delivered a big machine to the park, she got on the phone to historical societies in the area: Waupaca, Willow River, and Westfield—all of whom offered to help with the protests. Three members from the Link Lake Historical Society also volunteered to march, but Emily had warned them to wear dark glasses and otherwise disguise themselves so they would not be recognized.

Still, when Emily heard about the defacing of the mine map at the village hall, she was disturbed. She had told all the volunteers to do absolutely nothing that was illegal. "You break the law and all you do is turn the town's sympathy toward the sand mine," Emily had said. She was quite certain that none of the local historical society members would deface anything; it wasn't something a historical society person would do. Breaking the law and doing something like defacing a map was not an appropriate action, even when emotions were high in opposition to a sand mine coming to Link Lake.

Emily wondered who might do it, but she couldn't think of one person in Link Lake who would do such a thing. As Emily considered all that had been going on in the last couple days, she wondered if the protestors marching would change any minds. And she wondered what further action the Link Lake Historical Society could take to save the Trail Marker Oak.

That afternoon, Emily drove by the park to check on the marchers. She chuckled when she saw two sheriff's cars and a police cruiser parked on one side of the road that trailed by the park, with protestors walking on the other side. The deputies, the police, and the protestors all appeared to be enjoying the pleasant late summer day.

37

Oscar, Fred, and the Protestors

So what's new?" asked Fred Russo as he pulled out a chair at the Eat Well and sat down opposite his friend Oscar Anderson."

"Geez, Fred, you been asleep? There's a bunch of new stuff going on. Things are really poppin' around here."

"So what's happening? Been asleep, only up for couple hours. Good to get your rest, especially when you're older. I read that in a magazine, think it was *Reader's Digest*. Yup, that's where it was. That's where it said we old codgers ought to get at least eight hours of sleep every night. And I try to do that. You ought to try that too, Oscar. You'd feel better. You wouldn't be so damn ornery in the morning," said Fred as he held up his cup for Henrietta to fill with fresh coffee.

"Fred, I don't wanna hear your goofy theories on how much sleep I oughta get. This town is about to explode. Ain't you noticed what's goin' on?"

"I did see some folks walkin' back and forth in front of the park entrance. Looked like they were soakin' up a little sun and getting some exercise."

"Fred, you just don't get it. Those folks are protestors. They were carrying signs that said, 'Stop the Mine.'"

"Really? I didn't look at the signs. Figured they was welcoming folks to the park."

"Geez, Fred. You are dense. These are people that believe our park should be left just as it is and has been for more than a hundred years. These are our kind of people, Fred," said Oscar.

"Our kind of people? I doubt that. I didn't see you marching."

"I think I would've marched had I been a little younger and didn't have this bum leg. I think I would have been right out with those folks telling the world that Link Lake doesn't need no damn sand mine," said Oscar, leaning a bit toward his friend as he spoke quietly.

"Oscar, people in this town may be against things from time to time, but when they protest, they don't walk back and forth all day carrying a sign. There's a better way to protest than what they are doing," said Fred, taking another sip of coffee.

"Maybe so, Fred. But folks carrying signs get people's attention. We're talkin' about it, aren't we? Got our attention."

"Let's be straight about this. Them walkin'-all-day sign carriers got *your* attention. I didn't think much about it."

The two sat quietly for a few minutes, enjoying their coffee.

"Something else happened yesterday," began Oscar.

"Oh, and what would that be? Somebody's dog bite you on the leg?"

"Fred, how do you come up with those dumb ideas? No damn dog bit me on the leg."

"So what happened then? Hard to think of anything more serious than a dog chewin' on your leg."

"You know that big map of the park that's posted on the bulletin board outside the village hall? The one that outlines where the sand mine will operate?"

"Yeah, what about it? I looked at it a time or two. Nice map. Colorful."

"Well it's not very colorful now."

"So what happened to it?" asked Fred.

"Someone spray painted a huge *X* across the map. Ruined it. Paint slopped all over the bulletin board too. Whole thing's a mess."

"Well, Oscar. That was probably another one of them protestors that you seem to have kinship with that did it. What'd I tell you? I bet there's a bunch of people mad as hell about that."

"I don't agree with it. Don't agree with it at all," said Oscar. "It was an illegal act. I do not approve of illegal acts no matter how much a person is opposed to something. I hope the person who did it is arrested."

"Okay, Oscar. Let me get this straight. You think it's a good thing to spend your time walking back and forth in front of a park carrying a sign. But it's a bad thing to paint over a map?"

"Fred, sometimes I don't understand you. You ever read the Constitution? You ever read down through those amendments?"

"You think I've got time to sit around reading the Constitution? I've got lots of better things to do with my time."

"Fred, you're just like a bunch of people in this country—you don't know your rights."

"And now, I suspect I'm going to hear an Oscar Anderson speech on the Constitution and its amendments," said Fred.

"Nope, you are not, except for me tellin' you something about the right of people in this country to protest. It's in the First Amendment. But people don't have the right to deface a sign. That's breaking the law," said Oscar.

"Well, fine and dandy. But I just don't think marchin' all day is gonna do any good in stopping that old sand mine company from coming to town and cutting down the Trail Marker Oak. And painting over the map is just gonna make people mad," said Fred.

"It's a damn mess, Fred. A damn mess. I thought things were gettin' better with the outstanding Fourth of July celebration and Trail Marker Oak Days. Thought things had quieted down. But I guess not. Things can't get much worse. Little Link Lake is torn right in two—those thinkin' the sand mine is the best thing for Link Lake since sliced bread and the rest of us who can't see destroying history on the road to progress."

"That's a pretty fine speech you just made there, Oscar. That line about destroying history on the road to progress, that's notable."

"Well, thank you, Fred. But it's only a statement of fact. Doesn't do much for helping Link Lake dig out of this quagmire of a mess it's in."

"Wonder what's gonna happen next." said Fred.

As they had done every morning since the eagle cam had been showing the development of the bald eagle family in the big nest at the park, they spent a few minutes before they left the Eat Well watching the big screen that was just above the cash register.

149

"Really interesting to see how fast those little eagles grow. Those two little ones look nearly big enough to leave the nest," said Oscar.

"At least the eagle cam is one thing everyone in this town can agree on," said Fred.

38

Don't Give Up

FIELD NOTES
Link Lake Update

By Stony Field

My contacts in little Link Lake, Wisconsin, have just informed me that the Alstage Sand Mining Company that earlier signed a lease with the Village of Link Lake to mine sand in their village park is now preparing to begin operations. You will recall that one of the sticking points in the entire affair is an old bur oak that has historical significance as it was a trail marker that pointed the way for the Native Americans and early settlers to the area. Trail marker trees were the road signs of their day. Both the land and the old oak were sacred to the Native Americans.

The Link Lake Historical Society, along with many other citizens, is adamantly opposed to destroying the Trail Marker Oak for the sake of economic development. According to these historians, to even consider mining sand in a park that has served the community for more than a hundred years is blasphemous.

The historical society points to the recent highly successful Fourth of July celebration and Trail Marker Days as ways of attracting people to Link Lake and thus improving the economic situation of the community without doing harm to its historical artifacts.

It appears that the Alstage Sand Mining Company plans to go ahead with its operation no matter how much the community complains or objects. The narrow and rather misguided views of the Economic Development Council and the village's docile mayor and village board have generated hard feelings in this little community.

Don't Give Up

I have been informed that representatives of the Link Lake Historical Society, as well as representatives from nearby historical societies, have joined the renewed protest marches at the park. May their efforts be recognized for what they are: citizens showing their unhappiness for local government officials who have gone amok in their zeal to create jobs without consideration for anything else. The weak-kneed village board made a bad decision when they signed a lease with the Alstage Sand Mining Company. It is not too late to reverse their decision.

39

Explosion

*T*he explosion shook Karl Adams's bed, rattled the windows in his cabin, and brought him wide awake from a deep sleep where he had been dreaming about old people dancing around the Trail Marker Oak and singing a song that he didn't recognize. Karl sat up in bed, rubbed his eyes, and wondered if he had really heard an explosion or if that had been a part of his weird dream. When he heard the scream of sirens, he knew the explosion was real. He glanced at the clock sitting on the scarred table by his bed: 5:00 a.m. He pulled on his clothes and decided to find out what had exploded with such force that the entire cabin had shook.

It was about an hour before dawn—the eastern sky showed hints of the sunrise. Karl turned and glanced in the direction of the park and saw a reddish glow in the sky. He climbed into his car and headed for the park. Once there, he was stopped by the upraised arm of a Link Lake police officer, his patrol car parked across the road, blocking the way.

Karl rolled down his window. "What's going on?" he asked.

"Something blew up in the park. Made one helluva noise. Shook the whole town. Woke up a bunch of people."

"I was one of them. Think it had something to do with the new sand mine?"

"Might be. Some folks ain't too happy about having a mine in the park. They ain't happy at all. All these outside protestors in town. That didn't help either."

"So I've noticed," said Karl. "I'm with the Alstage Sand Mining Company and was curious if any of our equipment was involved."

"Tell you what, I'll give Henry a call—he's chief of our volunteer fire department. He's right there with his crew. He'd know."

The young police officer talked into his radio. "Say Henry, guy here with me says he's with the mining company, wants to know if any of the mining equipment was involved in the explosion."

The police officer listened to the response, then turned to Karl.

"Henry says there was some kind of a machine here—and it was blown all to hell. Those were Henry's very words. He said some of it's still burning and there's a big hole in the ground caused by the explosion. He doesn't have any idea what caused the machine to blow up. Appears nobody was hurt. Appears just the machine blew up and burned. Henry said something else that's not good. The eagle nest was destroyed. The one with the eagle cam. Henry said he found a pair of dead eagles and a dead eaglet. He said the other little eagle was alive but hurt. Terrible what happened."

Karl turned his car around and drove toward Link Lake until he found a place to park. He took out his cell phone and called Emerson Evans.

"Big problems here in Link Lake. Somebody just blew up the drilling machine that you delivered a few days ago," said Karl when he reached Evans.

"What'd you just say?" Evans asked, not believing what he was hearing. The ringing of his cell phone had awakened him.

"Somebody blew up the drilling machine. To quote the fire chief, 'it was all blown to hell.'"

"I thought you had everything under control, everything cool?" Evans shouted into the phone.

"So did I," said Karl. "But when people saw that big drilling machine move in, everything went south. A bunch of protestors showed up, marching back and forth in front of the park. Mostly older people carrying signs. I wasn't too worried about them. Then something else happened."

"And that was?" asked Evans, not at all pleased with what he was hearing from the man who was supposed to be smoothing the way for the mine opening.

"Somebody spray painted the map I put up at the village hall."

"Didn't you realize that things have turned? I thought that's why we hired you, to keep an eye on things."

"Well, I . . . I," Karl stammered. "I didn't see it coming. Things seemed to have calmed down."

"Didn't see it coming? A defaced sign and bunch of protestors seem to suggest a turning point!"

"I've seen protestors before, lots of them. Defaced posters and maps too," said Karl.

"But how many times have you seen a million-dollar machine blown up? Tell me that!" Evans was yelling and Karl held the phone away from his ear.

"I'd think you'd better come over here," said Karl quietly.

"You damn betcha I'm coming over there—I'll be there this afternoon. Don't say anything to the press; don't say anything to anybody. Sounds like we'll have to play hardball from here on out."

"One more thing," said Karl.

"Yes," said Evans.

"The blast that blew up the drilling machine also blew down a bald eagle nest and killed three eagles and hurt a fourth one."

"Good God, Karl. You know what that means, don't you? Those dead eagles will bring the federal Fish and Wildlife Service people into Link Lake faster than I can get there. That's the last thing we need, a bunch of feds prowling around our mine site. Anything else you haven't told me?"

"No," said Karl.

"Well, I should hope to hell not. We got ourselves a real mess in Link Lake. I'll meet you at the mine site this afternoon. I'll give you a call when I'm a few minutes out of town."

Karl drove back to his cabin feeling totally defeated. Just when he thought everything was working out better than he had hoped for, it all fell apart. He also couldn't remember when he'd gotten such a tongue-lashing.

Karl shaved, showered, and headed to the Eat Well Café for breakfast. At 6:30 a.m. the place was nearly filled with people, all talking loud, and all talking about the explosion that rocked the town. The smell of fresh coffee and bacon frying woke up Karl's taste buds, but his ears were tuned in to the variety of conversations he was hearing.

"Heard it was a terrorist bombing—you know them terrorists are just about everywhere, looking for things to blow up. Surprise that nobody got killed. That damn explosion shook my house so bad it about busted the windows. Never heard nothin' like that, 'cept when I was in the army.

Heard them kind of noises then." It was an older gentleman at the counter who was talking, waving his coffee cup in the air as he spoke.

At a table in the corner, just beyond where Karl was enjoying his platter of eggs, bacon, and coffee, Karl overheard Oscar Anderson and Fred Russo deep in conversation.

"Oscar, did you hear that bomb go off this morning, the one everybody is talkin' about?"

"Geez, Fred, who said it was a bomb? I heard it was an explosion of some kind—heard one of the volunteer firefighters say he thought the Alstage Mining drill had just blown up—that it may have had a gas leak of some kind. I did hear it go off, way out at my farm. Woke me up. Time to get up anyway."

"Sure as hell sounded like some kind of bomb. I heard it go off too," said Fred.

"Fred, just because it sounded like a bomb doesn't mean it was a bomb."

"Sounded like a bomb to me," Fred said as he took a long sip of coffee.

"Let's say it was a bomb. Who'd wanna blow up a drilling machine?"

Fred paused a minute before answering. "Maybe one of them Arab terrorists? They like blowin' up stuff."

"Good God, Fred. Do you think some Arab terrorist is gonna come all the way to Link Lake to blow up some damn mining machine?"

"You just never know, Oscar. This old world is changin' so fast I can't keep up with it. Wouldn't surprise me if some terrorist did it."

*K*arl Adams finished his coffee, walked up to the counter, and paid his bill. Henrietta recognized him and smiled.

"Pretty exciting around here this morning," said Karl.

"That explosion was really something. Shook my house. Rattled the windows," said Henrietta.

"Who do you suppose did it?" asked Karl.

"One of them protestors. It's got to be one of them protestors. Police should round them all up and arrest them," said Henrietta as she handed Karl his change.

40

Reaction

*T*he explosion roused Marilyn Jones from a deep sleep. Not only had the sound startled her awake, but her entire house shook from the shock of the blast. Within a few minutes she heard sirens. She reached for her phone and called the Link Lake Police Department—she knew that Louise Konkel was working the overnight shift as dispatcher. Louise had once worked for Marilyn as a waitress at the Link Lake Supper Club.

"Link Lake Police Department," a perky, wide-awake voice said.

"Louise, this is Marilyn Jones. What's going on?"

"I don't really know. Lots of folks heard an explosion a few minutes ago and immediately the 911 calls began coming in."

"I heard it," said Marilyn. "The blast shook my house. Where'd it happen?"

"At the park. Jimmy, our night patrol officer, is over there right now. Fire department is also on the scene."

"Did Jimmy say what blew up?"

"He guessed it was the big drilling machine that the mining company brought in a while ago."

"Oh," said Marilyn. "Thank you."

Marilyn, now wide awake, walked to her kitchen and started a pot of coffee. She glanced across the waters of Link Lake and saw a bright sun slowly creeping above the horizon. Everything was peaceful and quiet. Except on the other side of town there was pandemonium. A fire was raging and people were awake and wondering what the explosion was all about. What had blown up and what caused it?

Marilyn was thinking, *I'd guess some radical kook blew up Alstage's drilling machine. One of those protestors who march in front of the park every day. I suspect the bomber was encouraged by that damn Stony Field. He just can't quit sticking his nose into our town's business. You'd think he'd have enough to write about in other parts of the world.*

What is happening to this country? Here we're trying to improve Link Lake and people get all worked up when they see some changes coming their way. There's a bunch of folks around here that want things to stay just the same. Members of the historical society, that bunch with old Emily Higgins goading them on, are so stuck in the past that they wouldn't recognize progress if they stepped in it. Don't touch anything. Don't cut down an old tree. That damned Trail Marker Oak has evoked so much sympathy. You'd think it was a famous person. It's just a damned old oak tree that'll probably die by itself in a few years. And Stony Field—why does he think he should stick his nose into Link Lake's business?

The more Marilyn thought about the situation, the more agitated she became. But Marilyn wasn't one to just sit around and let things happen; it was her style to make things happen. She pulled on her clothes, jumped in her black Cadillac Escalade, and headed to the park. She had to know what had happened and once she did, she'd decide what steps to take.

*A*mbrose Adler had gotten up early that morning and was looking out his kitchen window when he saw a flash of light in the east and then heard a loud explosion followed by its echo. He'd never heard anything like it before. He snapped on his battery-operated radio and tuned it to WWRI, the station in Willow River.

Earl Wade, the early morning announcer, broke into one of Willie Nelson's tunes with a special announcement. "I just learned that there's been a loud explosion and a fire in Link Lake. The explosion apparently took place in the Increase Joseph Community Park on the edge of town. A part of the park was recently leased to the Alstage Sand Mining Company of La Crosse. So far there are few details, but apparently no one was injured in the blast. When we learn more, we'll share it." Willie Nelson came back on singing "On the Road Again," one of Earl's favorite early morning tunes.

Wonder what happened, thought Ambrose as he fired up his wood-burning cookstove, pulled the cast iron skillet from the oven where he stored it, and dropped in a hunk of butter, which began to sizzle as the fire warmed the stove top. He cracked a couple of eggs into the skillet and dropped in a few slices of smoked bacon. As he sat at his kitchen table, looking out over the fields where cattle once grazed, he continued listening to Earl and the early morning radio show. He wasn't a great fan of country music, but he tuned in the local station for the news and the weather. And Earl was good about keeping up with the news.

"I've got a little more information for you folks wondering about the explosion and fire over at Link Lake," Earl interrupted the music again. "Apparently a drilling machine belonging to the Alstage Sand Mining Company exploded and caused a fire that the Link Lake Volunteer Fire Department quickly extinguished. The cause of the explosion is not known. Fire Chief Henry Watkins has a couple of theories. He said there could have been a gas leak in the machine, which could have caused the blast. Or someone could have placed an explosive device on the machine. Henry said to remind our listeners that since the Link Lake Village Board approved the development of a sand mine in the park, lots of folks have been upset, none more than members of the Link Lake Historical Society. When I have more information, I will share it."

Ambrose sat back in his chair, running his fingers through his white hair. He was beginning to have second thoughts about his recent Stony Field column applauding the activities of those protesting the opening of the mine. He sincerely hoped that this had not been the trigger, but he also knew that there was always somebody out there willing to go too far, to take violent action in a misguided belief that what they were doing was the right thing to do. He made no mention in his column of taking any violent action or doing anything illegal. His motto was stand up for what you believe, but do it within the law.

He wondered what was really the cause of the blast that destroyed the Alstage drilling machine. Surely it couldn't be a member of the Link Lake Historical Society or one of the neighboring historical societies who had done it. Or could it? Ambrose thought he'd stop by the museum and talk with Emily Higgins when he went to Link Lake for supplies later in the day. If anyone had an idea of what happened in the park this early morning, she would.

Later that morning, when Ambrose was working in his garden, digging potatoes for his vegetable stand, he saw the Link Lake police cruiser pull into his yard. His mind immediately went into panic mode—someone had discovered that he was Stony Field and he was about to be interrogated about the blast at the park, maybe even arrested.

The young police officer got out of his car and walked toward the garden where Ambrose was working.

"You're Ambrose Adler?" the officer asked.

"Y . . . yes I am," stuttered Ambrose.

"Somebody told me that you understand wild animals. Is that so?" The young officer was very serious. Ambrose immediately wondered if he had broken some law concerning his pet raccoon.

"I . . . I've been told that," stammered Ambrose, taking his red hand-kerchief from his pocket and wiping the sweat from his brow.

"We've got a problem that I'm told you can help us with."

"W . . . hat kind of problem?"

"You hear about the explosion in the park early this morning?"

"I did," said Ambrose.

"Besides blowing up a mining machine, the blast blew apart the big bald eagle nest. Killed the big eagles, killed one of the little eagles, and injured the other little one. Blew up the eagle cam too."

"T . . . terrible," said Ambrose.

"I was hoping you could take care of the little eagle until the Fish and Wildlife Service gets here and they can decide what to do with it."

"Sure," said Ambrose, relieved that he now knew the real reason for the officer's visit.

Together they walked to the squad car and the officer removed a box from the backseat, where Ambrose saw a mostly grown bald eagle with one wing that appeared broken. He handed the box to Ambrose.

"Thank you for helping us out. We'll be in touch once I hear from the federal folks, who should be here in a few days. There's a big fine for killing an eagle, you know. They'll want to find out who the culprit is."

Reaction

Ambrose took the little eagle into his house and gently removed it from the box, talking to it all the time. At first the eagle struggled to get away, but as Ambrose talked to it, it calmed down and he was able to examine it. It indeed had a broken wing. Ambrose fashioned a splint for the wing and bandaged it. Then he put it back in the box and went into his office, where he spent an hour reading about eagles and especially what baby eagles ate.

He decided not to open his vegetable stand that afternoon. He needed to find out more about what was going on, what caused the explosion at the park, and who or what might have been responsible.

He stopped at the museum to talk with Emily Higgins. She said, "I'm certain no one from the Link Lake Historical Society had anything to do with the blast." Then she went on at length to lament the loss of three eagles and the camera. "People really liked watching that eagle cam," she said.

Ambrose told her that he was taking care of the injured eagle and asked her if she had any idea what caused the blast.

"Deputy from the sheriff's office said it was definitely a bomb and a good-sized one too. Pieces of the drilling machine were found a hundred yards from the site of the explosion. It's not going to help our cause one bit," said Emily. "What it will do is turn more people toward favoring the mining company. I heard that the machine that was blown up cost more than a million dollars."

"That much?" said Ambrose.

"Funny thing about it, the machine was far enough away from the Trail Marker Oak that the tree wasn't even scratched. Maybe that's a good sign of things to come."

The two old friends talked for a time about what they should do. Emily said that she hoped that Stony Field would write about something else for a while—to take some of the spotlight away from Link Lake. Ambrose agreed that it would be a good idea.

"But how can we get in touch with Mr. Field? Nobody seems to know where he lives."

Ambrose didn't comment, but to himself he was smiling and thinking, *If I ever get around to sharing that I'm Stony Field, Emily Higgins will be one of those most surprised.*

41

Perpetrators

Emerson Evans made record time driving from La Crosse to Link Lake. He was furious about what had happened at the mining site. How could anyone explain why a million-dollar drilling machine had been destroyed by some overzealous opponent of sand mining? And why had Karl Adams failed so miserably in placating the community, in bringing them around to supporting the upcoming mining operation? He needed answers and he needed them right away. His superiors in La Crosse were not happy, especially after receiving reports of how well everything was going in Link Lake and after pouring several thousand dollars into the community.

When Evans pulled up to the mining site, he spotted several police cars and yellow tape closing off the entrance to the park. Karl Adams got out of his car when he saw Evans arrive.

"What in hell is going on here?" asked Evans, a tall, thin, very intense man. There was no "good morning" or "how are you, Karl?"

"I don't know. Everything was cool until the drilling machine arrived— then all hell broke loose."

"So who blew up our million-dollar drilling machine? They caught the bomber yet?"

"No, they haven't. The sheriff is right over there." Karl pointed to a police cruiser with Sheriff written on the side. "Talk to him."

"You damn bet I will, but I'm talking to you first. Just what in the hell is going on here? You got any ideas? You're supposed to have your finger on the pulse of this community."

"I thought everything was under control."

"You thought. You thought! We pay you to know, not to think. So how did it all go down?" Evans was a little less red in the face, and his voice had come down from the near yelling he was doing when he first stepped from his car.

"Ever since the deal was struck between Alstage and the Link Lake Village Board, a half dozen or so protestors were marching in front of this park entrance every day. It seemed the locals mostly ignored them. Nobody seemed to know who they were, and everyone assumed they were some wide-eyed liberals from Madison who didn't have anything better to do."

"I get that part. We have protestors of one kind or another at nearly all of our proposed mine sites. But they usually don't blow up million-dollar mining machines."

"Nobody has said the protestors blew up the machine."

"Well, who else would? Tell me what else you know."

"Like I said, once people learned that a big machine had arrived, everything changed. Everywhere I went in the community, people were talking again about the mine and the fact that it looked like it was a sure thing that it would open in the park."

"Well, talk doesn't blow up a machine."

"I realize that, but right after the machine arrived someone defaced the big map of the mine site I put on the bulletin board at the village hall. And then the number of protestors grew to twenty or more."

"Then what?"

"Kaboom, was the next what," Karl said. "It shook the whole town, rattled the windows, and rattled a lot of nerves too. The explosion woke me up."

"The explosion also blew up a million-dollar machine," Evans said under his breath.

"Oh, and then there's the eagle nest," Karl said.

"Yeah, I remember. Blast blew the eagle nest all to hell and killed some eagles. You told me all that before. What I'm worried about is when those federal Fish and Wildlife people get here and start nosing around. Any feds here yet?"

"Not that I know about. I heard the injured eagle is being cared for by an old vegetable farmer who lives just out of town. An old guy who stutters and talks to animals. Met him once. Interesting guy," said Karl.

"Well, that's great," Evans said sarcastically.

"So what are we going to do about all this?" asked Karl.

"You're supposed to be our man on the ground. Don't you have an idea?"

"Well, I'd suggest we call a community meeting and explain everything that we know—we are the victims here, you know. On the plus side of this mess, blowing up one of our machines and killing some bald eagles might be just what we need to bring some of those people who opposed the mine to our side of the table. This should surely tip the fence-sitters in our direction," said Karl.

Evans was quiet for a bit, pondering what Karl had just said.

"That's the smartest thing you've said since I got here. I think you're right. We are the victims here. Nobody condones destroying private property. Let's make the most of what surely looks like a miserable situation on the surface," said Evans. He even had a hint of smile on his face.

Later that afternoon, Karl and Evans met with Marilyn Jones and Mayor Jessup to discuss their next steps. The mayor was especially agitated by all that was happening in his little, once quiet and peaceful town. Wringing his hands, he said several times, "Nothing like this has ever happened in Link Lake before." Obviously he didn't remember the story of the bank robbery back in 1900.

Marilyn Jones, with a steely look in her eye, said, "I think we should face this head on. We may be a small town, but we're also a tough town. Do you guys have a plan?" She was looking at Karl Adams and Emerson Evans.

"Yes, yes, I do have a plan," said Evans. "I suggest we call a general meeting and invite everyone in the community to come. We'll tell people what we know, ask the local police to say a few words about progress in catching the perpetrator or perpetrators, have both of you say a few words about the importance of a sand mine coming to Link Lake, then I'll wrap up—with the hope that we can turn a few fence-sitters toward our way of thinking." Evans made no mention that the plan really had been Karl's. Karl stood off to the side, saying nothing.

"We'll set up the meeting for tomorrow evening, at the community room in the library," said Marilyn, who was clearly buying into the plan.

Mayor Jessup stood silently by, wringing his hands. He was still mumbling, "Nothing like this has happened in Link Lake before. Nothing like this."

A half hour before the start of the meeting, the Link Lake Library community room was filled to capacity. People were standing four deep behind those with chairs and people were still coming through the door.

Marilyn Jones asked the mayor to chair the meeting, but he declined and suggested Marilyn was much better at this sort of thing than he was. Mayor Jessup stood at the door, greeting people as they arrived and thanking them for coming. "Typical politician," mumbled Fred Russo when he and Oscar Anderson arrived.

A few minutes after eight, the time set for the meeting, Marilyn Jones stood up, took the microphone, and said, "I'm Marilyn Jones, chairman of Link Lake's Economic Development Council. Welcome to this special meeting where we hope to bring you up to date on the unfortunate event that occurred yesterday in our wonderful Increase Joseph Community Park. We are all still numb from what happened. To think that someone would set off a bomb and destroy a valuable piece of equipment. I asked several people to say a few words about what happened and what will be the next steps. First, our esteemed Mayor Jon Jessup."

Mayor Jessup took the microphone from Marilyn and, still looking a bit unnerved by all that happened in the past couple days, began speaking. "Nothing like this has ever happened in Link Lake before. Our quiet little town is simply devastated. Absolutely devastated. I'm sure you all wonder whether the bomber has been caught. So here is Officer Jimmy Barnes, who was first on the scene of the explosion and has been working on the case with the help of the Ames County Sheriff's Department. Officer Barnes."

"Well, what we know is that a big machine from the Alstage Sand Mining Company blew up yesterday morning. We don't yet know for sure, but it would appear that someone or several people may have been responsible for the act. We continue to collect evidence and ask that if anyone in this audience heard anything or saw anything suspicious to call the Link Lake Police Department. Our office is devoting all its resources to apprehending the person or persons who committed this act. One more thing before I sit down. I'd like to ask Mr. Ambrose Adler to stand. I think you all know Ambrose, but I doubt that you know that he has agreed to take care of a baby eagle that was blown from its nest. We all appreciate that very much."

A reluctant Ambrose Adler rose to his feet to a round of applause from the audience as Marilyn Jones once more took the microphone. "Let me add my thanks, Ambrose," Marilyn said, but Ambrose knew that she really didn't mean it. He had never forgotten the role Marilyn had played in ruining his happiness with her sister, Gloria. And Marilyn had as little to do with Ambrose as possible, as she blamed him for tearing apart her family.

"Let's move on," Marilyn continued. "We are pleased to have with us Emerson Evans from La Crosse, who is an official with the Alstage Sand Mining Company."

Evans walked up to the podium and took the microphone.

"First I would like to introduce you to Karl Adams." Karl stood up and held up his hand. "Some of you know Karl; many of you probably have seen him around town and wondered who he was and what he was doing. Well, Karl works for us. And it was Karl, and a considerable sum of our company's money, I might add, that helped plan and finance several of your recent community activities."

Karl caught Emily's eye, and he immediately felt bad that his identity had to be revealed in this way, and that he had not told her the truth when he first met her. She was shaking her head in disbelief.

Oscar Anderson turned to Fred Russo and whispered, "So that's who that guy is. Wondered about that."

Evans continued, "Our company has so much looked forward to coming to Link Lake, opening a new, modern sand mine, and, I must say, adding several high-paying jobs to the community. We, like all of you, are disappointed with what happened yesterday morning. We lost a million-dollar drilling machine, but we are not deterred. We are still planning on opening the mine in October, as we earlier announced." Evans paused while many of those in the audience applauded.

"I know there are those who oppose a mine opening here. I understand that, but I also hope that it was not someone from the community responsible for destroying our machine. It is one thing to protest; it is quite another to destroy private property, especially property that is worth a million dollars." Another round of applause, with nearly everyone clapping this time.

"I know many of you are concerned about the destruction of the Trail Marker Oak tree. It's unfortunate that we have to remove it, but with the unique geology of your park, there is just no other way we can move our equipment in and out and haul the sand out of the mine without removing that old tree." Evans paused for a moment, noticing that several hands had gone up in the back of the room. Without recognizing them, he continued. "We have discussed the situation at our main office, and we have decided to do the right thing. With the lumber from that old oak tree, we will employ a craftsman to make benches, each with a brass plaque that will cite some of the history of that old tree. I don't know how many benches there will be, but there will be several and the historical society can place them around Link Lake as they choose."

More clapping from the audience, all but the members of the Link Lake Historical Society. They sat silently.

Billy Baxter from the *Argus* was one of those who had his hand up several times to ask a question, but he was not recognized. When the meeting was over, he pushed to the front to talk with Evans. "No comment," he said when Baxter asked him to say more about his company's plans for the sand mine in Link Lake.

42
Emergency Meeting

The day following the big community meeting, Emily Higgins called an emergency meeting of the Link Lake Historical Society.

"All of you were at the community meeting last night and heard what the Alstage mining people had to say," she started. "I must say I was shocked at what I heard. I was surprised to learn that Karl Adams works for the mining company. When he first came to town he stopped by the museum. He said he was interested in history, and I gave him a tour. I thought at the time that he was very nice young man. Now I think he was just trying to butter me up. I also didn't know that mining money helped with our Fourth of July and the Trail Marker Oak Days—all of that is more than a little disturbing to me. I had a feeling about what was going on, but didn't have it quite figured out."

"That bothered me too," said Oscar Anderson. "That mining company tried to buy us off."

"Sure looks that way, doesn't it," said Emily. "I've got to ask another question," she continued. "And I want a truthful answer."

The room became very quiet.

"Does any of you know who blew up the mining company's drilling machine?"

No response.

"I've got to know that none of the members of our historical society or the historical societies that helped us were involved with this illegal act. If a historical society member was responsible, our cause is lost. And if I hear

that a historical member was the culprit, I will turn that person in myself."
Emily stood ramrod straight, the sternest look on her face that anyone had
ever seen.

You could hear the old regulator clock tick as Emily waited for a reply.
Fred Russo finally broke the silence. "Emily, I can't imagine anyone from
our group or any other historical society would do such a thing. We're all
old enough to know better—besides, I don't think any of us is smart enough
to do it."

A few people chuckled.

"Okay, then," said Emily. "What do we do now? We surely can't continue our protest marches—I don't think the police would allow us even if
we wanted to."

"I just don't know what we can do," someone sitting in the front
row said. "Looks like no matter what we do the mining company will start
digging in October. And we'll be left with a few oak benches scattered
around town as reminders of the Trail Marker Oak."

"There's got to be some action we can take," said Emily. "This is not the
time to give up. We've got to keep fighting, but let's be clear. For heaven's
sake, no destruction of private property and no violence. All that does is
play into the mining company's hand—they'll claim they are victims and
some people will feel sorry for them."

Oscar Anderson held up his hand.

"Oscar," said Emily. "Do you have an idea?"

"I think this environmental writer, this Stony Field guy, could help us
out. Does anybody here know how to get in touch with him, to let him
know what a predicament we're in with this sand mine?"

"I surely don't know how to contact him," Emily said. "Anybody here
know how to reach him?"

Not one hand went up. Sitting in the back of the room was Ambrose Adler, who tried hard to attend all of the historical society meetings. He was the only one in the room who knew how to contact Stony
Field.

*W*hen Ambrose returned home that evening, he unlocked the door to his office, pulled back the chair at his desk, rolled a fresh sheet of paper into his Remington typewriter, and began typing.

FIELD NOTES
More Problems in Link Lake

By Stony Field

You will recall I have been writing about little Link Lake, Wisconsin, and the turmoil created when a sand mining company won the approval of the Link Lake Village Board to open a mine in the village park, and in doing so, remove a historic tree known as the Trail Marker Oak. The local historical society, with the leadership of its longtime president, Emily Higgins, put up a vigorous fight to overturn the village board decision.

Unknown to the majority of the citizens in Link Lake, the mining company sent in an undercover operative to "soften up the community" with good deeds and Alstage money. It nearly worked as people's minds turned from concerns about a sand mine coming to their community to having a good time with celebrations financed by the mining company.

But the focus on the mine and the realization that it was indeed going to open became real when the company brought one of their huge drilling machines to the park a couple weeks ago. The Link Lake Historical Society, in a last-ditch attempt to stop the mine and save the Trail Marker Oak, organized daily protest marches at the park, enlisting not only their own members but those of historical society members in neighboring communities to help with the effort. The marches were peaceful, people noticed, and I'm told citizens once more began discussing whether a sand mine was a fit for this little, rather bucolic community.

Then, much to the concern of everyone, both those for and those against the mine, unknown perpetrators blew up the drilling machine, claimed to be worth a million dollars by the mining company.

Readers of this column know that I have not been afraid to stand up and speak my mind about what I believe is right. But never have I suggested violence or the destruction of private property as an approach for protecting the environment.

Destruction of private property generally results in a backlash—in the case of Link Lake, my guess is those who were sitting on the fence or against the sand mine are now leaning toward accepting it. These folks have come to see the mining company as a victim of an illegal act—which it is.

In a well-attended community meeting, an official of the mining company took this very stance—that the company is a victim. Even though the company lost an expensive piece of equipment, in the long run it has gained from the destruction of the machine.

Perhaps we will never know who the perpetrator or perpetrators of this illegal act were, but I would point out to everyone reading this column that such actions usually result in the opposite of what is intended.

As a result of the unfortunate illegal act, the Link Lake Historical Society, which has led the opposition and had hoped to overturn the village board's decision, does not know which way to turn. My Link Lake informant tells me that some members of the historical society are ready to throw in the towel and accept the coming of a mine to their community.

As someone once said, "It's not over until it's over." When people believe in a cause and have evidence to back up their beliefs, then the rallying cry should be to keep trying. Another apt aphorism is "The pen is mightier than the sword."

So here is what I am suggesting to the readers of this column who want to stand behind the members of the Link Lake Historical Society in their fight to save their Trail Marker Oak and prevent a sand mine from coming to their village park: Write letters to the editor of your newspapers. Send letters to the Link Lake Village Board and the mayor of Link Lake. Write to Marilyn Jones, chairman of the Link Lake Economic Development Council, and express your dismay with their support of a sand mine in a village park. Write civil, thoughtful letters. But write. The future of Link Lake, Wisconsin, depends on it.

43

Cooling Off

After the community meeting, both Emerson Evans and Karl Adams agreed to allow things to cool off a bit before the company resumed preliminary exploratory drilling at the proposed mining site. Evans returned to La Crosse, and Karl stayed on in Link Lake, working with the Ames County Sheriff's Department to help determine the cause of the explosion. The sheriff's department brought in a specialist to help determine the type of explosive device used, which they thought might lead them to the perpetrator. After an extensive search of the area that resulted in no evidence of explosive materials, and the inability to locate witnesses who might have seen something suspicious in the park the day previous to the explosion, the investigation reached a dead end.

The village brought in a tractor with a front-end loader, filled in the crater made by the explosion, and planted the area with grass seed. Park visitors soon returned, children played on the playground equipment, and picnickers enjoyed the view of the lake on sunny summer afternoons. No protest marchers were in evidence.

A Fish and Wildlife Services officer, Gretchen Kimberly, arrived to investigate the killing and injuring of the bald eagles and the destruction of the eagle nest, all federal offensives. Trying to put the incident in some kind of context, she talked with Emily Higgins from the historical society, who along with the nature club at Link Lake High School had sponsored the highly popular eagle cam.

"All I know," Emily told her, "is when the machine blew up the camera blew up, the nest blew up, and the eagles were killed."

"Any idea who did it?"

"Nope, nobody seems to know. Sheriff's office and the local police are baffled. Terrible to see what happened to that eagle nest, and to think three eagles were killed. Just awful."

Officer Kimberly next stopped by the supper club to talk with Marilyn Jones; Karl Adams happened to be in Marilyn's office as well. After introductions all around, Kimberly asked, "Why was the bald eagle nest destroyed? And who did it?"

"That's easy," said Marilyn with anger in her voice. "Some wild-eyed, save-everything historian did it—but nobody's talking. I tell you, if the historians ever get control of things in this country we'll all starve to death. What a bunch of obstructionists they are. We're trying to bring jobs to little Link Lake. What are they trying to do? Save a damn old bur oak tree that'll probably die in a few years anyway."

"Can we get back to the eagle nest?" asked Kimberly.

"Well, sure. It's obvious. Whoever blew up the Alstage drilling machine killed the eagles. Why aren't more people talking about the machine that blew up? It was worth a million dollars. What's an eagle nest worth?"

Officer Kimberly left the last question hanging. "You, sir," said Officer Kimberly, as she turned to Karl, "what do you know about all this?"

"Not any more than you've probably picked up by talking to the sheriff and our local police, which I assume you've done," said Karl.

"Yes, that's where I started. But I'd like your take on what happened."

Karl explained his role as advance man for the mining company and said he believed the community had quieted down from the early debates about whether a sand mine should come to Link Lake.

"Everything changed when our company brought in a drilling machine to do some preliminary exploration," Karl said.

"How so?" the officer asked.

Karl went on to explain the defacing of the map, the increase in the number of protestors, and then how he was awakened by an explosion that shook the cabin where he was living.

All the while the officer was taking notes.

"What can you tell me about the eagle nest and the dead eagles?"

"Not much, except as the military is prone to say, the eagles appear to be collateral damage. One of the little eagles survived—you knew that, right?"

"Yes, I heard a vegetable farmer just out of town knows how to take care of wild animals."

"Tell you what," said Karl. "I'll take you out to his farm. I was out there for a thresheree a few weeks ago. I know him slightly."

*W*hen Officer Kimberly and Karl Adams arrived at the Ambrose farm, they stopped at the little roadside vegetable stand. A young boy sat behind the little counter.

"Can I interest you in some fresh vegetables?" he said. "We picked them just this morning; nothing better than fresh-picked garden vegetables."

"What is your name, young man?" asked Karl.

"It's Noah Drake," he said, smiling. He grabbed up an empty paper bag and was prepared to fill it with vegetables.

"We need to talk with Mr. Adler. Do you know where he is?"

"He's up at his house." Noah pointed to the house at the end of the driveway. "He said he wasn't feeling well this afternoon and he asked me to tend to the vegetable stand."

"Thank you," said Karl. "Sell lots of vegetables."

"I'll try," said Noah.

Karl knocked on the door.

"Y . . . yes?" said Ambrose when he opened it.

"I'm Karl Adams and this is Gretchen Kimberly with the Fish and Wildlife Service."

"Come in," said Ambrose, standing aside as they entered his modest but tidy kitchen.

"Ambrose, you probably don't remember me, but I talked with you at the Trail Marker Oak Days, and I was out here for the thresheree," said Karl.

Ambrose looked carefully at Karl. "Yes, I . . . remember. What can I do for you?" he asked, trying hard for the words.

"Officer Kimberly is here about the little eagle," said Karl.

"Yes," joined in Kimberly. "We so much appreciate that you were able to take in this injured bird."

Cooling Off

"Glad to do it," said Ambrose as he walked to a far corner of the kitchen and picked up a cage he had built to house the injured bird.

As Ambrose was retrieving the eagle, Karl's eye caught a framed photograph of a young woman hanging on the wall next to the door. He looked carefully at the photograph and thought, *There's something very familiar about that woman.*

Ambrose handed the cage to Officer Kimberly with a big smile. "This little guy is doing well," he said.

"Thank you so much for taking such good care of him," said Officer Kimberly. "I'll take him off your hands. We have an eagle rehabilitation center in Dubuque, where they'll take him until he can be released back in the wild. You've done a great thing, Mr. Adler." She shook Ambrose's hand. "A very important thing."

Karl and Officer Kimberly put the caged eaglet in the back of the officer's car and headed back toward Link Lake. As they drove, Karl couldn't get the photograph he saw on Ambrose's wall out of his mind. He thought, *I can't believe it. But that woman looks a lot like my mother did when she was young. There is a striking resemblance.*

44
Quiet Time

*L*egions of Stony Field fans wrote hundreds of letters to the Link Lake Economic Development Council, to the Link Lake Village Board, and to the mayor. All pleaded, many insisted, some even threatened—and all had one message. "Reverse your decision. Tell the Alstage Sand Mining Company to get the hell out of Link Lake," as one writer bluntly put it. The letters, which arrived in bundles and boxes, were mostly unopened and unread. The village officials, with the backing of the Link Lake Economic Development Council, had made up their minds. Since the ruckus over the blown-up drilling machine and the killed eagles, village officials dug in. As one of them said, "By God, we make our own decisions. We sure as hell aren't going to listen to those wild-eyed liberal agitators that this tailender Stony Field stirs up on how we run our village."

Other than the letters pouring in from all parts of the country, which only a few people knew about, the Village of Link Lake was mostly back to its quiet, bucolic self. Ambrose Adler continued brisk sales of vegetables at his stand with the able assistance of Noah Drake. The Link Lake Supper Club, with its new Lake Coffee Bar, became increasingly popular as bicyclists traveling the bike trail through town stopped for coffee, some pastries, and free Wi-Fi.

About the only change at the Eat Well Café was customers could no longer watch the eagle cam that had become one of the popular attractions. After a few days of discussion about the explosion, the destruction of the eagle nest, and the apparent inevitability of a sand mine coming to the park, most early morning customers at the Eat Well turned to other topics such as wondering who the next president was going to be and whether there was any rain in the forecast.

But not Fred Russo and Oscar Anderson.

"Fred, I don't like it. Don't like it one bit," said Oscar.

"You complaining about your coffee again, Oscar? I happen to think the coffee is pretty damn good," said Fred.

"I'm not talkin' about the coffee. I'm talkin' about a feeling I've got."

"Oh, so now you wanna talk about Old Arthur. You know I got enough of Old Arthur for both of us, you don't have to tell me about yours," said Fred.

"Dammit, Fred, it's not my arthritis that's keeping me awake these days."

"Something keepin' you awake, huh? Know what, I got this damn whip-poor-will that sits right outside my bedroom window and calls 'whip-poor-will, whip-poor-will' all night long."

Oscar laughed then picked up his coffee cup and took a long drink.

"Remember that column Stony Field wrote asking people to write to the mayor and the village board and some other folks? Have we heard if they got any letters? No, we have not. We don't know if they got one letter or five hundred. I don't trust that bunch. Don't trust any of 'em," said Oscar.

"So?" said Fred. "Who cares?"

"I, for one, care. And I'll bet Emily Higgins and the rest of the historical society membership cares. Those backers of the sand mine have put a lid on things, and I don't like it. Don't like it one bit," said Oscar. "I've got a feeling this whole thing is not over—we got us a few weeks before October, which is when the mine is supposed to open. Lots could happen between now and then."

"Like what?" asked Fred.

"I don't know," said Oscar. "But I got a feeling. Got a strong feeling."

"Say, Oscar," said Fred, changing the subject. "You see that Karl Adams fellow lately? Used to eat breakfast here every morning."

"I suspect he went into hiding," said Oscar, chuckling. "A bunch of folks here in Link Lake were fooled by this guy, him not telling us that he worked for the mining company. People around here don't like to be fooled. You bet they don't."

Karl Adams

Since the big community meeting when everyone learned that Karl Adams worked for the mining company, he ate breakfast every morning at Marilyn Jones's new Lake Coffee Bar, where he didn't have to worry about running into any of the locals. The coffee bar customers were mainly bicyclists passing through town and a growing group of Milwaukee and Chicago people who owned second homes on the lake.

Most mornings Marilyn joined Karl over breakfast. She had become quite impressed with Karl and the contributions he had made toward both the enhanced Fourth of July celebration and the wildly successful Trail Marker Oak Days. She realized that a number of people in Link Lake were unhappy with Karl, especially when they learned that he worked for the mining company. It was Marilyn who suggested to Karl, "If I were you, I would lay low for the next several weeks, until things quiet down a bit more at least."

Karl was smart enough to figure that out for himself, thus he seldom appeared downtown but spent most of his time at his cabin and at the coffee bar.

A couple weeks after Stony Field's column asked people from around the country to write letters to the backers of the sand mine, Marilyn confided in Karl that they had received several thousand. Outside of the village board, the mayor, and the executive committee of the Economic Development Council, no one knew this and Marilyn wanted to keep it that way. Marilyn told Karl that Billy Baxter from the *Ames County Argus* had inquired about how many letters they had received. Marilyn told him they had gotten a few, but not enough to warrant doing a story.

Karl Adams

Karl listened to all of this but didn't respond. He was not one to keep secrets from people—he believed they had a right to know what was happening in their community. But then he quickly reminded himself that he had done the same thing; he had people believing he was someone different from who he really was. He felt more conflicted than he had ever remembered feeling. There was something about little Link Lake that was getting to him, crawling under his skin, making him examine things about his life that he had not thought about before. *Maybe it's because I'm getting older. Maybe that's why I am feeling as I do these days.* But never before had he felt that he was being dishonest with people. He had always prided himself in being an upfront what-you-see-is-what-you-get sort of person.

Before he had signed the contract with Alstage, he had done considerable research on the company—some of these companies had broken zoning and environmental laws and he did not want to work for any of them. But the Alstage Sand Mining Company appeared to have abided by all the laws and regulations as they developed mines. Even with all of the controversy the proposed mine created in the Link Lake community, the mining company was not dishonest about any of it—or at least it didn't appear so. They had been right up front from the very beginning of the negotiations with the village; they had even contributed several thousand dollars toward the village's summer events. And what did they get for all of their efforts? A million-dollar machine blown to bits. *I was the one that was being dishonest by not telling people from the beginning that I worked for the mining company. I was the dishonest one, not Alstage.*

After his mornings at the Lake Coffee Bar, he returned to his cabin and spent most afternoons fishing and thinking. These late summer days were not the best for fishing, but he did manage to catch the occasional largemouth bass and usually a bluegill or two, all of which he returned to the lake.

His thoughts took him in two directions. When he wasn't pondering whether he'd been dishonest by not letting people know who he really was, he couldn't stop thinking about the photograph that he saw hanging on Ambrose Adler's wall. It reminded him so much of his mother as he remembered her when he was a little kid growing up in California. As the years

179

passed, he had not been close to his mother—she was always working hard at her job, and he traveled the country. He realized now that it had been several months since they'd talked, and he decided to give her a call one evening after he had returned from fishing.

"Mom, it's Karl."

"Oh, Karl, it's so good to hear from you. Where are you?" Karl's mother had given up trying to keep track of her widely traveled son.

"I'm in Hicksville, Wisconsin," answered Karl. "In a little village called Link Lake. I'm staying in a cabin on the lake, quite a nice place."

"Where did you say you were?" his mother asked again.

"Link Lake, Wisconsin. Have you ever heard of the place?"

"No, I guess I haven't," said his mother after another pause. "What are you doing there?"

"Oh, I'm working for this mining company that's planning to build a sand mine in the village park. It's been quite a struggle. Lots of people are opposed to having a sand mine in the park. One of the problems is there is an old oak tree that people claim is historic. They call it the Trail Marker Oak."

"Oh, really," his mother said quietly.

"Then there's this environmental writer who has stuck his nose into the fray. Do you know of a writer called Stony Field?"

"Yes, yes, I do. Everyone knows about Stony Field," his mother replied.

"Well this Field guy has gotten people all steamed up in opposition to the mine. It's quite a mess. It's an interesting place, though. It's grown on me. I met this old farmer, named Ambrose Adler, a strange old guy who grows vegetables and talks to animals. But he's interesting. He stutters so badly I can hardly understand him. But there's something about the guy that I like."

"He does sound interesting," his mother said quietly. "And a little different."

"And you know what? He has a photograph hanging on his wall that reminds me of how you looked when I was a little kid."

"Oh, Karl," his mother said. "It's been a long time since you were a kid—how could some old photo remind you of me? Have you met anyone else interesting there?"

Karl answered, "Let's see. Then there's this woman who owns the Link Lake Supper Club. Her name is Marilyn Jones and, well, she can best be described as a go-getter. Unfortunately, it seems she wants to take the village in a direction that many of the people don't want to go, especially those interested in preserving the history of the village and such things like this Trail Marker Oak. All that this Jones woman sees is jobs, jobs, jobs. She thinks preserving history gets in the way of progress. I mostly disagree with her on that point—but I've got to be careful with what I say, as I'm working for the mining company, and she was the person who convinced the village board and the mayor to bring in the mine in the first place."

"My, it certainly sounds like you've got your hands full," Karl's mother said.

"Everything really got tense a few weeks ago when somebody blew up one of the mining company's big drilling machines."

"Really! Who did it?"

"We don't know, but everybody is sure worked up about it."

"You better be careful, Karl. Maybe you should pack up and leave that place."

"I'll be fine, Mom. I've been in tight spots before. Trying to work through these situations is what I get paid for."

"Well, you be careful. You hear me?"

"I hear you, Mom, I'll be fine. Don't worry about me."

After he hung up, Karl thought, *Something's not right with Mom. She didn't sound like her old self. Is she having problems at work?* He was well aware that all newspapers were cutting staff and tightening down. *Is she worried about her job?*

46
Dry Weather

The rains in central Wisconsin had stopped in mid-summer, and now the hot August sun dried out the countryside and challenged the corn, soybeans, and vegetable crops that were not irrigated. Anyone who did not have irrigation, and that included small vegetable farmers such as Ambrose Adler, saw their pumpkins, squash, and cucumbers wither, their sweet corn leaves curl, and their potato vines turn brown. With no rain for weeks, Ambrose kept his vegetable stand open only three days a week as he didn't have enough produce to keep it well stocked.

The temperature each day climbed into the nineties, and only dropped into the seventies in the evening. To add to the increasingly dry conditions, a stiff southwest wind blew each day, helping to further dry the countryside, turning grass brown, drying up cow pastures, and even killing little trees, especially the pine trees that a few tree farmers in the area had planted in the spring. The air was filled with dust, dirty brown dust that was picked up by the wind and turned the sky the color of chocolate by late afternoon. Dust sifted through open windows and gathered on furniture. Dust gathered on the corn leaves, on the soybean leaves, on the goldenrods that struggled to bloom, on the brown grass alongside the highways, on the leaves of the oaks and the maples. Dirty brown dust everywhere.

Farmers in the Link Lake community who attended the Church of the Holy Redeemed and the Baptist and the Methodist churches prayed for rain on Sunday mornings and looked to the west every evening for an answer to their prayers. The dry weather continued. One week. Two weeks. Three weeks. Everyone kept their eye on the sky every evening, and they listened to the NOAA weather forecasts, watched the TV weather news, and heard nothing but the same forecast, day after miserable hot, dry, dusty day.

The talk at the Eat Well never strayed from the weather. Same conversation at every table every morning.

"Do you remember anything like this?"

"Reminds me of the 1930s."

"Will it ever end?"

"Damn dust is gettin' to me."

"Hot wind keeps blowin' every day. Every damn day."

Oscar and Fred talked about it.

"You remember back in the 1950s when we had a stretch of hot dry weather like this, Fred?" asked Oscar Anderson.

"I do. I remember cutting our second crop of alfalfa; first crop had been decent, but the second crop, well, I don't think we got more than 150 bales off of twenty acres. Worst damn yield of hay I ever had."

"That dry spell was a lot like this one. Hot sun every day. Damn old wind blowing out of the southwest that dried up everything that wasn't already dried up."

"Hate to change the subject, Fred, knowing how well we all like to complain about the weather, but you heard anything more about the sand mine?"

"Nope, ain't heard one word. Not one single word. All anybody talks about is the drought."

"You see any protestors at the park?"

"Nope, everything is quiet there since the big explosion."

"Well, I don't like it. I'll bet you my bottom dollar, Fred, that mining company is gonna come in here, cut down our Trail Marker Oak, start diggin' a big hole in the park, and stir up more dust than we got in the air right now. Read somewhere that these sand mines stir up a lot of dust— and dangerous dust, too. The kind that'll get in your lungs and raise hell with your breathin', eventually kill you."

"Really. I didn't know that," said Fred.

"Well, it's the truth. We're in for some tough times."

"Can't believe they could get much worse than they are right now, what with this drought and hot wind blowin' every day."

"You just wait, Fred. Just wait. What's goin' on right now is nothing compared to when that sand mine opens. You just wait and see if I ain't right."

The two old men sat quietly for a time, sipping their coffee. Fred ran his finger over the arm of the empty chair at their table, removing a coat of fine dust.

"When do you suspect it'll rain?" asked Fred, breaking the silence.

"Oh, it'll rain. Always does. Hope we don't have a big storm."

"Geez, Oscar. One minute you're complaining about how dry it is and the next you're worried that if it does rain we'll have a storm."

"Only speaking the truth, Fred. The truth that comes from eighty years of livin' in this place."

At six on a September morning the following week, it was already eighty degrees with a weather forecast of high nineties, maybe even one hundred degrees. Fred and Oscar had settled into their chairs at the Eat Well and said little or nothing since arriving. They sat staring out the window enjoying the cool air-conditioned room, for neither of them had air-conditioning in their farm homes.

Oscar broke the silence. "Do you know what I saw this morning on my drive in to town?"

"Let's see, you saw a dried-up cornfield, a dried-up soybean field, a few dead trees, and a deer walked across the road in front of you. Oh, you maybe also saw a bald eagle feasting on a road-killed raccoon. How am I doin'?" said Fred.

"I'll give you this, you got one helluva imagination."

"Got to be good for something."

"So you wanna hear about what I saw?"

"I suppose you're gonna tell me whether I wanna hear it or not," said Fred.

"Well, you wanna hear about it or do you just wanna sit there grumpin' and sippin' on your coffee and worrying about the drought?"

"Go ahead, I'm all ears," said Fred.

Dry Weather

"I saw a bank of clouds just off the horizon to the west."

"You saw a bank of clouds?"

"That's what I said. I saw a big bank of clouds just climbing over the horizon."

"So what's so great about that? Almost every day a cloud or two passes overhead, sometimes more than one or two, sometimes maybe three or four, or even eight or ten."

"Fred, what I saw isn't your everyday set of dry weather clouds. It looks like a storm is brewin'."

"Weather people didn't say anything about a storm. I listened this morning. All they said is there was a possibility of scattered thunderstorms. They've been sayin' that every day lately, but they never come. It never rains. Just never gets around to rainin' anymore."

"You mark my word, Fred. There's a storm a comin' our way."

"Your word is marked," said Fred, smiling. "I hope you're right though. We really do need a soaking rain. Can't remember when we had a good rain."

"You coming to the historical society lunch this noon?" asked Oscar.

"Nope, I'm gonna have to miss it this year. My back fence is fallin' down and my neighbor says I better get it fixed or he'll hire someone to fix it and send me the bill."

"Yeah, figured I'd stay home too. That fancy food doesn't agree with me."

47

Storm

*E*ach year, the Link Lake Historical Society held their annual late summer luncheon at the Link Lake Supper Club; this year was to be no exception. Emily would have preferred to hold the meeting elsewhere, but she knew of no other place close by that was as nice as the Link Lake Supper Club and large enough to hold the group. Emily Higgins and the planning committee had organized a special luncheon this year to commemorate all the hard work the members had done in helping the Link Lake citizens become aware of the perils of a sand mine coming to town and the travesty it would be to cut down the Trail Marker Oak. She had invited the members of the Link Lake High School Nature Club to come as well to applaud them for helping to put up the eagle cam, one of the most successful activities the historical society had ever supported. And of course a discussion of the cemetery walk and the bank robbery reenactment were on the agenda as well, with the appropriate committees giving reports and receiving praise for their efforts.

Emily had heard the weather forecast just prior to driving over to the supper club: "Possibility of severe thunderstorms for Ames County with high winds and hail." Like everyone else in Link Lake, Emily looked forward to some much-needed rain; she hoped the rains would come and the weather people were wrong about the high winds and hail. She saw the clouds boiling up in the west as she drove from the historical society headquarters down Main Street and then to the Link Lake Supper Club. She had seen clouds like this before; sometimes they resulted in strong storms, sometimes in rain, and sometimes nothing at all as the clouds moved north or south and passed Link Lake entirely.

With the invited guests, some fifty people were in attendance for the annual noon luncheon, one of the group's largest crowds in recent memory. Even Ambrose Adler had walked to Link Lake so he could attend the event.

Marilyn Jones remained in her office as the group enjoyed their luncheon and the conversation. When the dishes were cleared and fresh cups of coffee poured, Emily walked to the podium with a sheaf of notes in hand. Emily was well organized and planned everything down to the last detail. She didn't like surprises.

All Emily got to say was "Welcome," before a tremendous flash of lightning followed by a clap of thunder that rattled the supper club windows halted the proceedings. The lights flickered once and then went out. And the room was quiet.

Marilyn Jones burst from her office, her face pale.

"May I have your attention, please," she said in a loud voice. "I just heard on my weather radio that a tornado is headed our way. It touched down in Plainfield and will be here in fifteen minutes. Everyone gather in the middle of the room, away from the windows, and get under the tables," Marilyn yelled.

"Wait, wait," said Emily Higgins in her usual far-reaching voice. "I have a better idea. Some of you will remember that this place was once a stagecoach stop and roadhouse. What you don't know is the builders of this place also constructed an underground storm shelter. Follow me!"

Marilyn Jones stood with a mystified look on her face. She did not know the history of her supper club; indeed, she had never been interested in it.

"After me," said Emily as people, most of them with frightened looks on their faces, trailed behind her out a side door and a couple hundred feet away to a tangle of wild berry bushes.

"If I remember correctly, there should be a metal trap door right about here," Emily said. "I need a little help clearing away this tangle of berry bushes."

Several high school students stepped forward and began tugging and pulling at the berry bushes, while flashes of lightning and ear-splitting thunder continued to fill the air. The first big drops of rain began falling as Emily announced, "We've found it. Here's the trap door."

"It's rusted shut," one of the high school students said as he tugged on the latch.

Several other students helped him, and the door finally squealed open, revealing a set of stairs to an underground chamber. One after another, members of the historical society and the nature club slowly climbed down the soon to be quite crowded and very musty underground chamber. As the high school students, with the help of their teacher, slowly let down the metal door, the group could hear what sounded like the approach of a train. Louder and louder. And the ground began shaking.

It was completely dark in the crowded room until several people removed their cell phones from their pockets, providing a little light. Some began complaining about the cobwebs and the musty smell, but most concentrated on what they heard even though the sound was muffled by several feet of soil and an iron trap door. Three or four of the older members of the historical society had been in tornados before, and the sound of the wind brought back memories of devastating destruction, injury, and even death.

After a few minutes—quiet. Extreme quiet.

"Should we try the door?" one of the students asked.

"Let's wait a few more minutes," said Emily, "to make sure the storm has passed."

When the door was finally opened, and people crawled up the steps to the outdoors, they walked into a downpour of rain.

"Oh, my God," said Marilyn Jones when she saw the devastation to the supper club.

An enormous oak tree had fallen on the back part of the building, directly over her office. Had she been in her office she would have been severely injured, if not killed. The tornado tore the roof off the dining room; people saw pieces of roofing floating in the lake. An enormous white pine tree had snapped off and its trunk had pierced the front door of the supper club.

People stood in the rain, no one saying anything, not believing what they were seeing. Except for the falling rain, it was quiet. No wind. No thunder.

"Is everyone okay?" Emily Higgins asked.

Heads were nodding in the affirmative.

Marilyn Jones, with tears streaming from her eyes, found Emily and took her hand.

"Thank you, thank you," she said. "Thank you so much. Thank you for remembering the storm shelter."

"You are welcome," said Emily. Marilyn Jones gave Emily Higgins a big hug.

48

Aftermath

*H*istorical society members and representatives from the high school nature club stood in the rain, numb, staring at the destruction of the Link Lake Supper Club. In less than five minutes they heard the wail of sirens and soon the two Link Lake fire trucks appeared, followed by the squad car.

"Is anyone injured?" yelled Fire Chief Henry Watkins. "Is anyone hurt?"

"I . . . I don't believe so, Henry," answered Emily. "We're shaken a bit. But I believe beyond being soaked to our skins, we're okay."

Volunteer firefighters soon began dragging huge tarps from one of the trucks and with the assistance of historical society members and nature club students they began spreading the tarps over the exposed parts of the supper club, which was most of it, as the entire roof had been blown off.

Watkins walked over to where Marilyn Jones stood staring at the destruction.

"Are you okay, Miss Jones?" asked Watkins as he placed a spare firefighter's jacket around her shoulders.

"Everything is gone . . . all gone. Years of work . . . gone. Just like that, gone." Tears mixed with raindrops ran down Marilyn's face.

"I'm sorry," said Watkins. "The supper club took the worst of the storm; a few trees are down here and there around town and the power is out. But it looks like the tornado hit your building straight on and then skipped across the lake and disappeared. That's how these storms work."

"But we're all safe," said Marilyn. "I can't image how many of us would have been hurt if we'd stayed in the building."

"Where'd you go?" asked Watkins, not aware of any secure shelter nearby.

"See over there?" Marilyn pointed to a huge wild berry patch that seemed to have the middle torn out of it. "In that berry patch is an iron door leading to an old storm shelter that Emily Higgins knew about. Emily is the reason none of us was hurt."

"Well, you don't say," said Watkins, knowing full well, as did everyone in Link Lake, that Marilyn Jones had never had anything good to say about Emily Higgins.

As quickly as the storm arrived, it departed. The clouds cleared and the sun came out. The firefighters, historical society members, and the students worked for a couple hours, creating a temporary roof over the dining room with blue tarps.

"Thank you all so much," said Marilyn as everyone began drifting off toward their cars—the parking lot had not been touched by the tornado. After everyone had left, Marilyn, not knowing what to do, went back to the storm shelter, pulled open the trap door, and left it open, which provided a little light in the cramped space where everyone had sat out the tornado. She climbed down the stairs and with the added light of her cell phone looked around. On a little shelf in the back she spotted a metal box, covered with dust. She picked it up and once outside, she opened it. She took out photos of when she and her sister Gloria were little girls. There were early photos of the supper club, and there were photos of her parents, wedding photos they appeared to be, taken in front of the Trail Marker Oak. She also found a newspaper clipping, with a wedding photo, and the caption, "Fred and Barbara Jones, longtime visitors to Link Lake from Chicago, were married this past Saturday in front of the Trail Marker Oak at Increase Joseph Community Park in Link Lake. This old tree has become a popular place for young couples to marry, as some believe that the tree, which was a guidepost for earlier travelers, would point the way toward a happy marriage as well."

Marilyn thought, *My parents knew about this storm shelter. They must have carried this box into the shelter before another storm. And they were married in front of the Trail Marker Oak—I never knew that. I can't let anybody see this. I did not know my parents had such a connection to that old Trail Marker Oak. I just can't believe it.*

Ambrose Adler started walking toward his farm. He remembered another tornado that had torn through the north side of Link Lake back in the 1970s, uprooting many trees and destroying three cattle barns just out of town. There were no injuries. At least not serious. The storm hit in the middle of the night, around midnight. Old Jesse DeWitt was driving home from the Link Lake Tap with a little more than he could handle. On the back road to his farm, which is where the tornado first struck, a tree limb came crashing down, piercing the windshield of his old 1950 Chevrolet and ending up on the seat right beside him. People found him in the car the following morning muttering something about how God's wrath had nearly struck him down. After that fateful night, Jesse DeWitt never took another drink.

Ambrose also thought about the close call they had just had. Without Emily Higgins knowing about the old storm cellar there certainly would have been injuries, even deaths, when the roof blew off the supper club and debris and broken glass were flying everywhere. Ambrose was also surprised and even a little amazed at the kind words Marilyn Jones had for Emily. *Have we seen a Marilyn no one has seen before?* Ambrose thought. *Is there more to this woman than the hard-driving businessperson she likes to portray?*

Ambrose continued walking. He smelled the freshness that followed a welcome rain. The wildflowers and grasses alongside the country road had, with the heavy rain, already seemed to lift their heads and renewed their growth. Ambrose's gait was slower these days than it had been as recently as a year ago. He was often short of breath and had to stop and rest for a few minutes before continuing on. Someone from the historical society would have been more than happy to give him a ride home, but he refused, saying he enjoyed the walk. He did enjoy the walk, but every trip it seemed was becoming more of a challenge.

As he walked along, he also wondered if the storm had struck his place. He didn't know what he would do if it had. But as he rounded a turn and could see his place in the distance, everything appeared normal. The tornado had completely missed the Adler farm.

49

Storm Stories

The day after the storm, Marilyn Jones had an insurance adjuster on site, and the following week a construction crew began replacing the roof and repairing the other tornado damage. Village crews plus volunteers soon had the downed trees in the village cut up and hauled away. The power had come on a few hours after the storm and the Village of Link Lake mostly returned to normal. Of course the stories about the tornado continued, often enhanced with each telling. Emily Higgins, tough-minded, history-focused Emily, had become a local hero for remembering the storm shelter near the supper club. The *Ames County Argus* ran a feature story on the storm, with many photos and the headline, "Link Lake Historian Saves Lives."

The story read:

Emily Higgins, octogenarian head of the Link Lake Historical Society, has become a local hero. Moments before the tornado struck the Link Lake Supper Club, Higgins remembered that when the supper club was a roadhouse and stagecoach stop, early owners had built a storm shelter. Most people of Link Lake did not know about the shelter, but Emily did. Everyone at the supper club that fateful noon safely rode out the storm in the old underground shelter.

Fire Chief Henry Watkins said, "Without Emily Higgins's knowledge and quick thinking, many people would have been injured and some even killed when the storm took the roof off the supper club."

Link Lake Supper Club owner Marilyn Jones said, "We all owe a lot to Emily Higgins. I am grateful for all she did to prevent injury and save lives."

For several days, Oscar Anderson and Fred Russo had something to talk about at their early morning coffee gathering.

"Fred, I just heard this tornado story yesterday," said Oscar Anderson. "It's secondhand but it seems worthy of repeating."

"Worthy, huh? Does that mean it's not true?"

"I don't know anything about the truth of it, but it sure is a good story."

"So how long are you gonna keep me waitin'?"

"Well it goes like this. When everybody got down the stairs into that old long-forgotten storm shelter and they let the metal trap door down—"

"So what's worthy about all that?" asked Fred.

"Just hold your horses, Fred. I'm getting to the good part.

"I got 'em under control," said Fred, with a big smile on his face.

"So that big old iron door is now closed and the tornado is bearing down—some folks said it sounded just like a freight train roarin' through town. That old iron door begins to rattle. Pressure of the storm must have done it, and you know what, Fred?"

"Geez, Oscar, you sure take a long time gettin' to the nub of a story. What's the point—so far about everything you've said I've heard before."

"Bet you didn't hear this part, Fred. Bet this part is new."

"So what is it? My coffee's gettin' cold waitin' for you to get to the point of your tale."

"That old iron trap door wasn't just rattlin' up and down, just makin' noise. It was rattlin' 'Nearer My God to Thee.'" Oscar smiled from ear to ear when he said it.

Fred, unaccustomed to applauding Oscar's stories more than necessary, burst right out laughing, nearly spilling the cup of fresh coffee Henrietta had just poured for him.

"I suspect that's how some people felt, alright," said Fred, gaining his composure. "I got a story for you too, and this one I know is true because I heard it right from the fellow who saw it."

"And what did he see?" asked Oscar, wanting to go along with Fred's tale as he had been patient with his.

"Well, this guy who lives in Chicago has a place on the other end of the lake. Really nice place. A big log house. Had it built a couple years ago. More money in that place than either of us is worth."

"So?"

"I see this guy the other day at the Link Lake Tap and he's telling how he was sitting on his deck watchin' the storm boil up out of the west. He then sees this tornado drop down out of the clouds and begin tearin' apart the supper club."

"So?" says Oscar again.

"So when he sees that twister a comin', he hightails it to his basement."

"So?"

"You keep sayin' 'so?' and I'm gonna forget what the punch line is," said Fred, frowning.

"I'll keep quiet."

"Good. Well, when he comes out of his basement, he looks around and he has no damage whatsoever. But he sees somethin' that he's not seen before."

"And that would be?" asked Oscar.

"That would be one of the tables from the supper club's dining room sitting right on his pier. Not a scratch on it. His pier is a good mile away from the supper club. Isn't that somethin'?"

"Well, that surely is somethin'. He givin' the table back to the supper club?"

"How the hell do I know? That ain't got nothin' to do with the story."

"Seems like the right thing would be to give the table back to Marilyn Jones."

"Oscar. What am I gonna do with you?"

50
Another Drilling Machine

*T*he tornado completely missed Increase Joseph Community Park. Now in mid-September, the park began to look as it always did in early autumn, a little tired after a long, eventful summer. The once green grass had turned brown, except for the new grass planted where the explosion had occurred. Village workers kept that patch of new grass watered. There was almost no remaining evidence of the eagle nest that people from far and wide had watched in amazement before the explosion destroyed it.

The citizens of the Link Lake community were back doing what they always did in late summer. The merchants in town welcomed the last run of summer tourists. The antique store in the old mercantile had done a good business all summer, with more people visiting Link Lake than anyone could remember, and the store continued to do well, especially on weekends. The Eat Well Café was filled with breakfast customers every morning, and the Link Lake Tap was filled with customers every evening.

Karl Adams put up a new map of the mine site on the bulletin board by the village hall, with his fingers crossed that it would remain untouched. He was in close communication with his boss, Emerson Evans, at Alstage. He informed Evans that since the tornado, the village had seemed to forget about the upcoming sand mine. He also let Evans know that Marilyn Jones was busy putting her nearly destroyed supper club back together, and they likely couldn't expect her to help them much if new problems erupted.

"Karl, one more thing. In a few days we'll be delivering another drilling machine to the site. Let's sure as hell make sure that this one doesn't get blown up."

"Thanks for letting me know," Karl said, "but aren't you going to let the mayor and the village board know too? Didn't we learn anything from what happened in this town with the other drilling machine? You try and sneak another machine in and these people and the whole village will blow up. I don't think I'll be able to put a damper on it either."

"Well, we're bringing in another machine and don't you tell anybody. You hear?" ordered Evans as he hung up the phone.

Karl thought, *What in the world should I do? Tell the people of Link Lake another drilling machine is on its way and risk losing my consulting job? Or not tell them and feel that I've once more not been upfront with a group of people I've come to respect and admire?*

Alstage officials continued to press both the Link Lake Police Department and the Ames County Sheriff's Office for updates on who had been responsible for the destruction of their first machine. Each time the response was, "We're still working on it."

The construction crew working on repairing the Link Lake Supper Club, under the watchful eye of Marilyn Jones, had only a little landscaping to do and they would be finished. The supper club had been open for limited business for the past week; the Lake Coffee Bar had been in operation for more than two weeks—it being the first repaired.

People were beginning to think about winter, which, as Emily Higgins pointed out, was "just around the corner and ready to blow into town like an uninvited guest." It was a quiet time. Just as everyone in Link Lake looked forward to the arrival of the summer visitors each spring, they looked forward to their departure in the fall. But nobody would say that out loud, as Link Lake wanted to maintain an image of being open for visitors—as well as open for business, as Marilyn Jones kept reminding everyone. Of course visitors meant business, especially for establishments like Marilyn's. She couldn't wait for the sand mine to begin operations. She knew that once people got over the idea of having a sand mine at the park the community would once more prosper, as it had in the past. But she was more conflicted about her thoughts these days, especially since the tornado had raised havoc with her establishment. She kept coming back to what Emily Higgins had done just before the tornado struck. Emily had saved lives and avoided lots of injury when she remembered the storm shelter that had been built when the forerunner of the supper club, a stagecoach stop and roadhouse, had been built. Marilyn thought, *I hate to admit it, but this is an example of where Emily Higgins's love of history made a difference—a dramatic difference.* Marilyn also couldn't get her mind past the materials she had found in the storm shelter: photos and newspaper clippings of her parents and the story of their marriage in front of the Trail Marker Oak.

Marilyn sat in her new office at the supper club thinking about all this one early morning when her phone rang.

"Ms. Jones?"

"Yes, this is Marilyn Jones."

"Ms. Jones, this is Officer Jimmy Barnes."

"Yes, Jimmy. What can I do for you?"

"I don't know if you heard that the mining company hauled in another drilling machine last night. And not only that, they've got armed guards posted all around the mining site. I checked the guards and they've got all their permits in order, so they are legal."

"Thanks for letting me know, Jimmy," Marilyn said. She put down the phone, the red rising in her face. She immediately punched in the numbers for Karl Adams's cell phone.

"This is Karl," a tired voice responded.

"Did you know your mining company brought in a new drilling machine last night?" Marilyn said, a little too loudly.

"Yes, that's right. They're planning to do some test drilling as soon as tomorrow. The company thought it best to deliver it in the night, with the hopes that people wouldn't know about it until they were well into the testing."

"So you didn't tell anybody that the machine was coming?"

"Well . . ." Karl hesitated. "I tried to tell Emerson Evans that he should let people know the mining company was doing this. But he said no."

"You didn't even tell our police department?" Marilyn said, her voice rising even more.

"I guess I should have. Officer Barnes saw them unloading the machine at the park and they gave him a bit of a hard time, especially the armed guards. I guess he's not accustomed to seeing men wearing camouflage clothing and carrying assault weapons."

"Good God, Karl, just when I thought things had calmed down a little your damn company pulls a trick like this. At least you could have let me know ahead of time—given me a heads-up or maybe asked me what I thought of the idea. You could have done that."

"I thought you were too busy with the reconstruction of your supper club. I thought it best not to bother you."

"Not bother me! Not bother me!" Marilyn shouted into the phone. "When people in Link Lake see what you're doing, everything is going to hit the fan once more. What were you thinking?"

"I . . . I guess I wasn't thinking. Guess I should have let you know."

"Well, my guess is by this time every damn person eating breakfast at the Eat Well Café this morning is talking about it. And I'll bet you my last dollar that Emily Higgins is already organizing an emergency meeting of the historical society. What do you think we are? A bunch of country hicks?"

"I . . . I," stammered Karl. "If I would have to do it over again, I would have let you know. I screwed up."

"Well, I've got to talk to the mayor and the executive committee of the Economic Development Council. Dammit, Karl, I thought you were smarter than this. A lot smarter."

"It wasn't my idea to keep this a secret," said Karl quietly.

51

Eat Well Café

*F*red Russo had already been sitting at his place at the Eat Well for nearly ten minutes before his friend Oscar Anderson arrived.

"Geez, you get lost this morning?" asked Fred, when Oscar arrived, out of breath. He tossed his John Deere cap on the chair next to him.

"No, I did not get lost. But I did have an interesting experience on my way in."

"It seems you often have an interesting experience. You see a buck deer in the road, or maybe a fox, or a bear? Lot of bears around these days. We didn't have any bears, now they're here. Big buggers, too. Guy on the other side of Link Lake had a picture on his trail camera. He said that old bear would go four hundred pounds. Now that's a lot of bear. So what did you see on the way in?"

"Well, I thought I would stop at the park to see what was going on."

"So what possessed you to do that? Why'd you stop at the park this time of day?"

"Didn't you get a phone call from Emily?"

"The phone rang, but I didn't get there in time. What'd she have to say?"

"Emily said that the mining company moved a drilling machine into the park last night and brought along with them some armed guards. By the way, she's calling an emergency meeting of the historical society for seven tonight, at the museum meeting room."

"Middle of the night, huh? And armed guards, too?"

"Yup, so I thought I'd stop at the park and see for myself. See what was goin' on."

"And?" said Fred.

"Hold on, Fred, I'm gettin' there."

"Well, I hope so. Ain't got all day hearin' you march around the bush without tellin' me what's in it."

"Well, I park my pickup alongside the road by the park entrance. I get out and walk over toward the Trail Marker Oak, wonderin' if they'd cut it down already."

"Did they?"

"Nope, that old oak was standin' there just as proud as could be, like nothin' had ever happened or was gonna happen to it."

"None of what you said sounds all that exciting."

"I haven't got to the exciting part."

"And?"

"Well, like I said I was walking across the road toward the Trail Marker Oak when this guy jumps out from behind that old tree and yells, 'Halt!' Well I just about dropped my drawers."

"What kind of guy?"

"He was dressed in that camouflage stuff that army guys wear these days, even had a kind of mask across his face. Never saw anything like it. Scared the hell out of me."

"So what'd the guy say, besides 'Halt'?"

"Oh, what I didn't tell you is he was carrying one of them big old assault rifles, the kind you see guys on TV using."

"He point it at you?"

"Nah, not quite. But he was ready to. I think he was ready to do what he thought needed doin'."

"I'll bet he thought you were some kind of terrorist dressed up like an old farmer." Fred laughed when he said it.

"Fred, it isn't funny. That guy meant business. And before I could say anything, two more guys jumped out of the bushes that looked just like the first one. The first guy then said, 'I'd suggest you move along. This is Alstage Sand Mining Company property.'"

"He said that?"

"Yes, he did. And I almost said that he was full of it, that this was a public park and he should stand aside. But you know, Fred, you don't argue with three guys ready to point their assault weapons at you. You bet you don't. So I turned around, walked back across the road, climbed in my pickup, and drove here. I haven't run up against guys carrying big guns like that since I was deer huntin' twenty years ago, got lost, and stumbled onto this guy's property that he patrolled with a thirty-ought-six. Scared the hell out of me then. But these guys at the park looked even more dangerous. These bastards mean business."

"Looks like them mining folks are gettin' serious," said Fred.

"More than serious. Things are gettin' downright scary. What in hell is happening to Link Lake? Think you can make the meeting at the historical society this evening?

"I'll be there," said Fred.

"We gotta do somethin' about this. We can't have guys dressed like commandos and carryin' assault weapons scarin' the hell out of Link Lake citizens. It's just not right. Link Lake is not like that. Never was, and never should be."

"Say, Oscar," said Fred with a big smile on his face. "You have to stop at home and change your underwear after that little encounter? Is that the real reason you were late this morning?"

Oscar smiled. "See you at the meeting tonight."

52

Meeting

I believe you all know why we are here," said Emily Higgins as she called the Link Lake Historical Society meeting to order. She began by sharing the information she had gotten from a variety of sources, including what she had heard from Officer Jimmy Barnes and from Oscar Anderson, who chimed in to elaborate on his story, making it considerably more exciting than the reality of what had happened.

"We now have a drilling machine in the park, along with armed guards carrying big rifles that, according to Oscar, appear ready to shoot with the slightest provocation," continued Emily.

"Is there anything at all we can do?" asked someone from the back row.

"I don't know," answered Emily, "but that's why I called this meeting, to see if we can come up with something. There must be something we can do."

"Is the Trail Marker Oak still safe?" someone else asked.

"Oscar stopped by the park this morning, and he said it was still standing. In fact Oscar said one of the armed guards was hiding behind it. Isn't that right, Oscar?" Emily said as she nodded toward him in the front row.

"Yup, that's right. Scared the bejeebers out of me when this guy with a gun jumped out from behind that old oak," said Oscar.

"What if we organize a group to protest at the park, like we did before?" someone asked.

"I wouldn't recommend it. I think that's what the mining company expects us to do—that's one of the reasons they have the guards. Somebody might get hurt," said Emily.

Meeting

"I think the only hope we have is to let Stony Field know what's happening," said Fred Russo. "If Stony Field knew about what was goin' on, what he'd write in his column might make a difference. Might put a stop at least to this armed guard nonsense. Looks like there's no stoppin' the sand mine though. They're hell bent on goin' ahead with the project."

Someone else suggested that Emily talk with Karl Adams, perhaps go out to his cabin on the lake and see what he could do to help.

"I doubt that would do any good. What could he do? He's just small potatoes in that big Alstage Sand Mining Company," said Emily.

After an hour or so of lamenting, complaining, and wringing hands, the group disbanded and headed toward home. Ambrose Adler had sat in the back row and had taken in the entire conversation. He knew what he must do when he returned home that evening.

Once back at his house, he gave a few treats to Ranger and Buster, unlocked the door to his secret office, and pulled up to his big, dependable Remington manual typewriter. He rolled in a fresh sheet of paper and began typing.

FIELD NOTES
Gestapo Tactics in Link Lake

By Stony Field

As readers of this column know, I have been following developments in the little Village of Link Lake, Wisconsin, since their village board signed a lease for the Alstage Sand Mining Company to open a sand mine there in October. You will recall that a company-owned million-dollar drilling machine was mysteriously destroyed earlier in the summer. So far no person or persons have been arrested for that illegal act. Many readers also remember watching the park's resident bald eagle family on the town's eagle cam; three of the eagles were killed in the blast that destroyed the drilling machine.

Just this week, the Alstage Company, in the dark of night, secretly brought in a replacement drilling machine. And along with the drilling machine, they brought in hired guns, security guards wearing military clothing and carrying military-type weapons. I understand why the company would want security given what happened to the first drilling machine. But military-type men with military-type weapons for little Link Lake?

Everyone in the village was as disturbed by what happened to the first drilling machine as was the mining company. But guards armed with assault weapons seems more than a little overreacting.

If the mining company ever wants to arrive on the good side of the citizens of Link Lake, they'd better quit acting like bullies and begin acting like good neighbors. So far, the famous and very historic Trail Marker Oak still stands. But its future looks more and more uncertain.

Ambrose removed the sheet from his typewriter, folded it, and placed it an envelope addressed to Stony Field Column, P. O. Box 4678, Los Angeles, CA, the same address where he had mailed the column these many years.

As he often did, Ambrose included a little handwritten note. "*Gloria,*" he wrote in his careful script:

Is there any chance you could come out to Link Lake one of these days? As you can tell from my columns, the village is torn apart over this sand mining business. And I have not been feeling well. I'd sure like to see you.

You would be amazed how much little Link Lake has changed since you left. Your sister, Marilyn, is still as headstrong as ever— but since the supper club was nearly destroyed in a tornado, she seems to have mellowed a little. It may just be my imagination, but I think she is not the Marilyn you remember, the one those of us interested in preserving history and the environment have always found difficult to work with. I may be wrong about all of this, of course. It may just be wishful thinking on my part to believe she has changed.

There is something else on my mind these days. All these years I have successfully kept secret who Stony Field really is.

Now as I get older, I don't want to die and have people thinking that all I've been is a stuttering old vegetable farmer who refused to accept modern conveniences. I've been doing a lot of thinking about when and how I should let people know that I am Stony Field. Do you have any thoughts about this? I suspect it will create quite a stir when people find out Stony's true identity.

I would surely look forward to seeing you once more after all these years.

Much love,
Ambrose

53

Stony and Ambrose

With all the rain that accompanied the tornado, Ambrose's garden perked up and he once more began selling late-summer crops such as tomatoes, sweet corn, potatoes, broccoli, onions, and more in his roadside stand. He worked in his garden each morning and opened up the stand after his noon nap, around one thirty or so, keeping it open until four in the afternoon. Noah Drake was back in school, and although the boy stopped at the stand nearly every afternoon on his way home, he was not able to help out as much. He did manage to come on Saturdays to help with the garden harvesting, digging potatoes, picking tomatoes and zucchini, and pulling onions. Ambrose found harvesting his garden crops increasingly difficult. He could work only for a few minutes and then he had to sit down and catch his breath, especially if it was a warm day.

Business at the stand had been brisk on this September afternoon. In fact, Ambrose wished he had brought more potatoes and zucchini to the stand—he had some extra sitting on his kitchen table, but he didn't have enough energy to walk back to the house for them. Just then Noah Drake appeared on his bike on his way home from school.

"Hi, Ambrose," said Noah as he leaned his bike against the side of the vegetable stand and looked for Ranger. "How's it going?"

"Pretty well," said Ambrose. "B . . . but I need a favor."

"Sure, what can I do?" said Noah, always ready to help.

"I am out of p . . . potatoes and zucchini. Have more on the kitchen table."

"Sure, I'll fetch them for you," said Noah. He hopped on his bike and rode down the dusty driveway to Ambrose's house, climbed off his bike, and went inside. Noah knew that Ambrose never locked his outside doors. He found a couple of small pails on the kitchen table, one filled with zucchini and one with potatoes. He picked them up and turned to go back outside when he noticed the door just beyond the kitchen table, one that was always closed, stood open. Always curious, Noah put down the vegetables and peered into the room. What he saw both surprised and intrigued him. He knew that Ambrose was an avid reader, but he had no idea that the old farmer had such a vast collection of books. One entire wall of the room consisted of bookshelves. He began pulling a few off the shelf: John Muir, *The Story of My Boyhood and Youth*; Henry David Thoreau, *Walden*; Loren Eiseley, *The Immense Journey*; and Aldo Leopold, *A Sand County Almanac*. There were many, many more. Noah was astounded at what he was seeing. He glanced at another wall and saw that it was covered with framed awards, *Stony Field, Outstanding Environmentalist Award of the Year*; *Stony Field, Nature's Way Award*, and at least ten more. Noah then saw an open scrapbook with past Stony Field columns carefully arranged by date. He thumbed through it and was amazed at how many there were. Noah glanced around the messy office and saw piles of newspapers and magazines, as well as books that had not found their way to the shelves. It was a room like he had never seen before, certainly different from the other rooms in Ambrose Adler's home, which Noah had seen many times.

It didn't occur to Noah what he had discovered until he glanced at the old upright typewriter sitting on the scarred desk. Noah glanced at the partially typed page in the typewriter. It read:

FIELD NOTES
Link Lake Sand Mine about to Open

By Stony Field

The truth of what he was seeing hit Noah Drake like the kick of a horse. Stony Field was Ambrose Adler. He absolutely couldn't believe it, but the evidence was all there. He saw the wastebasket near the desk, reached in, and grabbed a crumpled-up piece of paper. He smoothed out the paper and saw the typewritten words:

Stony and Ambrose

FIELD NOTES

Gestapo Tactics in Link Lake

By Stony Field

As readers of this column know, I have been following developments in the little Village of Link Lake, Wisconsin, since their village board signed a lease for the Alstage Sand Mining Company to open a sand mine there in October. You will recall that a company-owned million-dollar drilling machine was mysteriously

Carefully, Noah folded the sheet of paper and put it in his pocket. He engaged the lock and pulled the office door shut. He did not want his friend Ambrose to know that he had been snooping where he didn't belong. Once outside Ambrose's house, it hit Noah what he had discovered. *I know who Stony Field is. I know something that almost no one else knows—in the whole country. And this piece of paper I have in my pocket is proof. But who should I tell? Maybe nobody. I should keep Ambrose's secret. Friends don't tell others about the secrets they know.*

Noah quickly hurried back to the vegetable stand with the extra produce. When he arrived, Ambrose thanked him for helping him out. Noah said, "I've got to go on home. Pa said he had some extra chores for me tonight."

Noah was ashamed to admit he had snooped into Ambrose's secret room and had discovered the answer to questions that thousands of people across the country and in many foreign countries were asking: who is Stony Field and where does he live? Noah now had the answer, but he didn't know what to do with the information, if anything.

Meanwhile, Ambrose sat thinking once again whether it was time to disclose who he really was. *If I reveal that I am Stony Field, will it divide the community even more?* he wondered. *Those supporting the mine and the jobs it will create have been mad as hell about my recent columns.*

When he closed up his vegetable stand for the day, he had sold about all the vegetables he had on hand, including the new supply of zucchini and potatoes. He slowly shuffled down his driveway toward home, Ranger and Buster walking along behind him. Little did he know that this would likely be the last day that he would be able to do so without somebody watching, somebody wanting to talk with him, somebody wanting to snap his picture, someone wanting to get in his face about the things he had written.

54

Revelation

*W*hen Noah Drake arrived home that afternoon and saw his dad working in the machine shed, he hurried out to help him.

"Where have you been?" his dad asked. "There's work to be done around here. You know I don't put up with people being late."

"Sorry, Pa," Noah said. "I stopped to help Ambrose with his vegetable stand."

"You spend too much time with that old codger. I want you here when there's work to be done," Lucas Drake said in his gruff voice.

Noah didn't respond. Try as he might to please his dad, he always came up short. Noah couldn't remember when his father had ever said a kind word to him, praised him, said he had done a good job. All Noah could remember was being criticized. But now he knew something that would surely evoke some praise from his dad.

Without thinking of the consequences, Noah blurted out, "Pa, I found out something today that you will never believe."

"What?" asked Drake, a man of few words but with strong opinions.

"Ambrose Adler is Stony Field.".

"What did you say?"

"I said Ambrose Adler is Stony Field."

"Can't be. That stuttering old vegetable farmer is too dumb to write the stuff that Stony Field writes."

"Pa, Ambrose is Stony Field, no matter what you say about him. Ambrose writes all those columns."

"Well, that just can't be so. You must be wrong."

"Pa, I got the facts. Ambrose is for certain Stony Field." Noah went on to explain how he had talked with Ambrose on his way home from school and Ambrose had asked him to fetch some extra vegetables from the house. Then he went on to describe that he had been in Ambrose's office, which had always been locked. He told about the books, papers, awards, and typewriter.

"And," said Noah, "look at this." He handed the folded sheet of paper to his father, who unfolded it and carefully read the words.

Lucas Drake rubbed his hand over the stubble of beard on his chin. "Well, that old bastard. That damn old bastard," he said. "And to think he lived just down the road from us all these years and we didn't know that he was doing all this damn writing. Stirring up people across the country and making it about impossible for some of us to make a living. Good God, if we'd do what Stony Field writes we should do, everybody would starve to death. That damn old fool Ambrose is a menace, a damnable menace."

"Pa, he's just an old man who has a pet raccoon and raises vegetables," Noah said. He quickly realized he should never have told his dad what he had learned. He had deceived his best friend.

"Son, don't you understand? Old Ambrose would have you think he's just a stutterin' old dirt farmer. Sure as hell fooled me all these years. Bet the old bastard doesn't even stutter."

"Pa, he does so stutter. I worked for him all summer. He can hardly spit out a sentence without tangling it up. And besides that, I think he's kind of cool."

"Kind of cool? Kind of cool?" said Drake, raising his voice. "Guys like that are dangerous. He's got folks in Link Lake so screwed up with his columns about the sand mine coming in that half of the people don't know if they're for it or against it."

"I like him," said Noah quietly.

"Like him? He's not to be liked. Young man, you will have nothing to do with that old bastard anymore. Don't let me ever catch you stopping at his place again. Good God, and to think he's our neighbor. What in hell kind of neighbor writes some damnable column about saving the environment, paying no attention to those who need jobs and reminding us commercial farmers, the ones who are making a difference in this country, that we're somehow ruining the land? What in hell does he know about ruining the land? The little farming that old bastard does won't matter one way or the other. Who does he feed? A handful of people who stop by his decrepit little vegetable stand. How many do I feed? Well, think about it. I farm a thousand acres."

Lucas Drake and his son stood quietly for a few moments. Then Drake broke the silence. "I've got to do something about this. I've got to let people know about Stony Field. And now that we know who he is and where he lives, maybe we can do something about what he writes. Son, you've done a great service. A great service to your country." He clapped his son on the back, pulled a cell phone from his pocket, and punched in some numbers.

"Marilyn," he said, "have I got news for you. I am immediately calling an emergency meeting of the Ames County Eagle Party."

55

Eagle Party

Marilyn Jones couldn't believe it. She sat quietly for a few moments, trying to make sense of what she had just heard. Could it be true that old Ambrose Adler, who stuttered so badly that no one could understand him and who lived as a subsistence farmer, was the famous environmental writer, the person who had given her Economic Development Council so much grief over the development of the sand mine?

Lucas Drake had explained to her how his son, Noah, had stumbled onto Ambrose's secret writing room and was dead certain about Ambrose being Stony Field. He even had a partially typed piece of wastepaper from one of Stony Field's columns.

Once Marilyn had decided that what she had heard was true, she became furious. She of course had known Ambrose Adler since she was a little girl. She had mostly ignored him, until her sister, Gloria, had taken up with him. She was rather proud to have shared with her parents the details of Ambrose and Gloria's dating, and that the couple had even spent a night together at Gloria's apartment. Marilyn knew she had helped convince her parents that they should not approve the couple's marriage. She just couldn't see having a stuttering dirt farmer as a member of the family. But she wasn't proud that her interference had resulted in her sister moving to California, never to return.

Marilyn drummed her fingers on her desk. *Why wasn't I able to figure out that old Ambrose was really Stony Field? The evidence was right there in front of me. How else could Stony Field have known so much about what was going on in Link Lake? How else could he have known about the Trail Marker Oak and the sand mine? It was because he was here. He was attending the meetings. We all ignored him—we all believed he was a harmless, bearded old stuttering vegetable farmer. I knew he spent time at the library. I knew he was no dummy. But a writer? A nationally known environmental writer?*

She slapped her open hand on her desk. She was furious with herself but now, being the strong-minded and usually clear-thinking business-woman that she was, she wondered what she should do next. Surely, once the world knew the true identity of Stony Field and where he lived, people would be traveling to Link Lake in droves to see the real Stony Field, to interview him and see where and how he lived. And, she quickly surmised, some would come to see the old Trail Marker Oak and the site of the sand mine that Stony had written about in his columns. *What else is going to happen to me?* she thought. *Bombs, tornadoes. And now the real Stony Field revealed. Is this part of God's plan for me? Do I really have no control over my life? Am I merely a puppet in God's hands, doing his will? What will he want me to do next?*

She knew what she must do. She had to let the Economic Development Council know as soon as possible, as Stony Field had been a thorn in their side from the day they began discussing bringing jobs to Link Lake. And she looked forward to attending the emergency meeting of the Ames County Eagle Party that Lucas Drake was calling. The Eagle Party tended to disagree with almost everything that Stony Field wrote. The party saw him as a great deterrent to the nation's progress, if not the world's progress.

That evening, the community room at the Link Lake Library was filled with members of the Ames County Eagle Party. They did not yet know the purpose of the meeting, but they trusted Lucas Drake enough to come out when he suggested they should meet.

"Thanks for coming on such short notice," said Drake as he got the group's attention. "We have an extremely important situation on our hand. I need your advice on how we should proceed."

Some fifty Ames County Eagle Party members, including several members of the Link Lake Economic Development Council, most of whom belonged to the party, were in attendance. All were well aware of the problems the Village of Link Lake had as the Alstage Sand Mining

Company was making preparations to begin operations in October. Eagle Party members had not been directly involved in the fussing and fuming about the mine and were surprised when Drake said, "We have just learned the true identity of Stony Field, the national environmental writer who, to put it mildly, is not a friend of the Eagle Party, nor is he a friend of the Link Lake Economic Development Council."

The room was so quiet you could hear a lone mosquito buzzing in the back of the room, looking for a likely victim.

"I've just found out Stony Field lives right here in the Link Lake community," continued Drake. "And he is someone nobody would ever have guessed would be a famous writer. Ambrose Adler is Stony Field. My neighbor, that old stuttering vegetable farmer, has been fooling us for years."

"Are you sure?" asked someone in the back. "This sounds preposterous."

"I'm positive," said Drake. He took a few minutes to explain how he lived just down the road from the Adler farm, and how his son, Noah, had by accident stumbled upon the secret room where Ambrose did his writing.

"I've got solid evidence here in my hand," said Drake, waving a sheet of paper above his head. "I've got here a draft copy of one of Stony Field's columns that my son fetched from old Ambrose Adler's wastebasket. This is the smoking gun that proves Ambrose is Stony Field."

"But are you absolutely sure?" someone else spoke up. "I happen to know Ambrose Adler; I've bought vegetables from him. That man can't speak a sentence without tangling it up, he stutters so bad."

Marilyn jumped in, "Just because someone stutters doesn't mean they can't write. It doesn't mean they can't think straight."

"You defending that old bastard, Marilyn?" asked Drake.

"Certainly not. But I am stating a fact. Just because Ambrose Adler stutters doesn't mean he is stupid."

"He sure writes some stupid stuff," someone in the front row said, followed by laughter.

"Okay, what are we gonna do about it, now that we know who the real Stony Field is? You are the first to hear the news; we've told no one else. What should we do next?" asked Drake.

There was buzzing in the room. A hand went up. "I say we call the sheriff and have him arrested," said an angry person standing in the back.

"On what grounds?" chimed in Marilyn.

"On pretending to be someone he is not. Isn't that called impersonation?"

"I don't think that's illegal," said Marilyn.

"Well, it sure as hell sounds illegal to me. That old bearded stuttering bastard has fooled thousands of people for years. It sounds illegal to me. Let's call the sheriff. That's one thing we can do."

"Any more ideas?" asked Drake, trying to ignore the previous speaker and looking around the room for someone holding up a hand.

"Well, I have an idea," he said. "I know one way to shut him up. I suggest we call the *Los Angeles Journal* that syndicates his column and tell them that unless they quit sending the Stony Field column around the country, people will cancel their subscriptions. That should get everyone's attention. And we should call the *Ames County Argus* and suggest the same thing. We'll shut off that old bastard before he does any more harm to this country."

As soon as his father left for the Eagle Party meeting in town, Noah Drake climbed on his bike and pedaled to the Adler farm. Ambrose was sitting on the porch, in an old rocking chair, Ranger and Buster at his feet.

Noah parked his bike and walked up to the porch.

"Hi, Noah," said Ambrose, pleased to have some company on this pleasant September evening. The crickets had begun singing shortly after sundown, a sure sign that autumn was on the way, but otherwise it was peaceful on Ambrose's porch. The rocking chair squeaked as Ambrose rocked slowly back and forth.

"I have something to tell you, Ambrose," said Noah as he looked down at his shoes.

"Here, sit down," Ambrose said, motioning to an empty chair next to the rocker.

Noah took off his cap and sat down. He continued to look at his shoes.

"Nice evening," said Ambrose. Ranger walked from Ambrose's rocker to the chair where Noah sat. Noah reached down and petted the little animal.

"I did a terrible thing," Noah blurted out. He continued looking at his shoes. Ambrose didn't say anything but looked at his friend, who didn't look back.

"You forgot to lock your office door this morning," Noah began. He looked out toward Ambrose's barn, still avoiding looking at his old friend. "And I looked inside. And I know I shouldn't have. I shouldn't have done that," Noah said quickly, his bottom lip quivering.

Ambrose reached over and put his hand on Noah's arm. "I . . . I," Noah hesitated. "I figured out that you are Stony Field, the writer." The words gushed out of Noah like a person who turned on a hose and water poured out in a rush.

"It's okay," said Ambrose in a quiet voice. "It's okay."

Tears ran down Noah's face. "I'm so sorry," said Noah. "So sorry. And one more thing. I told Pa. I shouldn't have told him," Noah sobbed. His entire body was shaking. "Pa is off at a special meeting in town right now to talk about you, to talk about Stony Field."

Ambrose continued to pat young Noah on the arm. The little raccoon, sensing Noah's discomfort, rubbed against Noah's leg.

For what seemed like forever, the two friends sat quietly listening to the crickets and feeling the cool night air. Ambrose, his hand still on Noah's arm, said, "Look at me."

Slowly Noah turned his tear-stained face toward his old friend. "I . . . was going to tell folks myself," said Ambrose, smiling.

"You were?" said Noah. "You really were?"

"Yup. Don't have to now."

56
Phone Calls

*I*n her office at the supper club, Marilyn Jones looked up the phone number for the editorial desk of the *Los Angeles Journal* and gave it to Lucas Drake. "Are you sure you want to make this call, Lucas?" Marilyn asked. "Can you imagine what's going to happen when the country finds out that Stony Field lives right in the Link Lake community?"

"Marilyn, you're going soft on us," Drake replied. "People need to know who Stony Field really is so they can put a stop to his liberal nonsense. Let the chips fall where they may. Ambrose Adler deserves all that he's going to get, the old bastard. To think he's fooled us all this time. Unbelievable. We gotta stop him. We gotta figure out a way to do it before he does any more damage to this country. One way to do it is to cut off the snake's head right in his nest. And that nest would be that damnable *Los Angeles Journal* that's been sending his columns all over the country."

The next morning, Drake fussed and fumed and waited for ten o'clock to roll around before he punched in the numbers for the *Los Angeles Journal*.

"*Los Angeles Journal*," said a pleasant voice upon answering the phone. "How can I be of help?"

"This is Lucas Drake calling from Link Lake, Wisconsin," Drake said, trying to keep his fury under control. "I would like to speak to Stony Field's editor."

"Sorry, but she is not available just now. May I take a message?"

"Are you sure she can't come to the phone? What I have is pretty darn important for her to hear."

"Yes, I am quite sure. Please give me your message and I'll pass it on to her."

"Well, you tell her that this Stony Field guy who's been a mystery all these years—well, some of us in Link Lake know who he is." Drake paused for a moment. "You got all of that down?"

"Yes, sir, I do."

"Well, here's the kicker. Stony Field is really an old dirt farmer who lives on a little farm just outside of Link Lake, Wisconsin. His name is Ambrose Adler and he stutters so bad you can hardly make out what he says." Another pause. "You got that? Stony Field is really Ambrose Adler who lives near Link Lake, Wisconsin."

"Yes, sir. I've got it down. But are you sure you have it right?"

"Miss, you're damn right I got it right," said Drake, unable to control his anger anymore. "You folks have gotta stop those Stony Field columns, and I mean right now. You got all that?"

"Yes, I've got it all."

"Well, I hope so. I never did trust big city newspapers, not one bit. Most of them are in cahoots with those damn Democrats. A bunch of damn liberals. Ruining this great country of ours, sending it right down the tubes. Dirty shame too."

"Sir, thank you for the information. And thank you for calling the *Los Angeles Journal.*" The line went dead.

"Well, I'll be damned," said Drake. He thought, *That newspaperwoman just hung up on me. I had more to say if she'd have listened. But those damn liberals never did know how to listen. Especially to somebody who makes sense. Wonder if she'll do anything about what I told her or just make sure that nobody sees the message. That's the way those liberals work. When they hear about something they don't agree with, they hide it.*

After he cooled down a bit, Lucas Drake punched in the numbers for the *Ames County Argus.* "Connect me to Billy Baxter," he said.

"And who shall I say is calling?"

"Lucas Drake."

Brief pause. "Lucas, it's Billy Baxter," said the editor.

"You know who I am, don't you?" said Drake.

"Sure, you've got that big farm out by Link Lake, and you are chairman of the Ames County Eagle Party," said Baxter. "How's the corn doing this year? Price looks pretty fair?"

"The corn is doing just fine. But I'm calling because I've got some news for you and a request from the Eagle Party."

"Okay, shoot," said Baxter.

"We've figured out who the writer Stony Field really is."

"You have? Well, that would be news."

"Are you ready for this? Stony Field lives right outside of Link Lake."

"You sure about that?" said Baxter, using his journalist's show-me-the-evidence voice.

"You damn bet I'm sure," said Drake, his voice rising.

"Well, who do you think Stony Field is?"

"Dammit, Baxter, you listen to me now. I don't think, I *know* who the bastard really is."

"Well?" said Baxter.

"Stony Field is really Ambrose Adler, that old vegetable farmer who stutters so bad nobody can understand him."

"I know Ambrose Adler. What you're saying is a little hard to believe."

"There you go, you're just like those other damn liberal newspaper people, afraid to face the truth when it stares you right in the face."

"What evidence do you have?" Baxter asked. "Can you prove that Ambrose Adler is really Stony Field—which does sound a little far-fetched?"

"So you don't believe me. You can't take my word?"

"I didn't say I didn't believe you, but I do need evidence. It's the way we journalists work."

"Okay, let's say I've got a piece of paper in my hand that came out of old Ambrose's wastebasket, and it's the beginning of one of them damnable Stony Field columns. Would that be the kind of evidence you'd like to see?"

"Where'd you get the piece of paper?"

"Well, that's privileged information."

"So somebody broke into Ambrose Adler's house and rummaged through his wastepaper basket and stole a piece of paper from it."

"Good God, Baxter. The piece of paper was in his wastebasket. He was gonna throw it away."

"So you've got this piece of paper and you figure that's enough to prove that Ambrose is Stony Field."

"I got lots more. Lots more. He has a secret office in that run-down old house he shares with a pet raccoon. He's got books piled everywhere, and newspapers and magazines, and awards hanging on the wall. He's Stony Field alright."

"So you broke into his house and saw all this stuff?"

"I swear on a stack of Bibles, I did not break into his house."

"Then how did you learn about all this, about him having a secret office?"

"That is privileged information," said Lucas Drake again. "Now you listen to me. We had a meeting of the Eagle Party last night, and we all agree that we've got old Ambrose Adler nailed on this one."

"Well, it would make quite a story. Who else have you told?"

"I called the *Los Angeles Journal* and told them—that's the paper that sends that damn column all over the country, you know."

"Yes, I know," said Baxter.

"One more thing," said Drake, his voice rising again. "The Eagle Party is adamant about this. We all agree that you must immediately stop running the Stony Field column, and if you don't, every one of us—and there are a bunch of Eagle Party members in Ames County—will cancel our subscriptions to your newspaper."

"What?" said Baxter, incredulous at what he just heard.

"You heard me right, Baxter. Stony Field and his ilk are sending this country toward ruination. He's got to be stopped, and you are one of the people who can do it," Drake said as he hung up.

Billy Baxter sat back in his chair. He wondered if Lucas Drake was right, that Stony Field has been living right here under their noses all these years. He sure sounded like he knew what he was talking about. And he sure didn't want to talk about how he got the information. That part sounded a little fishy. Then there's the fact that some Eagle Party members were quick to say things that when checked out weren't true. And the audacity of the Eagle Party to believe they can shut off somebody's writing by threatening to cancel subscriptions. He'd heard that one before.

Baxter's first inclination was to drive out to Ambrose Adler's farm and talk to him about what he just learned. But Baxter knew Adler and he also was well aware of the Eagle Party's reputation for sometimes going off half-cocked with rumors and innuendos. He thought he'd wait for a bit before doing anything more. After all, Ambrose Adler was one of the oldest residents of the community and he deserved some respect.

57

Los Angeles Journal

Do you have a minute?" asked Cassandra as she poked her head in Gloria's office.

"Sure, what's up?"

"Got a strange phone call from a place called Link Lake—I think the caller said it was in Wisconsin. Anyway, this gruff-sounding fellow said he had an important news tip. He said it was about Stony Field, and he wanted to talk with you. I told him you were busy."

"Who was this guy?"

"He said his name was Lucas Drake. And the more he talked the angrier he sounded."

"What'd he have to say?"

"Well, he thinks he knows who the real Stony Field is."

"Really? Who does he think it is?"

"He said Stony Field is an old vegetable farmer named Ambrose Adler who lives near this place called Link Lake and that he stutters so bad most people couldn't understand him."

The color drained from Gloria's face and she nearly dropped the cup of coffee she was holding.

"You all right?" asked Cassandra, surprised.

"Sure, sure, I'm okay." Gloria set her coffee cup down on her desk. "Are you certain that's the name this Drake used, Ambrose Adler?"

"I'm certain. I wrote it down right here." Cassandra showed her notepad to Gloria.

"Well, this is really something," Gloria said after a brief pause. "People have been wondering for years who Stony Field really is. Did Drake say anything else?"

"Well, he was yelling something about how he is a founding member of the Eagle Party and we'd better quit running that liberal Stony Field column or we'll suffer the consequences."

"I guess we've heard that before," said Gloria. She was trying hard to keep her emotions under control, to not let Cassandra know how troubling this news was. She wondered how Lucas Drake had figured out the puzzle that had stumped people for more than four decades.

Cassandra closed her pad and returned to the receptionist desk, leaving Gloria thinking about how to handle the story. She knew the disclosure would cause a firestorm among the media. She also knew that as soon as the story broke, hundreds of newspeople would flock to little Link Lake and try to learn more about Stony Field—and Ambrose Adler.

She knew from Ambrose's recent note that he was thinking about revealing that he was Stony Field. But she wondered, *Will Ambrose be able to handle all of this attention, especially now that his health has been in decline?*

She decided on a course of action. She would write a brief story explaining who the real Stony Field was and provide a little background information about Ambrose Adler and his longtime interest in nature and preserving the environment. She would also write about his lifelong speech impediment, and how some people dismissed those with problems such as Ambrose's as also being mentally incompetent. She would point out that Ambrose as Stony Field had won a national reputation for his clear thinking and creative writing about a variety of contemporary environmental issues and that having a speech impediment did not interfere with his thinking, his research, or his writing.

She would write the story right away so that it could get into the afternoon edition of the paper. She buzzed Cassandra and asked her to clear her calendar for the next three weeks and book a flight for tomorrow to Appleton, Wisconsin, as she had a meeting today she could not miss. She then turned to her computer and began writing the story. It was one of the hardest she had ever had to write.

Identity of Stony Field Revealed

By Gloria Adams, associate editor

When Gloria completed the story, she reached for her phone and punched in some numbers. After a few moments she said, "Good morning, Karl."

"Mom, is something wrong?" Karl Adams said.

"I'm fine, Karl. But I need a favor. Would you pick me up at the Appleton airport tomorrow evening? My plane comes in at seven thirty."

"Sure, but . . . but why are you going to Appleton?" Karl asked.

"I'm not. I'm coming to Link Lake."

"Why?" was all Karl could think to say.

"I'll explain on the way from Appleton. See you tomorrow evening."

58

Reaction

The news that Ambrose Adler was the famous environmental writer Stony Field swept through the Link Lake community faster than a wildfire in California. Before any news had appeared in the media, it seemed everyone in the village and those living nearby knew about it, and every last person was totally amazed. The Eat Well Café discussion was about nothing else.

"Well, Fred, would you have ever guessed that our old fellow farmer was a writer?" asked Oscar Anderson.

"Nope, he sure had me fooled, and I've known the old bugger since he was a little kid," said Fred Russo. "I just couldn't believe it when I heard the news. Just couldn't believe it."

"How do you suspect old Ambrose feels about all this?" asked Oscar. "His health isn't all that good. Got a bad heart, you know."

"Well, I can imagine he doesn't think much of the idea, after all these years of keeping it a secret," said Fred. "Who would have guessed that Ambrose Adler is Stony Field—I mean who would have suspected that a guy who stutters was such a famous writer?"

"I heard the Drake kid who worked for him this summer stumbled onto his secret office," said Oscar. "Kind of too bad it happened. What I know about Ambrose Adler is he tried to keep to himself, always did things the old way, bothered nobody, had only a handful of friends, and beyond having a big garden, he apparently did a whale of a lot of writing."

"You know what, Oscar? When you think about it, he always came to the historical society meetings. He never missed any kind of community gatherings. He often stopped at the library. Those should have been clues that maybe old Ambrose was up to something beyond just sitting in the back row and never saying anything," said Fred. "You never saw him sleeping at a meeting, and sometimes he even took some notes. Nobody else was doing that."

"Fred, once you take a look at Ambrose with his mussed-up clothes, his long beard, and his old-fashioned way of living, and the fact that he had one helluva time spitting out even a handful of words, you would never guess he could write a sentence. And you know what? That old buzzard has written hundreds of columns and thousands of words—and has won awards besides, lots of awards. I just can't believe it," said Oscar, shaking his head. "Just can't believe it."

"Wonder what's gonna happen when everybody learns about this?" asked Fred. "Stony Field's column is one that everybody reads, but a goodly bunch of folks hated his guts. Every time they read one of his columns they seem to hate him more. We've got a bunch of people right here in Link Lake who have no time for Stony Field—Marilyn Jones, Mayor Jessup, the Reverend Ridley Ralston, most of the members of the Link Lake Economic Development Council, and every darn one of those crazy Eagle Party members, especially old Lucas Drake. I've heard Lucas Drake is just spittin' nails and trying to figure out a way of getting back at his neighbor."

"I don't like it. Don't like how things are shaping up one bit. Here we've got this damn sand mining company that's already drilling test holes in our park. They plan to cut down the Trail Marker Oak and begin serious digging in a few weeks. And then this Stony Field thing. We're gonna have a circus around here when the country learns where Stony Field lives," said Oscar.

"So whatta we gonna do about it?" asked Fred.

"Tell you what I'm gonna do. I'm gonna stop by Ambrose's place and offer to help him in any way I can. All hell's gonna break lose in a few days, and he'll need some help, no question about it. And I'm gonna suggest to Emily Higgins that the members of the historical society be prepared to give Ambrose a hand. Tell you the truth I really feel sorry for him," said Oscar.

"Count me in to help out as well," said Fred. "Ambrose Adler may be a tad different in his looks and actions, but he's a good old guy. A darn good old guy."

59
Billy Baxter Responds

*B*illy Baxter waited to act on the Stony Field situation—he wanted to see a confirming story in the *Los Angeles Journal*, which syndicated the Field column each week, before he would include a story in his paper. Meanwhile he traveled to Link Lake and to the Increase Joseph Community Park to gather updated information about the Alstage Sand Mining Company's recent activities. He heard a new drilling machine had been delivered, along with armed guards. He knew his readers would appreciate an updated story on the mining company's plans and present operations, especially since other counties in Wisconsin such as Crawford and Trempealeau had been examining their procedures for permitting the development of sand mines.

He stopped his car in the parking place near the Trail Marker Oak, got out, and was immediately confronted by an armed guard holding an assault rifle.

"Please climb back in your car and move along, sir," the guard said in a gruff voice. He held his rifle in front of him, his finger on the trigger guard, ready to use it at the slightest provocation; at least it looked that way to Billy Baxter.

Baxter pulled out his identification that indicated he was a journalist and held it up for the guard to see. "I'd like to talk with someone who can update me on mining operations," Baxter said quietly but firmly.

"I have my orders," the guard said. He was tall, well over six feet, with a camouflage mask covering the lower part of his face. "I am to let no one pass."

"But don't you understand? I am the editor of the *Ames County Argus*," said Baxter.

"Sorry. I don't care if you're the king of England, nobody gets by me."

"You're sure about that?" asked Baxter, stuffing his credentials back in his pocket and fishing out a camera. Before the guard could react, Baxter had taken his picture.

"Give me that camera," the guard ordered.

"Over my dead body," said Baxter, who ran to his car, roared the engine, and sped down the road. *I've got a different story than I thought I'd get, but it will surely get people's attention when I run it with the picture of this armed guard.*

Back at his office, before he began writing the mining story, he checked the AP Exchange website and saw the story he was waiting for. Lucas Drake had it right about Stony Field. This would certainly be first-page news in the *Argus*, and that's where the story would appear, along with the story about armed guards at the mining site and his inability to talk with anyone about mining plans.

He read the story published in the *Los Angeles Journal*, but rather than using it as it was written, he decided to write a separate story, using the facts he had at hand, but also writing about Ambrose Adler as a farmer who had a pet raccoon, a vegetable stand, and a way of life that did not include such taken-for-granted conveniences as electricity, automobiles, tractors, and even telephones. He would mention that Stony Field columns were often controversial, but they were always well researched and well argued—and well written. He decided to quote from several recent columns, especially those that took the Village of Link Lake's officials to task for being taken in by promises of jobs without taking into account the importance of historical artifacts like the Trail Marker Oak and the potential harm to people and to the environment once the mine began full operations.

In addition to the front-page story, Baxter also decided to write an editorial about the Stony Field situation. He had not forgotten Lucas Drake's threat to cancel his subscription to the paper and Drake's encouragement that everyone else should do so unless the paper quit publishing the Field column.

Billy Baxter Responds

Stony Field in Link Lake

By Billy Baxter, editor

The *Ames County Argus* recently learned that our very own Ames County resident Ambrose Adler, a farmer living near Link Lake, is really the famed environmental writer Stony Field. For several decades, the Stony Field column has been a weekly feature in several hundred newspapers, both dailies and weeklies across the country, including the *Ames County Argus*.

No matter what you may think about the content of his writing, everyone must agree that Stony Field causes people to think about things they may not have thought about before. Without doubt we need more of that in this country. We should be extremely proud to have in our midst such a skilled writer, such a competent researcher, and such a fine advocate for the environment.

On the other hand, there are those who are so upset with Stony Field and his writing, especially now that they know who he really is, that they have threatened to drop their subscriptions to this paper, and indeed to each and every paper that they may subscribe to that carries the Field column. It is their right to not agree with Stony Field's writing, but he, like they, and everyone else living in this country, has the right to state his opinion. Let me remind these angry Field column opponents of what the First Amendment of the Constitution of the United States has to say about this matter:

Amendment I

Congress shall make no law respecting an establishment of religion, or prohibiting the free exercise thereof; or abridging the freedom of speech, or of the press; or the right of the people peaceably to assemble, and to petition the government for a redress of grievances.

As much as some of us would like to see certain speech eliminated (for some, Stony Field columns), our Constitution assures us that we have the right to speak out, to share our opinions, and likewise, we also have freedom of the press, which means the press can do likewise.

Let this always be so, as these are the freedoms, along with several others that provide the foundation for the United States of America.

Let's applaud the good work of Ambrose Adler (Stony Field) and be extremely pleased that we have had this skilled writer in our midst these many years.

60

Overrun with Attention

*H*oly moley," said Fred Russo when he pulled out a chair and sat down across from Oscar Anderson at the Eat Well. He looked around the crowded restaurant. "This place is packed to the gills."

"It sure is, and these aren't local folks either. I couldn't find a place to park my pickup, had to walk three blocks. Whole damn Main Street is parked full of cars and vans and buses. I told you it would be a circus when people found out who Stony Field really was and I was right."

"For once you nailed it, Oscar. I never saw so many bigwig newspeople in one place in my life. Let's see, I spotted CBS, NBC, ABC, CNN, Fox— each has a big old truck with one of them satellite dishes hanging on the top of it. Kind of interesting it is, aside from it messin' up everyday goings on in little Link Lake."

"You know what I saw, Fred? I saw that big-shot CNN guy with the fancy hair, that Klayborn Stitzer fellow who thinks he's up on about everything happening in the world. Well, I saw him talking to our esteemed mayor. The mayor looked like he was gonna wet himself he was so excited."

"Yup, Oscar, just look around this room. We are in the midst of grandeur. In this room are some of the finest journalists in the world," said Fred.

"Oh, calm down. My guess is these guys pull on their pants just about the same way that we do. I don't know about the women, don't know how they do it," said Oscar, who smiled when he said it.

"Know what, Oscar? I saw the CBS truck parked up there by the park and one of them big-shot reporters was talkin' with Emily Higgins while they stood in front of the Trail Marker Oak. I can imagine what they were talkin' about. Wonder what those gun-totin' guards thought about that.

Wonder what the Alstage Sand Mining people thought about it? I'm sure the last thing the mining company wants is this kind of attention, just when they're about to open their new mine," said Fred.

"I drove by Ambrose's place this morning. Fred, there were cars parked on both sides of the road for a quarter mile in each direction, and photographers stood elbow to elbow in his front yard, waitin' for a picture of the poor old guy. Sheriff's car was directing traffic. You'd think Ambrose was havin' an auction, for all the people that were gathered there. Too bad. Too damn bad this had to happen. I feel sorry for poor old Ambrose. Wonder how he's takin' it. I wanted to stop and talk with him, but I couldn't get near the place. Them damn photographers are something else. Like a bunch of wolves waiting to devour fresh meat. That's how I'd describe them. Like a pack of hungry wolves," said Oscar, who appeared to have forgotten about the cup of coffee in front of him.

"I'll bet Marilyn Jones isn't too pleased about all this either. She never liked Ambrose, especially when he was datin' her sister way back, lots of years ago. Did you remember that, Fred? Ambrose and Gloria Jones were plannin' on gettin' hitched and Gloria and Marilyn's folks put a stop to it, and Gloria left for California and never came back."

"Oh, yeah, I remember all that. But I'll bet you my bottom dollar that no one was more surprised that Ambrose Adler was Stony Field than Marilyn Jones. I'd sure like to have seen her face when she first got the news. Sure like to have been there," said Fred.

"Well, the Eat Well folks are not complaining; my guess is that they've never in all their years seen such business in their place as they're seein' right now. And my guess is that the supper club is doin' pretty damn well too. Talk about improvin' the economy in Link Lake. I wonder if the Economic Development Council has noticed the amount of money being spent in this town without one mining hole being dug. I wonder if they ever thought about that. My guess is that for years to come people are gonna flock to little Link Lake to see where Stony Field lived and worked. I betcha it's gonna happen, whether the village wants it to or not," said Oscar. "Mark my word."

"I have marked it," said Fred, finally picking up his coffee and taking a big sip. "Damn coffee is cold."

61

Karl and Gloria

Why is my mother coming to Link Lake? thought Karl Adams as he drove along Highway 10 on his way to the Appleton airport. *She's associate editor of the* Los Angeles Journal. *Why didn't the paper send a reporter, not someone of her stature, to cover the Stony Field story in Link Lake? What's going on?*

Gloria's flight was right on time. Karl waited at the baggage claim area for her, and after a few minutes, there she was. They embraced, talked briefly about the flight, found Gloria's luggage on the carousel, and then headed for Karl's car, neither saying anything. Once away from the airport, they headed back on Highway 10 toward Waupaca, and then Link Lake. Karl broke the silence. "Mom, why are you coming to Link Lake? Are you here to cover the Stony Field story? It's turning out to be a circus with media people here from all over the country."

"Yes and no," Gloria answered.

"What in the world does that mean?"

"Yes, I'm coming because of Stony Field. And no, I am not here to write a story about him."

"Now I really am confused," said Karl. "Why in the world would you come to Link Lake, Wisconsin, in the middle of nowhere just because a famous writer lives here?"

"Well, where should I begin? It's all kind of complicated."

"Mom, you are not sounding like your old self. What's going on?"

"Well," she began, "now that we know who the real Stony Field is, it's probably time that you knew who the real Gloria Adams is."

"What?" was all Karl could think to say.

"I suppose I should start at the beginning. First, you should know that my name has not always been Gloria Adams," she said.

"Huh?" said Karl, glancing at his mother beside him, her hands together on her lap, a strand of gray hair falling over one eye.

"I was born in Chicago in 1944 and moved with my parents to Link Lake in 1955, when they opened the Link Lake Supper Club. My parents were Fred and Barbara Jones and my name then was Gloria Jones."

"Wait, wait," said Karl, trying to take in all that he had just heard. "Your last name is not really Adams?"

"Oh, it's Adams alright, but I'll get to that part of the story later," said Gloria.

"Is . . . is Marilyn Jones your sister?" asked an incredulous Karl Adams after a brief pause. He was running one hand through his hair as he drove with the other.

"Yes, Marilyn Jones is my sister. I haven't seen her since 1966, when I moved to California when I had a breakup with the family."

"You . . . you haven't talked to your sister since 1966?"

"I talked to her once, when our folks died in a car accident in 1973. I told her she could have the supper club. Appears she has done quite well."

"Wow, I don't know if I can handle all this. Hard-driving, ultraconservative Marilyn Jones is your sister." A few hundred yards ahead, Karl spotted a rest area and he pulled in, stopped, and turned off the car.

"Okay, Mom, so Marilyn Jones is your younger sister?"

"She sure is, and I'm more than a little anxious about seeing her again, after all these years."

"I can't believe it. I can't believe it," Karl said as he ran his hands through his hair again.

"Is Marilyn well?"

"Oh, she's well alright. In fact she probably looks years younger than she really is. For all her faults, she's a darn good businessperson. She's got the Link Lake Supper Club humming. Had a little setback a few weeks ago when a tornado tore the roof off the dining room and smashed up her office, but she's got it all back in shape and doing better than ever."

"Well, that's good," said Gloria.

Both Gloria and Karl had gotten out of the car and were now sitting opposite each other on a picnic table that was on the banks of a little stream that ran by the rest stop.

After a couple minutes of silence, Karl said, "So my name is not really Karl Adams?"

"Oh, it's Karl Adams alright," said Gloria.

"Now I suppose you'll tell me that my father really isn't dead."

"That's right; your father is still alive."

"Oh, Mother. You are driving me nuts. What is going on with you? Why haven't you told me this before?"

Gloria reached across the table and put her hand on Karl's arm. The little stream sounded like little bells as it flowed over some rocks in the streambed. Karl, his hair mussed and his face red, sat staring at his hands.

"I'm sorry, Karl. So sorry it all happened this way. I had to tell you something when you were a little boy and you asked about your dad, and it was easiest to say he died in an accident."

"So where does my father live?"

"He lives in Link Lake," Gloria answered.

"In Link Lake, Wisconsin?" Karl said, raising his voice.

"Yes," Gloria said quietly.

"Do you think I may have met him?"

"Yes, I believe you have."

"I have? You think I've met my father."

"Your father is Ambrose Adler."

"Who?" said Karl, once more raising his voice. "Who?"

"Ambrose Adler."

"Ambrose Adler is my father? How could that be? How could that ever be?"

Gloria went on to explain how she and Ambrose had dated and had even been planning to get married when her parents violently objected, and she moved to California and began working for the *Los Angeles Journal*.

"The first thing I did when I got to California was to change my name from Jones to Adams. I didn't even know I was pregnant with you then," Gloria said. She had tears in her eyes as she continued her story. "I didn't want anyone to come looking for me, to find me and encourage me to come back home. And when you were born, I gave you the name of Adams as well. You were another one of my secrets, Karl."

A long pause.

"Okay, where does Stony Field fit into all of this?"

Gloria explained how she had kept in contact with Ambrose over the years, and when his parents died in 1971, she helped him start a weekly column, which her paper syndicated and she edited.

"Your father wanted no one to know that he was the author of the column, so he came up with the name Stony Field. I promised him I would tell no one who Stony Field really was, and I haven't. Neither of us could have predicted that the column would become so wildly popular."

She explained that Ambrose never accepted any of the money the column earned. Gloria had started the Stony Field Trust Fund that donated money to various environmental groups.

"I just can't believe it. My father is the famous environmental writer Stony Field. I can't believe it," said Karl.

"Your dad isn't feeling well these days, and he's been pondering letting people know that he is Stony Field. He wasn't quite ready to let people know when a fellow by the name of Lucas Drake called our newspaper and said he knew that Stony Field was really Ambrose Adler, and he had the evidence to prove it."

"Slow down, Mom, you're almost telling me more than I can handle." Karl was quiet for a moment, then he said, "You know from the moment I first met Ambrose Adler, I knew there was something familiar about him—mostly when I looked into his eyes. You know what, when I look in the mirror, I see the same eyes. I never made the connection, but I had a feeling."

"You do have Ambrose's eyes," said Gloria. "Those gray penetrating eyes that I never forgot. Whenever I looked at you, Karl, from the time you were a little baby, I saw Ambrose Adler, the only person I ever loved. You made life bearable for me, Karl." She put her hands on his.

"Something else, Mom. Do you remember when I told you I saw a photograph hanging in Ambrose's kitchen and I told you on the phone that it looked like you when you were younger? Remember that?"

"Yes, I remember."

"That photo really was you, wasn't it?"

"Yes, yes it was," said Gloria. "And you know, Karl, I don't have one photograph of your father. Not one. What does he look like now? He was rather handsome when he was a young man."

"Well, he has white hair, a white beard, walks a little bent over, but his gray eyes are still bright. He lives without electricity and all the rest that most of us take for granted. And he has a pet raccoon that seems to go with him everywhere."

"Sounds like my Ambrose hasn't changed much over the years. You didn't mention his stuttering."

"Oh, he still stutters, especially when he's anxious and there are several people trying to talk with him. But one-on-one he does pretty well."

"What's the deal with this sand mine coming to Link Lake?" Gloria asked, changing the subject.

"Ah, God, Mom, you should ask. I'm caught right in the middle of the worst community fight I've been in for all the years I've done this mining consulting work. Your sister, Marilyn, chairs the Link Lake Economic Development Council, and they, together with the village board's approval, lined up the Alstage Sand Mining Company to open a mine in the village park."

"Yes, I remember reading all of this in Stony's columns. What's the status of the mine?"

"Looks like they are right on schedule to open in October, in spite of all that's going on. But lots of folks are opposed to it. Mom, it's a mess, and everything you just told me . . . well, I don't know what I'm going to do. Ambrose Adler is a member of the historical society that opposes the mine—and we both know that Stony Field has no time for sand mines and supporters of the mine hate Stony Field's guts. Mom, it's awful."

"Well, that's why I decided to fly out here," said Gloria. "Two of my favorite people are up to their ears in controversy—on opposite sides, it appears—and I thought I would come to see where I could help."

"Mom, I don't know what to do. You want me to drive you out to see Ambrose?"

"No, not tonight. It's too late. We'll go out tomorrow morning. I assume you've got an extra bed at your place?"

62
Barn Fire

At 6:00 a.m., both Karl and his mother were awakened to the sound of sirens. Karl had not slept well. His mind was a tangle of thoughts after hearing all that his mother had told him the previous evening. He was trying to accept the idea that Ambrose Adler was his father and that Marilyn Jones was his aunt. It was almost too much for a person to accept at one time.

He pulled on his robe, walked to the kitchen, and snapped on WWRI, the station that everyone in Ames County listened to for the news. "I've just gotten word that there is a barn fire west of Link Lake," said announcer Earl Wade. "I don't have any further details, but the Link Lake fire trucks along with those from Willow River are on the scene. I'll let you know when I have more details." The station resumed playing a Willie Nelson tune.

"What's going on?" Karl's mother asked when she came into the kitchen, pushing her gray hair back from her eyes.

"Radio said there was a barn fire west of Link Lake. Happens this time of the year—something about putting up hay that's not cured enough. Heard the county agent talking about that on the radio the other day."

Karl started the coffee pot. "Want some breakfast, Mom?"

"Sure, what have you got?"

"Not much. Some instant oatmeal. Some peach yogurt. Some toast."

"That will be fine," Gloria said, a big smile on her face. She sat down at the kitchen table.

When the toast and oatmeal were ready, Karl sat down opposite his mother.

"You don't look so great this morning," Gloria said, smiling at her son.

"Mom, you expect me to sleep after all you told me last night? I still can't believe that Ambrose Adler is my father. Just can't believe it. What must he think of me, working for a sand mining company that has disrupted this community more than it's ever been disrupted in the past? What must he think?"

"Oh, my guess is that he will be pleased when he learns he has a son who has done well."

"Ambrose doesn't know about me, doesn't know he has a son?" blurted out Karl.

"No, I never told him. I didn't think it would be right to burden him with anything else."

"So he must think I'm just another Joe trying to make a living."

"We're going to find out when I introduce you to him," Gloria said. "My guess is he is going to be mighty proud of this son he never knew he had."

"Mom, you got any more bombs you're going to drop on me?"

"No, don't think so," said Gloria, trying to keep a serious look on her face.

Their conversation was interrupted by Earl Wade's voice, as he cut in on a Johnny Cash tune. "I have further information about the barn fire west of Link Lake. The barn is on the farm of Ambrose Adler, who we all have just learned is the famous writer Stony Field. The firefighters found Mr. Adler unconscious in the barn; he had apparently sought refuge there from the many media people who have been trying to photograph and interview him. He has been taken by ambulance to the Link Lake Clinic. His condition is not known." Country music came back on the air.

"Oh my God," said Gloria, bringing her hands up to her face. "Oh my God!"

She and Karl quickly dressed and drove to the Link Lake Clinic, which already had media people filling the lawn.

"Please, let us through," said Gloria, pushing her way through the crowd of media people. Karl followed close behind his mother. At the counter, Gloria said, "We're here to see Ambrose Adler."

"Sorry, but he is to have no visitors beyond close family."

"We are close family," said Gloria.

The receptionist raised an eyebrow. "You're sure about that?" she said.

"Young lady, there is nothing I am more sure of," said Gloria, in a voice that had all the authority of a woman with years of executive experience.

"Room three," the receptionist said.

Gloria quietly eased open the door for room three and saw an old, white-haired, white-bearded man with his eyes closed, an oxygen mask over his nose and mouth and tubes in both arms. She, with Karl a few steps behind, walked up to the bed. Gloria took Ambrose's calloused hand in hers and whispered to him, "Ambrose, Ambrose, it's Gloria. It's Gloria."

Ambrose's eyes slowly opened. Then a tear appeared as he recognized the only person who had really cared about him, and who had moved away so many years ago.

"I'm here, Ambrose. I'm so sorry. So sorry about everything that's happened to you. So very, very sorry." For a long time, Gloria stood holding Ambrose's hand in hers, she saying nothing, he unable to speak because of the oxygen mask covering his nose and mouth.

After a few minutes passed, Gloria said, "I have somebody here to see you." Gloria motioned for Karl to stand beside her. "I believe you have met this man before. Ambrose, this is Karl Adams, and he's your son."

A strange look came over Ambrose's face, as if his mind was rolling back the pages of history to the time when he and Gloria were dating and enjoying each other's company and were planning marriage. And then the tears began running down his tired, wrinkled face.

Karl took his father's hand and held it in his, and father and son looked into each other's eyes for a long time.

"Dad, I'm so happy to meet you," Karl said, squeezing Ambrose's hand a bit. Ambrose squeezed back. Now tears were streaming down Karl's face as well. "So happy to meet you."

A nurse appeared in the room. "Folks, you'll have to leave. Mr. Adler needs his rest."

63

Reacquainted

At 3:40 that afternoon, Ambrose Adler breathed his last. His doctor said he suffered a massive heart attack that was triggered in part from excessive smoke inhalation from the barn fire. He was eighty-two years old.

Both Karl and Gloria were absolutely devastated when they got the news of Ambrose's death later that afternoon. *If only I hadn't been such a fool*, thought Gloria. *If only I hadn't let my pride, my guilt, and my anger control my life all these years. To think that I had only fifteen minutes with the man who has made the most difference in my life, the man who gave me a son. A man who, through his writing, made me so very proud.* "Oh, what a fool I've been," she sobbed as Karl, equally saddened by the news, tried to console his mother.

Karl had gone to the clinic when he got the news of his father's death and there met the Link Lake funeral director. "Do you know what kind of funeral you and your mother would like to have?" the man asked.

Karl told him that he didn't know, but he would check with his mother.

"Oh, I know what Ambrose wanted," she said. She was still sobbing. "He wrote me a note with detailed instructions."

Karl called the funeral home with the information he had gotten from his mother and turned to dealing with the media, who now had moved their attention toward Karl and his mother, hoping to interview one or both of them as soon as possible. Media cars, vans, and buses were parked along the road in front of the cabin that Karl had been renting, hoping to catch a photograph of him and his mother.

A surprise visitor arrived at the cabin in the early evening. She had elbowed her way through the hoard of photographers and reporters to the cabin door, where she politely knocked.

Karl came to the door.

"Marilyn," he said.

"May I come in? One of the media people said my sister might be here. Is that true? Is Gloria here?"

"Yes, yes she is." Karl walked toward the deck where Gloria sat, looking out over the lake. "There is someone here to see you."

"Who is it? I don't want to talk with anybody."

"Why don't you come and see," said Karl.

Gloria, her eyes red from crying, and her usually stylish gray hair tangled and twisted, slowly got up and walked toward the door, where she stared for a moment and then said, "Marilyn, is that you?"

Marilyn embraced her older sister, whom she had not seen for so many years.

"I'm so sorry to hear about Ambrose," Marilyn said. "So sorry."

They stood holding each other for a long while, neither saying anything.

"I'm so glad you came home," said Marilyn. "I wondered if we wouldn't see you once everyone found out that Ambrose Adler was Stony Field."

Karl had been standing in the background, not interfering with the two sisters, who had not seen each other for several decades and were trying to decide what to say to each other. Gloria broke the silence. "Karl," Gloria said. "Come over here please." Marilyn had a perplexed look on her face, a look that said, *How does my sister know this Alstage consulting engineer?*

"Marilyn," Gloria began, taking Karl by the arm. "This is my son, Karl."

"Your son?" asked Marilyn incredulously.

"Yes, your nephew."

Marilyn was absolutely speechless. Karl said, "I didn't know Mom had any ties to Link Lake. I didn't know that my father lived here. I didn't know that my father was Ambrose Adler."

"Gloria, why . . . why didn't you tell any of us about this? Why didn't you tell the folks? They would have loved knowing they had a grandson."

"I don't think so, Marilyn. Our parents hated Ambrose. They said he was a dumb, stuttering farmer. And besides, I was a single mother. A mother with a fatherless child. Back in the '60s, unmarried mothers were not well thought of. I changed my name and made up a lie about Karl's father being killed in an accident."

"Oh, Gloria," Marilyn said. "Oh, so many years we've wasted because of one little incident."

"Marilyn, it wasn't so little. Dad said he'd shoot Ambrose if we got married. I don't think that's something little."

"I don't think he would have done that. Dad wasn't like that."

"Well, I happened to think he would have. That's why I moved to California. I didn't want anything to happen to Ambrose. He was a good man. Lots of people didn't know that. And he was smart too. And a darn good writer. One of the best column writers the *Los Angeles Journal* had." Tears began to run down Gloria's face again.

64

Memorial Service

*B*ack in the spring, when the doctor told Ambrose his heart wasn't near as strong as it once was, he had penned a letter to Gloria:

My Dear Gloria,

I've just returned from the doctor, who told me my old ticker isn't up to par, and that I should slow down a bit. You know me; I'm not too keen on slowing down. But nonetheless, I thought that if something should happen to me, and I'm not planning on it, here is how things should be taken care of. I do not want a church service of any kind. I never set foot in a church and to do so when I'm dead wouldn't make a whole lot of sense. But it would be nice, if people were so inclined, to hold a memorial service at the Increase Joseph Community Park, in front of the Trail Marker Oak. And again, if it is not too much trouble, I'd like to have my ashes spread beneath that old tree. As much as your folks disliked me, I know how much they loved that old tree, as I do. I sincerely hope it outlives all of us.

Fondly,
Ambrose

Gloria and Karl set a date for a memorial service a week following his death, at the park and in front of the Trail Marker Oak. Gloria traveled to Willow River, met Billy Baxter, and asked him to put a note in the *Ames County Argus* about the event. She also sent an e-mail message to her own newspaper, the *Los Angeles Journal*, to mention the service. She asked Karl to let the people at the Alstage Sand Mining Company know that a memorial service would be held at the park, and the camouflaged guards with the automatic weapons should fade into the background during the service. Karl contacted Emerson Evans directly, and Evans reluctantly agreed. "But," he said, "I'm not very happy about having a memorial service at our mine site for the fellow that gave us the most grief about even having a mine there."

Karl explained that it was Ambrose Adler's last request, and the whole thing would be over in an hour or so. The service was scheduled for the last Sunday in September. It was likely one of the last events to be held in the park before the mine commenced operations on October 15.

Gloria and Karl expected a large crowd, but nothing of the order that turned out for the event. Five deputies from the sheriff's department plus a couple of state patrol officers and the entire contingent of Link Lake officers (two) were pressed into duty to direct traffic and, along with volunteers, park cars at the Link Lake High School. School buses and drivers were organized to transport people to and from the park site. Of course most of the media from across the country were still in Link Lake, which swelled the crowd and somewhat unexpectedly, but not surprisingly, representatives from almost all of the major environmental groups arrived in Link Lake to pay their respects to the one person who likely did more in his tenure as Stony Field, environmental writer, than any other single person in recent history to advance the cause of environmental protection. Gloria had met many of these people, as they knew she was Stony Field's editor. She recognized people from the Sierra Club, the National Wildlife Association, the National Audubon Club, the Nature Conservancy, and several more. None of them knew that her relationship with Stony Field was much deeper than editing his weekly columns.

Emily Higgins enlisted Earl Wade as emcee for the service. Wade walked up to the microphone and looked out over the crowd, which a state patrol officer who had helped with many large events had told him numbered well over a thousand people.

"Ladies and gentlemen," Wade began. "On this beautiful September day, when the maple leaves are just beginning to show color, and the waters of Link Lake are as blue as the sky above, we gather here to honor one of our own—Ambrose Adler—farmer, lover of wildlife, advocate of living life simply, and . . . and much to the surprise of all of us, a brilliant writer with legions of readers in this country and well beyond." Wade stopped for a moment and looked out over the lake.

"This is the kind of day that Ambrose Adler loved. He took time to enjoy the seasonal changes, to marvel at nature's splendor, to appreciate the beauty of the land, and at the same time he helped us remember how we are all tied to it. As he often said in his writing, 'We are people of the land.' How fitting it is that we take time from our busy lives to pay respects to this great man on such a beautiful day."

Wade adjusted his glasses and looked down at his notes. "Several people have agreed to say a few words about Ambrose." Folding chairs were lined up in front of the podium for those who had agreed to speak at the event.

"We'll start with Emily Higgins, president of our Link Lake Historical Society."

Slowly Emily made her way to the podium. She took a deep breath, looked out over the crowd, and began.

"I've known Ambrose Adler longer than anyone in this audience," she began. "Ambrose was often shunned by people in these parts. Shunned because people thought he was different. Shunned because he never troubled to hook up to electricity or learn how to drive a car. But mostly he was shunned because he stuttered, and because he couldn't speak well, people thought he had little to say. He sure fooled us, myself included. Who would have thought that my old farmer friend who lived so frugally, bothered no one, and put up with being a curiosity in this town all these years was the brilliant writer Stony Field? I guess he showed us—especially those who dismissed Ambrose Adler, ignored him, and sometimes even made fun of him—that everyone can make a contribution to society. Hats off to you, Ambrose Adler. You will not be forgotten."

The next speaker, introduced as Rex Oakley, a representative from the Nature Conservancy, took the microphone. He was tall, much taller than Emily Higgins. He adjusted the microphone and began.

"Who imagined that Stony Field had such humble beginnings and lived such a simple, uncluttered life? I for one thought that Stony Field was a college professor working on some campus in this great country, perhaps in a department of environmental studies, but no, here we have a true man of the soil. A man with limited formal education but with vast knowledge. Ambrose Adler lived his entire life connected to the land. He worked the land, but the land also worked him, for his writing clearly showed that he continued to learn, that he continued to gain new insights about nature and his relationship to it throughout his entire life."

Oakley continued, "I place Ambrose Adler in the company of other great lovers of nature with roots in Wisconsin: John Muir, Sigrud Olson, Wakelin McNeil, Gaylord Nelson, and of course Aldo Leopold. Ambrose, Stony Field, you are in good company."

Other speakers followed, each with another take on the tremendous contributions he, both as Ambrose Adler and as Stony Field, had made during his lifetime. No one from the Eagle Party attended the event, nor did anyone from the Link Lake Economic Development Council, including its president, Marilyn Jones, even though Gloria had hoped that she would come. When someone asked Lucas Drake if he was coming to the memorial service, he said, "Are you kidding? At last we're rid of that damned Stony Field and his socialistic writing."

Earlier in the week, when Emily Higgins saw Noah Drake riding his bike past the historical society headquarters on his way home from school, she had told him about the memorial service and asked him if he would read the last column that Stony Field was working on, the one he had not completed before he died. Gloria and Karl had found the draft copy on his desk, next to his old Remington typewriter that was so worn that several of the keys were bare.

"Pa said I should never see Ambrose Adler again," said Noah Drake when Emily Higgins asked him to speak. "But now that he's dead . . ." Noah hesitated, choking back tears. "I'll do it," he said.

After Earl Wade's brief introduction, Noah, but twelve years old, walked up to the podium. Wade adjusted the microphone for him and whispered, "Talk right into the mike."

Noah looked out over the vast audience. He had never seen this many people in one place before and for a moment he felt like turning around and running. He felt his hands shaking and his mouth go dry. In a quiet voice he said, "My name is Noah Drake. Ambrose Adler was my neighbor and my friend. He listened to me when I told him my troubles. He let me play with his pet raccoon. He didn't speak real good. But that didn't matter. He was like a second father to me. He . . ." Noah couldn't finish the sentence. He paused for a moment, trying to gain his composure.

"I've got the last column Ambrose Adler wrote. It's not finished. Miss Higgins asked me to read it, and I will." Noah's voice now got stronger. He read:

FIELD NOTES
Trail Marker Oak a Symbol

By Stony Field

The little village of Link Lake in central Wisconsin has torn itself apart these past few months as it debated and then protested a decision made by its village officials to allow a sand mine to open in its cherished village park. It's a debate that has occurred often in this country: what is more important? Economic development, or history and the environment? And why not all three of equal importance?

The debate in Link Lake has centered on an old bur oak tree. The mining company insists that it be cut down for it stands in the way of the only clear and easy access to the mine site. For some it is hard to imagine that a tree could be the center of a controversy. Why would it matter if this old tree is cut down? Why let one lone tree stand in the way of jobs and supposedly a better life for many people?

But that old tree, the Trail Marker Oak, once pointed the way for the Indians and the early settlers in the Link Lake community toward the Fox River and the trading post located there. Today it reminds the people of Link Lake of their past and it is a visible connecting link of the community to its history.

Memorial Service

Symbols like the Trail Marker Oak are important to communities, for they allow people to see their history in something tangible, not merely in what someone remembers and perhaps has written down—although that is of great worth as well. We must as a nation protect our historic symbols, for if we don't, we will lose touch with an essential part of our histories. And when we forget our histories, we forget who we are.

"That's as far as Ambrose got," said Noah as he folded the paper, stuffed it into his pocket, and stepped away from the podium. The applause would have continued even longer had not Earl Wade interrupted to say, "This concludes our memorial service for our friend and neighbor who has done so much for this community and for this great country. Thank you all for coming."

Noah Drake hopped on his bike and rode home, feeling more sad and lonely than he ever felt in his young life. When he stepped onto the porch at his farmhouse, a little animal appeared from the shadows. It was Ranger, Ambrose Adler's pet raccoon. The little animal trotted up to Noah and rubbed its back on Noah's leg. Noah reached down and petted it.

65

Trail Marker Oak

The whine of a chain saw assaulted the quiet of the new day as the mists rising from the waters of Link Lake slowly drifted west and the sun's first rays broke the horizon, illuminating the brilliant autumn colors of the maples and aspens, the oaks and the birches that clustered on the hillsides around the lake. Three men walked from their truck. One carried a chain saw; the other two carried axes. The chain saw operator, a burly man in his fifties, his face hidden under an orange safety helmet, revved the machine a couple of times like a teenager with a new driver's license and permission to drive his father's car alone for the first time. The men, all professional loggers, walked the short distance from their truck. The chain saw operator held the saw well in front of him, the saw sending off little spurts of chain oil. As the trio approached the old bur oak tree that they were ordered to cut this October day, they saw something emerging from the mist—something that surprised them. The chain saw operator shut off his machine and fished a cell phone out of his pocket to call his supervisor. "Boss, we've got a problem."

Out of the mists walked a line of people, holding hands, approaching the Trail Marker Oak, and then surrounding it, continuing to hold hands. And singing. Everyone was singing.

"We shall overcome," they sang. They sang in loud, melodious voices that carried from the park to the lake, singing that people heard in the Village of Link Lake. Singing that replaced the sound of heavy equipment the villagers expected to hear on this, the day construction of the Alstage Sand Mine was supposed to begin.

Trail Marker Oak

Armed guards, carrying rifles and looking menacing, were supposed to prevent this sort of thing. But where were they? Not a one in sight. Only loggers, one with a chain saw, and enough people to encircle the Trail Marker Oak with a few left over. And a newspaper reporter. Billy Baxter, with camera and notepad, as surprised as the loggers, as he had come expecting to record the cutting down of this historic tree. In his notepad he wrote down the people he recognized, the people who were holding hands and circling and protecting the Trail Marker Oak and singing. And he was both shocked and amazed at who he saw holding hands and singing together that old Civil Rights song that tugged at the hearts and minds of so many.

"We shall overcome. We shall overcome. We shall overcome someday."

Upon returning to his Willow River office, Billy Baxter immediately began typing the story that he knew would make its way across the country. He wrote:

Old Oak Tree Brings People Together

By Billy Baxter, editor

Sometimes something as simple as an oak tree can bring people together, even longtime bitter enemies. As many people know, the little Village of Link Lake in central Wisconsin has been the center of attention since the revealing of the identity of the nationally known environmental writer Stony Field as a simple-living vegetable farmer by the name of Ambrose Adler. Persons unknown, but obviously someone who disliked Stony Field and his writing, burned Adler's barn and contributed to his death.

All of this took away from the issue that has torn little Link Lake apart since the day the village board signed a lease with the Alstage Sand Mining Company of La Crosse to open a sand mine in Increase Joseph Community Park.

On an early October morning, loggers hired to remove the historic Trail Marker Oak, and thus officially begin the mine's operation, faced something they had not anticipated, nor had this writer, who was there to record the event. From out of the early morning mist came a group of people who held hands and surrounded the tree and sang "We shall over-come" in voices that rolled across the waters of Link Lake on that still morning and hung in the air like the morning fog.

There Emily Higgins, outspoken foe of the sand mine and especially the mining company's plan to cut the Trail Marker Oak, held hands with Marilyn Jones, the original advocate for the mine. Marilyn Jones held hands with her sister, Gloria, who left the community many years ago in a family dispute. Gloria held hands with her son, Karl, who works for the Alstage Sand Mining Company as a consulting engineer. Also holding hands at the tree were well-known farmers from the area, Fred Russo and Oscar Anderson, plus several other historical society members.

In his many years as a newspaper reporter and editor, this writer has never witnessed anything quite like this. Obviously the Alstage Sand Mining Company did not begin operations on the planned date. Now the question appears to be, will the mine open? And can this collection of onetime adversaries continue to protect the Trail Marker Oak and prevent a sand mine from opening in their beloved park? Can they save an old oak standing on sacred sand, as Emily Higgins once asked?

Books by Jerry Apps

Novels in the Ames County Series
The Travels of Increase Joseph
In a Pickle
Blue Shadows Farm
Cranberry Red
Tamarack River Ghost
The Great Sand Fracas of Ames County

Nonfiction
The Land Still Lives
Cabin in the Country
Barns of Wisconsin
Mills of Wisconsin and the Midwest
Breweries of Wisconsin
One-Room Country Schools
Wisconsin Traveler's Companion
Country Wisdom
Cheese: The Making of a Wisconsin Tradition
When Chores Were Done
Country Ways and Country Days
Humor from the Country
The People Came First: A History of Cooperative Extension
Ringlingville USA
Every Farm Tells a Story
Living a Country Year
Old Farm: A History
Horse-Drawn Days
Campfires and Loon Calls
Garden Wisdom
Rural Wit and Wisdom
Limping Through Life
The Quiet Season

Audio Books
The Back Porch and Other Stories
In a Pickle

Children's Books
Eat Rutabagas
Stormy
Tents, Tigers, and the Ringling Brothers
Casper Jaggi: Master Swiss Cheese Maker
Letters from Hillside Farm